Dedicated to all the caregivers out there:
those who care because they want to,
those who care because they have no choice,
and especially medical professionals during the COVID-19 pandemic,
every single one

The Heart Principle

Titles by Helen Hoang

THE KISS QUOTIENT
THE BRIDE TEST
THE HEART PRINCIPLE

The Heart Principle

HELEN HOANG

CORVUS

First published in 2021 in the United States of America by Berkley,
an imprint of Penguin Random House LLC.

First published in 2021 in Great Britain by Corvus, an imprint of Atlantic Books Ltd.

10 9 8 7 6

A CIP catalogue record for this book is available from the British Library.

Paperback ISBN: 978 1 83895 080 4
E-book ISBN: 978 1 83895 081 1

Printed and bound by CPI Group (UK) Ltd, Croydon CR0 4YY

Corvus
An imprint of Atlantic Books Ltd
Ormond House
26–27 Boswell Street
London
WC1N 3JZ

www.corvus-books.co.uk

THE HEART PRINCIPLE

Part One

Before

ONE

Anna

THIS IS THE LAST TIME I'M STARTING OVER.

That's what I tell myself, anyway. I mean it every time. But then, every time, something happens—I make a mistake, I know I can do better, or I hear, in my head, what people will say.

So I stop and go back to the beginning, to get it right this time. And it's really the last time *this* time.

Except it isn't.

I've spent the past six months doing this, going over the same measures again and again like a rhinoceros pacing figure eights at the zoo. These notes don't even make sense to me anymore. But I keep trying. Until my fingers hurt and my back aches and my wrist throbs with every pull of the bow on the strings. I ignore it all and give the music everything I have. Only when the timer goes off do I lower my violin from my chin.

My head is spinning, and I'm parched with thirst. I must have turned my lunch alarm off and forgotten to actually eat. That happens a lot more often than I care to admit. If it weren't for the zillions of alarms on my phone, I might have accidentally ended myself by now. It's out of consideration for life that I don't keep any plants. I do have a pet. He's a rock. His name is, very creatively, Rock.

The alarm notification on my phone screen says *THERAPY*, and I turn it off with a grimace. Some people enjoy therapy. It's venting and validation for them. For me, it's exhausting work. It doesn't help that I think my therapist secretly dislikes me.

Still, I drag myself into my bedroom to change. Attempting to muddle through things on my own hasn't helped, so I'm determined to give this therapy thing a try. My parents would be disgusted by the waste of money if they knew, but I'm desperate and they can't mourn dollars they don't know I'm spending. I remove the pajamas that I've been wearing all day and pull on exercise clothes that I don't plan to exercise in. Somehow, these are considered more appropriate in public even though they're more revealing. I don't question why people do things. I just observe and copy. That's how to get along in this world.

Outside, the air smells of car exhaust and restaurant cooking, and people are out and about, bicycling, shopping, catching late lunches at the cafés. I navigate the steep streets and weave through the pedestrians, wondering if any of these people are going to the symphony tonight. They're playing Vivaldi, my favorite. Without me.

I took a leave of absence because I can't perform when I'm stuck playing in loops like this. I haven't told my family because I know they wouldn't understand. They'd tell me to quit indulging myself and snap out of it. Tough love is our way.

Being tough on myself isn't working now, though. I can't try harder than I already am.

When I reach the modest little building where my therapist and other mental health professionals have their practices, I key in the code 222, let myself in, and walk up the musty stairs to the second floor. There's no receptionist or sitting room, so I go straight to room 2A. I lift my fist toward the door but hesitate before making contact. A quick glance at my phone reveals it's 1:58 P.M. Yes, I'm two minutes early.

I shift my weight from foot to foot, uncertain what to do. Everyone knows that being late isn't good, but being early isn't great either. Once, when I showed up early to a party, I literally caught the host with his pants down. And his girlfriend's face in his crotch. That wasn't fun for any of us.

Obviously, the best time to arrive somewhere is right *on* time.

So I stand here, tormented with indecision. Should I knock or should I wait? If I knock early, what if I inconvenience her somehow and she's annoyed with me? On the other hand, if I wait, what if she gets up to go to the bathroom and catches me standing outside her door grinning creepily? I don't have enough information, but I try to think of what she'll think and modify my actions accordingly. I want to make the "correct" decision.

I check my phone repeatedly, and when the time reads 2:00 P.M., I exhale in relief and knock. Three times firmly, like I mean it.

My therapist opens the door and greets me with a smile and no handshake. There's never a handshake. It confused me in the beginning, but now that I know what to expect, I like it.

"It's so good to see you, Anna. Come on in. Make yourself comfortable." She motions for me to enter and then waves at the cups and hot water heater on the counter. "Tea? Water?"

I get myself a cup of tea because that seems to be what she wants and set it on the coffee table to steep before I sit in the middle of the sofa across from her armchair. Her name is Jennifer Aniston, by the way. No, she's not *that* Jennifer Aniston. I don't think she's ever been on TV or dated Brad Pitt, but she's tall and, in my opinion, attractive. She's in her mid-fifties is my guess, on the thin side, and always wears moccasins and handmade jewelry. Her long hair is a sandy brown threaded with gray, and her eyes . . . I can't remember what color they are even though I was just looking at her. It's because I focus in between people's eyes. Eye contact scrambles my brain so I can't think, and this is a handy trick to make it look like I'm doing what I should. Ask me what her moccasins look like.

"Thank you for seeing me," I say because I'm supposed to act grateful. The fact that I actually *am* grateful isn't the point, but it's true nonetheless. To add extra emphasis, I smile my warmest smile, making sure to wrinkle the corners of my eyes. I've practiced this in a mirror enough times that I'm confident it looks right. Her answering smile confirms it.

"Of course," she says, pressing a hand over her heart to show how touched she is.

I do wonder if she's acting just like I am. How much of what people say is genuine and how much is politeness? Is anyone really living their life or are we all reading lines from a giant script written by other people?

It starts then, the recap of my week, how have I been, have I made any breakthroughs with my work. I explain in neutral terms that nothing has changed. Everything was the same this week as the week before, just as that week was the same as the week before it. My days are essentially identical to one another. I wake up, I have coffee and half a bagel, and I practice violin until the various alarms on my phone tell me to stop. An hour on scales, and four on music. Every day. But I make no progress. I get to the fourth page in this piece by

Max Richter—when I'm lucky—and I start over. And I start over. And I start over. Over and over and over again.

It's challenging for me to talk about these things with Jennifer, especially without letting my frustration leak out. She's my therapist, which means, in my mind, that she's supposed to be helping me. And she hasn't been able to, as far as I can tell. But I don't want her to feel bad. People like me better when I make them feel *good* about themselves. So I'm constantly assessing her reaction and editing my words to appeal to her.

When a deep frown mars her face at my lackluster description of the past week, I panic and say, "I feel like I'm close to getting better." That's an outright lie, but it's for a good cause because her expression immediately lightens up.

"I'm so happy to hear that," Jennifer says.

I smile at her, but I feel slightly queasy. I don't like lying. I do it all the time, though. The harmless little lies that make people feel nice. They're essential for getting along in society.

"Can you try skipping to the middle of the piece that you're struggling with?" she asks.

I physically recoil at the suggestion. "I have to start at the beginning. That's just what you do. If the song was meant to be played from the middle, that part would be at the beginning."

"I understand, but this might help you get past your mental block," she points out.

All I can do is shake my head, even though inside I'm wincing. I know I'm not acting the way she wants, and that feels wrong.

She sighs. "Doing the same thing over and over hasn't solved the problem, so maybe it's time to try something different."

"But I can't skip the beginning. If I can't get it right, then I don't deserve to play the next part, and I don't deserve to play the ending," I say, conviction in every word.

"What is this about deserving? It's a song. It's meant to be played in whatever order you want. It doesn't judge you."

"But people will," I whisper.

And there it is. We always come to this one sticking point. I look down at my hands and find my fingers white-knuckled together like I'm pushing myself down and holding myself up at the same time.

"You're an artist, and art is subjective," Jennifer says. "You have to learn to stop listening to what people say."

"I know."

"How were you able to play before? What was your mindset then?" she asks, and by "before" I know she means before I accidentally became Internet famous and my career took off and I went on an international tour and got a record deal and modern composer Max Richter wrote a piece just for me, an honor like nothing else in the whole world.

Every time I try to play that piece as well as it deserves—as well as everyone expects me to, because I'm some kind of musical prodigy now, even though I was only considered adequate in the past—*every time*, I fail.

"Before, I played just because I loved it," I say finally. "No one cared about me. No one even knew I existed. Other than my family and boyfriend and coworkers and such. And I was fine with that. I *liked* that. Now . . . people have expectations, and I can't stand knowing that I might disappoint them."

"You *will* disappoint people," Jennifer says in a firm but not unkind voice. "But you'll also blow others away. That's just how this works."

"I know," I say. And I really do understand, logically. But emotionally, it's another matter. I'm terrified that if I slip, if I fail, everyone will stop loving me, and where will I be then?

"I think you've forgotten why you play," she says gently. "Or more precisely, *who* you play for."

I take and release a deep breath and unclasp my hands to give my stiff fingers a break. "You're right. I haven't played for my own enjoyment in a long time. I'll try to do that," I say, offering her an optimistic smile. In my heart, however, I know what will happen when I try. I will get lost playing in loops. Because nothing is good enough now. No, "good enough" isn't right. I must be *more* than "good enough." I must be *dazzling*. I wish I knew how to dazzle at will.

For a second, it looks like she's going to say something, but she ends up touching a finger to her chin instead as she tilts her head to the side, looking at me from a new angle. "Why do you do that?" She points to her own eyes. "That thing with your eyes?"

My face blanches. I can feel my skin flashing hot and then going cold and stiff as all expression melts away. "What thing?"

"The eye wrinkling," she says.

I've been caught.

I don't know how I should react. This hasn't happened to me before. I wish I could melt into the floor or squeeze myself into one of her cupboards and hold the door shut. "Smiles are real when they reach your eyes. Books say so," I admit.

"Are there lots of things that you do like that, things that you read about in books or have seen other people do so you copy them?" she asks.

I swallow uncomfortably. "Maybe."

Her expression turns thoughtful, and she scribbles something down on her notepad. I try to see what she's written without looking like I'm peeking, but I can't make anything out.

"Why does it matter?" I ask.

She considers me for a moment before saying, "It's a form of masking."

"What's masking?"

Speaking haltingly, like she's choosing her words, she says, "It's when someone takes on mannerisms that aren't natural to them so they can better fit in with society. Does that resonate with you?"

"Is it bad if it does?" I ask, unable to keep the uneasiness from my voice. I don't like where this is going.

"It's not good or bad. It's just the way things are. I'll be able to help you better if I have a clearer understanding of how your mind works." She pauses then and sets her pen down before forging ahead to say, "A lot of the time, I believe you tell me things just because you think that's what I want to hear. I hope you can see how counterproductive that would be in therapy."

My desire to crawl into her cupboard intensifies. I used to hide in tight places like that when I was little. I only stopped because my parents kept finding me and dragging me out to whatever chaotic event they had going on: parties, big dinners with our enormous extended family, school concerts, things that required me to wear itchy tights and a scratchy dress and sit still in silent suffering.

Jennifer sets her notepad aside and crosses her hands in her lap. "Our time is up, but for this next week, I'd like you to try something new."

"Skipping to the middle and playing something fun," I say. I always remember her to-do items, even when I know I won't actually do them.

"Those would be great things to do if you could," she says with an earnest smile. "But there's something else." Leaning forward and watching me intently, she adds, "I'd like you to watch what you're doing and saying, and if it's something that doesn't feel right and true to who you are, if it's something that exhausts you or makes you unhappy, take a look at *why* you're doing it. And if there isn't a good reason . . . try not doing it."

"What's the point of this?" It feels like going backward, and it doesn't have anything to do with my music, which is all I care about.

"Do you think there's a chance that maybe your masking has spread to your violin playing?" she asks.

I open my mouth to speak, but it takes me a while before I say, "I don't understand." Something tells me I won't like this, and I'm starting to sweat.

"I think you've figured out how to change yourself to make other people happy. I've seen you tailor your facial expressions, your actions, even what you say, to be what you think I prefer. And now, I suspect, you're trying, unconsciously perhaps, to change your music to be what people like. But that's impossible, Anna. Because it's art. You *can't* please everyone. The second you change it so one person likes it, you'll lose someone who liked it the way it was before. Isn't that what you've been doing as you go in circles? You have to learn how to listen to yourself again, to *be* yourself."

Her words overwhelm me. Part of me wants to yell at her to stop spouting nonsense, to get angry. Another part of me wants to cry because how pitiful do I sound? I'm afraid she's seen right through me. In the end, I neither yell nor cry. I sit there like a deer in headlights, which is my default reaction to most things—inaction. I don't have a fight-or-flight instinct. I have a freeze instinct. When things get really bad, I can't even talk. I fall mute.

"What if I don't know how to stop?" I ask finally.

"Start with small things, and try it in a safe environment. How about with your family?" she suggests helpfully.

I nod, but that doesn't really mean agreement. I'm still processing. My head is in a haze as we wrap up the session, and I'm not entirely aware of my surroundings until later, when I find myself outside, walking back home.

My phone is vibrating insistently from my purse, and I dig it out to see three missed calls from my boyfriend, Julian—no voice messages, he hates leaving voice messages. I sigh. He only calls like this on those rare occasions when he's not traveling for work and wants to meet for a night out. I'm exhausted from therapy. All I want to do right now is curl up on my couch in my ugly fluffy bathrobe, get delivery, and watch BBC documentaries narrated by David Attenborough.

I don't want to call him back.

But I do.

"Hey, babe," Julian answers.

I'm walking down the sidewalk alone, but I force a smile onto my face and enthusiasm into my voice. "Hi, Jules."

"I heard good things about that new burger place by Market Square, so I made us a reservation at seven. Gonna try to make it to the gym, so I gotta go. Miss you. See you there," he says quickly.

"What new burger pla—" I begin to ask, but then I realize that he's already hung up. I'm talking to myself.

I guess I'm going out tonight.

TWO

Anna

CONFESSION: I DON'T LIKE GIVING BLOW JOBS.

That's probably not a good thing to be thinking while I have my boyfriend's dick in my mouth, but here we are.

Some women enjoy this act, and I figure their enjoyment drives them to excel at their craft. For me, however, it's tiring, monotonous work, and I doubt I'm great at it. My mind often wanders while I'm down here.

For example, right now, I'm going over what Jennifer said in therapy earlier today. *I'd like you to watch what you're doing and saying, and if it's something that doesn't feel right and true to who you are, if it's something that exhausts you or makes you unhappy, take a look at why you're doing it. And if there isn't a good reason . . . try not doing it.*

As Julian guides my head up and down, I think about how my jaw aches and I'm tired of sucking—is he even concentrating? It's been a long day, and after smiling and being bubbly for him throughout dinner, my endurance is shot. But I keep going. His pleasure is supposed to be my pleasure. It shouldn't matter if it takes forever.

Please don't take forever.

Naturally, this train of thought leads me to remember that line everyone's mom tells them at some time during their youth: *If you keep making that face, you'll look like that forever.* Ladies and gentlemen, if I'm going to be stuck with this sucking face for the rest of my life, you might as well kill me now.

He finally finishes, and I sit back, rubbing at the blower's wrinkles around my mouth. They're set deep into my skin, and I know from experience that it'll take several minutes for them to go away. My mouth is full, and I force myself to swallow, even though it makes me shudder. When we first started dating, Julian told me that it hurt his feelings when women didn't swallow, that it made him feel rejected. As a result, I've probably swallowed gallons of his semen to safeguard his emotional well-being.

He kisses my temple—not my mouth. He refuses to kiss me on the mouth after I've gone down on him, and tonight I don't mind. When he kissed me earlier, he tasted like a hamburger. Tucking himself back into his pants and zipping up, he flashes a smile at me, grabs the remote to turn the TV on, and rests against the headboard. He is the picture of relaxation and contentment.

I go to the bathroom and brush my teeth, making sure to thoroughly floss and use mouthwash. I don't like the idea of having sperm stuck in between my teeth or wriggling on my tongue.

As I'm crawling back onto the bed to take up my regular spot next to him where I usually surf social media on my phone while he watches sitcoms, he pauses the TV and gives me a thoughtful look.

"I think we need to talk about the future," he says. "About how we want to move forward."

My heart jumps, and the fine hairs on my skin stand up. Is this . . . a proposal? Whatever excitement I feel at the prospect is outweighed by sheer terror. I'm not ready for marriage. I'm not ready for the changes that would bring. I'm barely handling the status quo.

"What do you mean?" I ask, making sure to keep my voice neutral so I don't give away my ambivalence.

He reaches over and squeezes my hand affectionately. "You know how I feel about you, babe. We're great together."

I put on my best smile. "I think so, too." My parents love him. His parents love me. We fit.

He caresses the back of my hand before sighting a bit of lint on my T-shirt, picking it off, and tossing it to the carpet. "I think you're the one for me, the one I'm going to marry and have kids and a house with, all of that. But before we take that final step and settle down, I want to be sure."

I don't know where he's going with this, but still, I smile and say, "Of course."

"I think we should see other people for a while. Just to make sure we've ruled out other possibilities," he says.

I blink several times as my brain struggles to shake off its shock. "Are we . . . breaking up?" Just saying those words makes my heart pound. I might not be ready for marriage, but I definitely don't want our relationship to end. I've invested a lot of time and energy to make this work.

"No, we're just putting our relationship on pause while we consider other options. We started dating exclusively when I was still in grad school, remember? Should you buy the first car you test-drive on the lot? Or should you test-drive a few more to make sure that first car is really as great as you think?"

I shake my head, quietly horrified that he's comparing proposing to me with buying a new car from a dealership. I'm a *person*.

Julian sighs and reaches over to squeeze my leg. "I think we should really take some time apart, Anna. Not breaking up, just . . . seeing other people, too."

"For how long? And what are the rules?" I ask, hoping that this will make sense if I learn more.

He focuses on the frozen image on the TV as he says, "A few months should be good, don't you think? As for rules . . ." He shrugs and glances at me quickly. "Let's just go with the flow and see where things go."

"You're going to have sex with other people?" An unpleasant feeling pools in my stomach at the thought.

"Aside from you, I've only been with one other person. If we're going to get married, I want to do it without regrets. I don't want to feel like I'm missing out. Doesn't that make sense?" he asks.

"You'll be okay if *I* sleep with someone else?" I ask, hurt and not even sure why. He makes it sound so reasonable.

He smirks slightly. "I don't think you'll sleep with someone else. I know you, Anna."

I glower at his confidence.

"What? You don't like sex," he says with a laugh.

"That's not true." Not entirely. I've orgasmed with him twice. (Twice in five years.) And even when I don't like the sex itself, I do like to be close to him, to feel connected to him.

It makes me feel less alone. Sometimes.

Smiling, he takes my hand and squeezes it. "I just need to know what else is out there," he says, returning to the main point of this conversation. "Because when we marry, I want it to be forever. I don't want to get a divorce two years later, you know? Can you see where I'm coming from?"

I look down at our joined hands. I know I should say yes or nod, but I can't quite bring myself to do it. His proposal makes me inexplicably sad.

"I'm going to leave," I say, pushing his hand away from mine and getting up from the bed.

"Oh, come on, Anna. Stay," he says. "Don't be like this."

I rub at the wrinkles around my mouth that still haven't entirely gone away. "I need some time before—" I stop speaking when it occurs to me that he's not going to wait until I'm ready to go through with this plan of his. He never asked for my permission. He's already decided. I can be on board, or I can lose him. "I need to think."

Against his continued protests, I leave. In the elevator, I sag against the wall, overwhelmed and on the edge of tears. I take out my phone and type a text message to my closest friends, Rose and Suzie. *Julian just told me he wants us to see other people for a while. He thinks I'm the one he wants to marry, but before he settles down, he wants to be sure. He doesn't want to have regrets.*

It's late, so I don't expect them to answer right away, especially Rose, who's in a different time zone. I just needed to reach out, to feel like I have someone I can go to when things are crashing down around me. To my surprise, my screen instantly lights up with messages.

OMG WTF?! I WILL KICK HIS ASS, Rose says.

WHAT A DICK!!!!! Suzie says.

Their instant outrage on my behalf startles a laugh out of me, and I cradle my phone close. These two are precious to me. That's a bit ironic since we've never even met in person. We connected through social media groups for classical musicians. Rose plays violin for the Toronto Symphony Orchestra. Suzie, cello for the Los Angeles Philharmonic.

I'm glad you two are upset, I tell them. *He acted like he was being so reasonable, and it made me question myself.*

THAT'S NOT REASONABLE, Rose says.

It's not! Suzie agrees. *I can't believe he said that!!!*

The elevator door opens, and I rush through the posh lobby of Julian's building (his parents bought him his condo as a graduation gift when he got his MBA from Stanford's business school). I text as I walk home. *I asked if he was going to sleep around, and he dodged the question. Pretty sure that means sex is on the table. Is it closed-minded of me that I hate that?*

I would not be okay with that at all, Rose says.

Suzie replies, *Me neither!!!!*

I don't know what to do now. Other than, you know, go out and have revenge sex with a bunch of random guys, I say.

I expect them to laugh in response, but instead, the group chat goes eerily still for several moments. Cars pass by, their engines extra loud in the quiet of night. Frowning, I check if I've lost cell reception—there's one tiny bar. I hold my phone up higher just in case that will get me an extra micro-bar of connectivity.

I get a text from Suzie first. *Maybe you should take advantage of this opportunity to see other people.*

I agree with Suz. It would serve him right, adds Rose.

I'm not saying you need to sleep with anyone, but you could turn this around. See if HE is right for YOU. Someone else might be a better fit, Suzie says.

That makes so much sense, Suz. Think about it, Anna, Rose says.

I can't help making a face as I type my response with my thumbs. Meeting new people isn't my favorite. *I haven't dated in five years. I think I forgot how. To be honest, I'm scared.*

Don't be scared! Rose tells me.

Dating can be fun and kind of relaxing, Suzie says. *It's not an audition or anything. You're just seeing if you and this other person are a fit. If you don't like them or something embarrassing happens, you never have to see them again. There's no pressure. Every time I dated a new person, I learned a little more about myself. There's no incentive to try to be someone else, you know what I mean?*

Also, from someone who's done it many times, one-night stands can be empowering. It's how I learned to demand what I want in bed and not be ashamed. 100% recommend, Rose says, adding a winking emoji at the end.

You almost make me regret getting married, Suzie replies.

Rose's advice strikes a chord with me, though I'm not exactly sure what it is that resonates. I know this is one of those conversations that I'll be replaying in my head for days and analyzing from different angles.

My old-fashioned apartment building comes into sight, Victorian rooftops and tiny iron balconies with well-tended planter boxes. Home. Suddenly, I'm aware of how drained I am on every level. Even my thumbs are tired as I type out a last set of messages. *I need to think about this. Just got home. Going to call it a night. Thank you for talking to me. I feel better. Sorry to bother you so late. Love you guys.*

It's no bother. We love you! says Suzie.

Anytime! LOVE YOU! Good night! says Rose.

THREE

Quan

I MIGHT BE AN ADDICT.

A running addict. If my mom caught me doing drugs, she'd chase after me with a clothes hanger—she wouldn't catch me, though. I ran yesterday for three hours, and I'm at it again today even though my left knee's been acting up. I just can't seem to stop. Lately, it's the only thing that keeps my mind off stuff.

When I turn onto my street, my head is calm and the only things I want are a cold drink of water and ice for my knee, but Michael is waiting outside my apartment building. He's got sunglasses on, his hair is perfect, and he looks like he's ready for a fashion shoot. It's kind of disgusting.

"Hey," I say, using the front of my T-shirt to wipe the sweat from my face. "What's going on?" It's a Saturday, and he's always got stuff going on with his wife, Stella. It's weird for him to be here.

Michael pushes his sunglasses to the top of his head and gives me a direct look. "You haven't been picking up, so I started to worry."

"I must have forgotten it on Do Not Disturb again." I pull my phone out of the holder strapped to my arm, and sure enough, there are a bunch of missed calls. "Sorry."

"This isn't like you," Michael says.

"I forgot," I say with a shrug, but I'm purposefully missing the point. I know what he's getting at. I just don't want to talk about it.

He doesn't let me avoid the topic, though. "So, did you hear from the doctor? What did they say?" His face is creased, and I notice now that he's got bags under his eyes.

I guess that's because of me, and I'm sorry for it. He's really tried to be there for me over the past two years. Some things I just have to do alone, though. I squeeze his arm and smile reassuringly. "It's official, I'm good. Completely recovered."

He narrows his eyes. "Are you lying because you don't think I can handle the truth?"

"No, I'm really all better," I say with a laugh. "I'd tell you if I wasn't." Aside from my rickety knee, I've never been healthier. Things could have been much worse, and I know how lucky I am. I'm more grateful than words can describe.

But big life events change people, and the truth is I'm different now. I'm still figuring everything out.

Michael surprises me with a crushing hug. "You motherfucker. You had me so scared." He pulls away, laughs in between deep breaths, and swipes at his eyes, which are suspiciously red. The sight makes my own eyes prick, and we're about to have some kind of emotional man moment when he grimaces and rubs his palms on his pants. "You're all wet and gross."

I smirk, relieved that the intense moment has passed, and barely resist the urge to smother him with my sweaty armpit. Two years ago, I would have done it without hesitation. See? I'm different.

He probably wants to talk, so I sit down on the steps outside my building and motion for him to join me, which he does. For a while, we sit side by side and enjoy the afternoon, the cool air, the rustling of the leaves in the trees that line the street, the occasional passing car. It's kind of like when we were kids and used to sit on the front porch of my house and watch the homeless guy walk by in nothing but a T-shirt. Seriously, why wear a shirt if you're going to leave your dick hanging out?

"I'd invite you up to my place, but it stinks. I think it's my dishes." I haven't done the dishes in . . . I don't know how long. Pretty sure they're growing mold. Recently, I've been eating out a lot due to pure laziness and dish avoidance.

Michael chuckles and shakes his head. "Maybe you should hire a cleaning person."

"Eh." I don't know how to explain that I don't feel like having to deal with a stranger in my apartment. I'm a people person. Strangers don't usually bother me.

"What does your doctor say about dating . . . and other stuff? Are you cleared for that?" Michael asks, casting a carefully neutral glance my way.

I rub the back of my neck as I say, "I've been good to go for a long time. Some guys even get back at it a couple weeks after surgery, but that's kind of extreme. That would hurt, you know?"

"You're good now, though, right?"

"Yeah." More or less.

"So are you seeing people again?" Michael persists.

"Not really." From the look on his face, I know he understands that I really mean "not at all." My body feels personal in a way it never did before. Getting naked with someone was never a big deal in the past. *Sex* was never a big deal. Plus, I was good at it, and that's always a confidence booster. But now I'm scarred and slightly damaged. I'm not what I was.

Michael gives me a long look before he kicks at some rocks on the pavement. "I've thought about how you might be feeling. I can't say I really know, because it's not happening to me. But have you thought about maybe just ripping the Band-Aid off?"

"You mean like stripping down and riding naked through SF on Naked Bike Day?" I ask.

Michael grimaces like he's in pain. "Can you even ride anymore after everything?"

I give him a disgusted look. "You're doing it wrong if you ride sitting on your balls."

He laughs and scrubs a hand wearily over his face. "Sorry, you're right. And no, Naked Bike Day isn't what I meant. I was thinking that maybe, if you're uncomfortable about being with someone again, maybe it would help to just do something really casual that doesn't matter. Like a one-night stand, you know? Just to get the first time over with. And by 'first time,' you know what I mean."

"Yeah, I know. I've been thinking about doing something like that, too." It's just that the idea of it leaves me feeling hollow, which isn't like me. Casual sex has always been my thing. No strings attached. No expectations. No promises. Just fun between consenting adults.

"I have a friend who—"

My whole body cringes, and I don't wait for him to finish before saying, "Thanks, but *no*, thanks. I don't want to be set up with anyone." Least of all Michael's female friends. They try to hide it because he's taken, but they're all in love with him. I don't want to be some weird kind of consolation prize. And what kind of prize would that even be with me like I am? "I know how to meet people."

"But will you actually go out and do it?" Michael asks. "From what I can see, all you do is work and run now."

I shrug. "I'll reinstall my dating apps. It's easy." And kind of boring. It's always the same thing—messaging hot chicks, recycling the same witty lines, arranging a time and place, meeting and flirting and all that, the sex, and then going home alone after.

Michael gives me a skeptical look, and I make an exasperated sound and unlock my phone.

"Here, I'll do it right now. You can watch." I download a bunch of apps, some that I've used before, some that I haven't.

Michael points at one of the apps and arches his eyebrows. "Pretty sure that one's only used by prostitutes and drug dealers now."

"You're shitting me." It's a famous app that everyone was using two years ago.

He shakes his head emphatically. "There's this whole code that they speak to avoid cops and detectives and everything. I wouldn't really recommend that app for you. It'll get awkward. Do you need tips on pickup lines or anything? You're kind of scaring me."

I delete the app and give him an insulted look. "I had cancer, not amnesia. I remember how to have a hookup. And how do you even know about that app? You quit dating before I did."

Michael shrugs, cool as a cucumber. "People tell me things. *You* can tell me things. Anytime. About anything. You know that, right?"

"I know." I release a tight sigh. "And I'm glad you came. I need to move on. This will be good for me. So . . . thanks."

He smiles slightly. "I'm going to go, then. Stella's parents are coming over for dinner, and I haven't gone grocery shopping yet. Unless you want to come?"

"No, thanks," I say quickly. Stella's parents are nice and all, but they're so proper and wholesome that hanging around them always feels like a trip to the principal's office to me. I've spent too much time in principals' offices as it is.

"Let me know how it goes, okay?" Michael asks.

I feel stupid about it, but I give him a thumbs-up.

With a wave good-bye, he heads off. Only when he's disappeared around the corner do I recognize the hollow pang in my chest. I miss him. It's the weekend, nighttime is rolling around, and I'm super aware that I'm all by myself.

I open up one of my old apps and start editing my profile.

FOUR

Anna

THE NEXT MORNING, I AWAKEN ON MY COUCH IN THE SAME exact position as when I collapsed last night, too tired to go the extra distance to my bedroom. I slept like a corpse, and I basically feel like one today. My head aches, and my muscles are sore. It's like I have a hangover even though I missed the fun of actually getting drunk. Yesterday was too much. The looping hell of violin practice. Therapy. Dinner with Julian. The blow job. Our discussion.

Ugh, I'm in an open relationship now. I need to decide if I want to start dating. Groaning, I cover my face with a throw pillow. I should get up and start my day, but I have zero desire to do anything.

My purse vibrates against my thigh, and I plop a limp hand inside and half-heartedly fish for my phone. If my mom is yelling at me about something, I'm going to ignore her until lunchtime. I just can't deal with her right now.

It turns out it's not text messages from my mom. It's a picture of

Rose's fluffy white Persian cat in a pink tutu. She's only sent the picture to me because Suz is a late riser.

What do you think? she asks.

I laugh silently to myself as I reply, *You take your life into your own hands every time you do that to her.*

I know. I'm lucky I still have all my fingers. But she looks so pretty dressed up! she says.

She looks like she's plotting your murder, I tell her.

But she'll do it IN STYLE, she says, pausing briefly before she messages me again. *How are you today?*

I don't have energy to go into it, so I keep things simple. *I'm okay. Still processing. Thanks for asking.*

I really do think you should try dating. I meant what I said about it helping to empower me, she says.

I'm considering it, I reply, and because I don't want everything to be about me, I ask, *Are you exhausted today? You were texting past midnight your time.*

> *Yes, so tired. I couldn't sleep last night. I'm supposed to hear back from the producers for that special project on TV this week.*

I think you're going to hear good news. You're exactly who they need, I say.

> *I hope so! I really, really, really love this piece.*

Envy sparks in my chest at her remark, and I dislike myself for it. I wish I still loved music like she does, that it brought me joy instead of this suffocating pressure. I will be happy for her if this opportunity pans out, though. I'm not a complete monster.

How are you doing on the Richter piece? Any progress? she asks.

I hate talking about my progress on the Richter piece—because there never is any—so I keep my reply short. *Nope. But I'll keep trying anyway. I should get to it.*

Good luck! she says. *One of these days, everything is going to flow right out of you. You're just creatively constipated right now.*

I don't believe her, but I keep my reply light so that she doesn't turn this into a long motivational chat. *I hope so. Have a good one!*

I don't want to, but my bladder forces me to get up and plod to the bathroom. Bad instant coffee and half a bagel later, I drag myself to the secretary desk in the corner of my living room where my black instrument case resides. Rock sits next to the case, his painted smile aimed up at me, and I pet him once in greeting.

"You're such a good boy," I say. "The cutest rock I've ever seen."

His smile doesn't move, of course it doesn't, but I can tell he's pleased with the attention. If he had a tail, he wouldn't be able to control his wag. I recognize that it's possibly a bad sign that I've taken to anthropomorphizing a stone, but there's something about his crooked eyes and mouth that gives him an extra splash of character. After a moment, I can tell he wants me to get to business, and I sigh and focus on the instrument case.

My life is in this box. The best parts. And the worst, too. The highest highs and the lowest lows. Transcendent joy, yearning, ambition, devotion, desperation, anguish. All right here.

This is the ritual: I run my fingertips over the top of the case, undo the latches, and open it up. I retrieve my bow and tighten the horsehairs, apply rosin. I shut my eyes as I breathe the pine scent into my lungs. This is the scent of music to me, pine and dust and wood. I pull my violin out and tune the strings, starting with the A. The discordant sounds relax me. Adjusting the tension of the strings relaxes me. Getting the notes to ring true relaxes me, the familiarity, the everydayness, the illusion of control.

I begin with scales. Critics can say whatever they want about me artistically, but when it comes to my technical abilities, I have always been a strong violinist. It is because of these scales, the fact that I practice them for an hour every day, rain or shine, in sickness and in health. I set my timer and run through my favorite keys, the sharps, flats, majors, minors, the arpeggios, the harmonics. The notes sing from my violin effortlessly, fluidly, as slow or as fast as I want them to.

At the end of the day, however, scales are just patterns. They aren't art. They don't have a soul. A robot can play scales. But music . . .

When the alarm on my phone rings, I turn it off and step over to the music stand that I keep by the French doors leading to my small balcony, which overlooks the street below. The sheet music is sitting there, ready for me, but I don't really need to see it. I memorized the notes long ago. I see them in my sleep most of the time.

The top of page one reads "Untitled for Anna Sun, by Max Richter," and that title alone nearly makes me hyperventilate. There are probably violinists who would commit murder if it would inspire Max to write them something, and yet here I am, letting these pages gather dust in my living room.

I glance at Rock, and his smile looks a little stretched now, a little impatient. He wants me to get on with it.

"Okay, okay," I say. Taking a breath, I straighten my back, settle my violin under my chin, and bring my bow to the strings.

This is the last time I'm starting over.

Only nothing sounds right, and when I get to the sixteenth measure, I know that was all garbage. I'm not playing this with the right amount of feeling. I can *hear* it, and if I can, others will, too. I stop and start back at the beginning.

This is the last time I'm starting over.

But now I sound like I'm trying too hard. That's a horrible criticism to get. Back to the beginning.

This is *really* the last time I'm starting over.

But it isn't. I'm a liar. I start over so many times that when my alarm rings, telling me it's time for lunch, I've lost count of how many restarts I've had. All I know is I'm exhausted and hungry and on the edge of tears.

I put my violin away, but instead of heading to my kitchen to reheat the leftovers of yesterday's leftovers, I slump down to the floor and bury my face in my hands.

I can't keep going like this.

Something is wrong with my mind. I can see it when I take a step back and analyze my actions, but in the moment, when I'm practicing, I can never tell. My desperation to please others deafens me so I can't hear the music the way I used to. I only hear what's wrong. And the compulsion to start over is irresistible.

For that's the only place where true perfection exists—the blank page. Nothing I actually do can compete with the boundless potential of what I *could* do. But if I allow the fear of imperfection to trap me in perpetual beginnings, I'll never create anything again. Am I even an artist, then? What is my purpose, then?

I have to make a change. I have to *do* something and take control of this situation, or I'll be stuck in this hell forever.

Jennifer said I need to stop masking and people pleasing, that I should start with small things, in a safe environment. Her suggestion that I try it with family, however, is ridiculous. Family is *not* safe. Not for me. Tough love is brutally honest and hurts you to help you. Tough love cuts you when you're already bruised and berates you when you don't heal faster.

If I'm going to stop people pleasing, I need to try it with the very opposite of family, which is . . . complete strangers.

Pieces click into place in my mind one after the other, like pin tumblers in a lock when the proper key is inserted. Stop masking. Stop people pleasing. Revenge on Julian. Learn who I am. Self-empowerment.

Reckless resolve grips me, and I push myself off the floor and march into my bedroom to yank open my closet door. I have fifteen different black dresses in here, no low necklines, no high hems, perfectly decent dresses for a concert stage. I shove them aside and look for something that will show off my cleavage and thighs.

When I see the red dress, I go still. I purchased it for a Valentine's Day that Julian wasn't here to celebrate with me. The way things are going, I'll probably never get the chance to wear it for him. I'm not sure I want to anymore.

But I can wear it for me.

I take off my exercise clothes from yesterday that I've never actually exercised in and step into the dress. It's tighter than when I tried it on last, but it still fits. When I turn around, my eyes widen at how my butt has grown. A pity. Julian would love this, though he wouldn't approve of my methods. I didn't drink protein shakes and spend hours in the gym doing donkey kicks and squats. These curves are made of Cheetos.

I reach under my arm and yank at the price tag until the plastic snaps. I *will* wear this dress out. Maybe not today. But soon.

After retrieving my phone, I search the App Store for "dating apps" and install the top three.

FIVE

Quan

IT'S FRIDAY NIGHT, AND I'M UNWINDING FROM A LONG WEEK, with an entire pizza to myself, a cold beer, and this documentary about an octopus. I haven't had a social life in two years, so I've basically watched all of Netflix by now, even that series about the samurai assassin who gets paid to kill a cat. Lucky for me, the ocean fascinates me, and I think octopuses are cool.

But when the burned-out filmmaker befriends the octopus and they shake hand and tentacle, I don't know, I'm . . . sad. I find myself scrolling through the dating apps that I neglected all week. I've been matched with a bunch of people.

Tammy. Light hair, dark eyes, great smile, great body. She wants to have a big family, loves craft beer, and is training to be a special-ed teacher. I sigh. She's perfect—if I'm looking for a girlfriend. Which I'm not. Pass.

Naomi. Gorgeous brown eyes, mysterious smile, curves for days. A business executive who dreams of traveling the world with a special someone. I like everything about her, but that has serious relationship written all over it. Pass.

Sara looks like an honest-to-God Barbie doll and just wants a fun time. My interest is definitely piqued. Until I read further and see she's considering adding a seventh man to her harem. I've tried some wild shit in my day, but an eight-person orgy is not what I had in mind for my first time back, or ever, to be honest. Pass.

Savannah, pass. Ingrid, pass. Jenny, pass. Murphy? Wow, okay, Murphy is drop-dead gorgeous, volunteers at nursing homes, and—the kicker—is saving their virginity for true love. Pass.

Naya. Fran. Penelope. Pass. Pass. Pass.

I'm thinking I need to switch apps or narrow my search criteria when I come across Anna. Her picture is so sweet that I almost skip her on principle, but I keep looking because I can't help myself. She's got a self-conscious smile and dark eyes that manage to be soft yet penetrating. They draw me in.

In her profile, she says, "Looking to spend an uncomplicated evening with someone nice. Just one night, please." Under occupation and hobbies, it says, "Not applicable."

Her picture and profile seem so out of tune that I look back and forth a bunch of times, trying to understand how they belong to the same person. Based on her photograph, I'd say she's the serial monogamist type who should be looking for flowers and forever, not a meaningless hookup.

Maybe she's going through some life stuff and just wants to blow off steam. I can appreciate that. It's not so different from what I'm trying to achieve.

I shake my head at myself as I tap on the button to message her privately. With a profile like that, she's probably got hundreds of messages in her inbox already. I'm not the kind of guy who gives up without trying, though, so I give myself a moment to think, decide honesty is best, and start typing.

> Hey Anna,
>
> I like how direct you are. Right now I'm eating pizza and watching the last thing on Netflix that I haven't seen before. Free to talk if you want.
>
> Q

I send the message, turn my phone's screen off, and toss it onto the couch next to me. I'm not going to sit around holding my breath for her to respond to me. Instead, I bite into a fresh slice of everything pizza and switch my attention to the TV, where the octopus is getting chased by a small stripy shark. She jumps out of the water, crawls over land—how boss is that?—and jumps back in, only for the shark to pick up where they left off. I'm so absorbed by the scene that I only notice the notification on my phone when I reach for my beer.

I wipe my hands and mouth on a haphazardly torn sheet of paper towel and pick up my phone. I have a message on the app.

> Hi Q,
>
> What are you watching?
>
> A

I look up at the screen just as the shark bites the octopus and shakes her from side to side, and I have to laugh, even though I feel horrible for the octopus. A documentary about a dude and an octopus, lol, I tell her, and yeah, maybe my face heats up a little. It would be cooler if I was watching *Star Wars* or *Deadpool* or something.

I loved that one! I watched it twice, she admits, and I can't help grinning. That was the last thing I expected her to say.

> This octopus rocks but I think the shark is going to eat more than just her leg this time.

Keep watching, she says.

So I do, and then I reply, I'm so impressed.

> Right? She's amazing. Maybe I need to watch a third time.

I hesitate a couple of seconds before pausing the video and suggesting, I'm at 1:05 if you want to watch the end with me.

She surprises me by saying, Okay. She even adds a smiley face.

We go through the process of syncing our videos, and soon we're watching together, separately. It's a weird experience for me. Kind of dorky—wait, *very* dorky. Let's not forget what we're watching here. Normally, people in our situation would be flirting right now. There'd be sexual innuendo, maybe even dirty photos. But I think I like this.

Oh, I love this part, she says.

When I see what she's talking about, I agree. She's playing with the fish, not even trying to eat them. I didn't know an octopus could be so cute.

Haha! Me neither, she replies, and I'm grinning all over again.

We continue this back-and-forth, and before long, the documentary is over and I kind of wish it wasn't.

Isn't that such a bittersweet ending? she asks.

Yeah, but it's a good ending, I say.

We both go quiet then, and I take a breath before asking, Do you want to trade phone numbers and take this off the app?

She doesn't reply right away, and I fidget as I wait. I'm nervous, I realize. I like this weird octopus-loving girl.

Yes, please. This interface is so confusing. I accidentally sent octopus comments to other people while we were watching, she says.

The crack of my laughter is loud in my apartment, even as something uncomfortable pushes at my chest at the idea that she's talking to other guys. Their responses were probably awesome.

> They were. One guy said he didn't sign up for this.
> The other said, "Baby, I only have two hands, but I'll
> use my feet if you want." I laughed so hard that
> someone's dog started barking outside.

A second later, she sends me her number, and I feel like I won the lottery. I don't think she gave her number to that other dude, even though he's willing to get fancy with his feet.

Off app, I text her the question, *Do you want to text or call?*

There's a pause before she replies, *Do you have a preference?*

I want to hear your voice, I answer.

Okay, she says.

But when I call her, the phone only rings a few times before the call disconnects.

Sorry, I'm nervous, she texts.

I'm cool texting. No worries, Anna. In the back of my head, I wonder if she's really a middle-aged man catfishing me from his mom's basement in his underwear. My gut tells me she's real, though.

Thank you. I've never done this before, she says.

Hey, it's been a long time since I've dated and stuff, so I feel a little awkward too, I admit.

Were you in a serious relationship too? she asks.

So that's it. She's coming out of a serious relationship and looking for rebound sex. I completely get it.

Nah, I had some health issues, needed surgery. Don't worry, I'm better now, I tell her, hoping she thinks "health issues" and "surgery" mean a torn ACL or something like that.

I'm glad you're better. She adds another smiley face, and it's stupid of me, but it makes me happy.

Thanks, I say.

So what do we do now? she asks.

> *Whatever you want, but usually trading phone numbers means we're planning to meet up soon.*

Do you want to meet tonight? she asks.

My eyes widen at her message. It's only a little past nine o'clock, but it feels too late and too soon at the same time. Late because we only have one night, and tonight is half over. Soon because I only just met her, and it's almost good-bye for good. *How about tomorrow night?*

Sure, that works for me, she says.

I send her a link to a local bar. *This place at 7?*

> *Sounds good!*

Great, I reply, and after a few seconds, I send her a smiley face.

We fall silent then. I want to keep talking to her, watch another movie, even if it's this weird documentary again, but I don't want to be annoying. And I don't want to act like this is more than it is. That's the beauty of it—that it's nothing.

It takes restraint, but I don't message her again all night.

SIX

Anna

THE FIRST THING I DO WHEN I WAKE UP SATURDAY MORNING IS check my phone for messages from him.

There aren't any. Of course there aren't. I'm not surprised. Really, I'm relieved. But I'm a little disappointed, too. Just the tiniest bit.

Still lying in bed, I read over our conversation from last night. That same giddy excitement fills my chest, and I smile as I bite my lip.

I did it. I met someone online, we talked, and then we set up a date. If I'm being honest with myself, it was kind of nice. He likes octopi! Better than that, I was able to be myself. I didn't pretend. For once, I feel like I'm in control of my life. It's a heady experience.

It took me forever to fall asleep last night because my mind wouldn't stop. I should be dragging today, but I'm buzzing with nervous energy instead. The hours fly by.

Halfway through my practice time, when I find myself starting over again and again just like usual, I impulsively set the Richter piece aside and decide to try something else, like Jennifer suggested. Clearing my mind and taking a series of deep breaths, I set my bow to the strings and let the opening notes of Vaughan Williams' "The Lark Ascending" sing.

This is my dad's favorite song. He requests I play it on his birthday and whenever we have family events or his friends are over, so the notes are deeply ingrained in my muscle memory. I'm not sure which pleases him more—the music itself or showing me off to people. It doesn't really matter to me. I just like making him happy.

The music slowly pours from my violin, fluttering erratically upward on changing currents of air. It transports me, so sweetly passionate that for a moment I get caught up in it. I forget time, I forget *me*. There's only this beautiful feeling of soaring over vast fields of open green. And I realize I'm playing, truly playing.

This is the reason I breathe.

I hear it then. My timing is just a hair off. It's been so long since I've played this song that my bow work is a bit sloppy. I can do better.

So I start over. It's such a signature piece that if it isn't just so, critics can be vicious. I won't give them an opening. I can outmaneuver them. I can be *more* vicious to myself than they are, and in so doing, I will win.

Art is war.

It's still not quite right, so I start over just one more time. I try harder to get the timing exact. And I hit it. The notes trill and climb like small wings beating on updrafts of wind. Only to snag. Not enough emphasis in that part.

I start over.

And I start over.

And I start over.

Until the alarm on my phone pulls me out, and I turn it off and stare blankly about the room. I'm back where I started. At the beginning. My throat aches, but I swallow the tightness away.

There was that brief moment when the music sang to me and I forgot to listen to the voices in my head. That's something.

I'm so close to beating this. I can feel it. The solution is right there. I can *see* it. If I can just wrap my fingers around it, I will unlock my mind, and everything will go back to how it used to be.

Determined, I put my violin away and prepare to battle in a different manner. I'm going to have a date tonight. I'm going to flirt. I'm going to have fun. I'm not going to torture myself by watching his reactions and trying to be what he wants. Inevitably, because I'm me, I will embarrass myself. And I'm going to try my hardest not to care about any of it. I have no reason to care—not beyond basic human decency, at any rate. This man is completely wrong for me. I have no intention of ever seeing him again. I don't need his respect. I don't need his approval. I don't need his love.

And that makes him perfect. With him, I will experiment with being brave.

I shower and shave my legs, brush my teeth, do all the hygiene things, and put on makeup and fix my hair, like I'm preparing for an important concert. I suppose tonight will be a concert of sorts, one where my performance is based entirely on improvisation. After putting on the red dress and stepping into my nicest high heels, I take a picture of myself in the mirror and send it to Rose and Suzie, along with the message *Going on a date. Wish me luck.*

Suzie replies first this time. *OMG, you look great! Have fun!*

WHAT?! WHO IS HE? WHAT DOES HE LOOK LIKE? TELL US EVERYTHING!!!!! Rose demands.

I smile with dry lips as I type, *Gotta go. So nervous I could barf. I'll tell you about it later.*

With that, I drop my phone into my purse and venture beyond the security of my apartment. I make a detour to the pharmacy, where my merchandise is confusingly located in between ovulation kits and men's diapers and the high school–aged kid at the cash register is too embarrassed to look at me as he rings up my purchase. Still, I arrive at the bar early enough to grab the last open booth with a view of the street.

I text him, *At the bar. Last booth on the right*, and then I settle in to wait. The bar has a rugged feel, with old barrels and photographs of farms decorating the walls. It's fairly busy, but the music isn't too loud and the lighting is comfortable. It's pretty easy to pretend confidence and ignore my nerves.

Through the window, I see a motorcycle pull up to the curb. The rider climbs off, pockets his gloves, and removes his helmet, revealing a cleanly shaven scalp that few men can pull off. It works for him, though. Together with his close-fitting motorcycle jacket, black pants, boots, and active build, he looks like a Marvel action hero—or villain. There's an undeniable edginess to him, something just a bit dangerous. Or maybe a lot dangerous. It's in the smooth way he moves, the strong but swift lines of his body, the air of steadiness about him.

My entire being goes still as recognition hits me. It's him. He's not just a profile on a website. That badass tattooed guy in the picture, the one who I thought was perfectly discardable because he's so far from being suitable for me. He's a real person with a life and a past and feelings. And he's here.

As I watch, he clips his helmet to the back of his bike. Close to another helmet that's strapped to the far end of the seat. Two helmets. It looks like he brought one for me.

For whatever reason, that sends a jolt of pure panic to my chest.

My anxiety grows when he digs his phone from his pocket, taps out a quick message, and my own phone, which is sitting faceup on the table, illuminates with the words, *Just got here.*

My muscles tense, and pinpricks of sensation wash over my skin. I tell myself this is just a meaningless date, a one-night stand. People do this all the time.

The problem is I don't know if *I* can do this. What if in trying to be true to myself, I'm unkind to him? He looks tough, but that doesn't mean he's made of stone. What if I hurt him?

When he disappears toward the front doors of the bar, this feeling of wrongness intensifies. It blows out of proportion. It explodes.

I can't control myself. I gather my things. And I run. There isn't a line for the bathroom, so I don't need to wait to lock myself in one of the stalls. Sitting on the toilet and hugging my phone and purse to my chest, I rock back and forth. I tap my teeth together, comforted by the feel of it. My face burns. There's a roaring in my ears.

My phone buzzes with messages, but I don't look. I don't want to see. I just want him to go away, so I can go home and pretend this never happened. I need to find a different way to solve my problem, but I'll do it later, when I can think.

I wait, counting seconds in my head. A minute goes by. Another. I lose track of my counting—I've never been good at remembering numbers—so I start back at one and simply focus on counting to sixty again and again.

When a good amount of time has passed and I get another text message, I'm calm enough to look at my phone.

Hey, I think I'm at the table is his first message.

Then: *Are you okay?*

Followed by: *I guess something came up.*

His most recent message says, *I'm heading out. Worried about you.*

I cover my eyes with a palm. Why does he have to be so nice? This would be easier if he was more of an asshole. Relieved, and guilty about it, I hurry from the bathroom.

And collide with him.

Firm chest. Solid body. Warm. Alive. Real.

This is horrible. Absolutely horrible.

His hands wrap around my upper arms for an instant as he puts space between us, and the shock of his touch reverberates through me.

"Hey," he says, his expression blank with surprise.

My lips form the word *hey*, but my vocal chords refuse to make a sound. His throat is directly at my eye level, and I'm staring straight at the swirling calligraphy inked into his skin.

Tattoos.

On his neck.

Neck tattoos.

I knew that he had lots of tattoos, but somehow it's different seeing him—*them*—in person. Classical musicians don't get tattooed like this. Or have shaved heads and ride motorcycles and look like sexy villains. None that I know, anyway. One probably exists somewhere. Part of me thought it would be an adventure to try something new and be with a guy like this tonight.

But this doesn't feel like an adventure.

This feels terrifying.

He's nothing like Julian, and Julian is all I've ever known.

"I was just going to . . ." He points at the door to the men's room, right next to the women's room, and his eyes twinkle as his lips curve into a smile, like someone's just told him a secret.

My frazzled brain malfunctions, and I can't catch my breath. He's disastrously gorgeous when he smiles. Something wonderful radiates from the heart of him, realigning the features of his rough exterior and making him beautiful.

"Have you been in there all this time?" he asks.

Too dazed to come up with a suitable lie, I confess, "I was scared."

His amusement immediately melts away to be replaced with concern. "Of me?"

"No, not of you, not exactly." In an effort to make him understand, words tumble rapidly from my mouth as I explain, "I've never done this before and I had all these ambitious plans but then I saw you and I started to worry I was taking advantage of you and I don't want to hurt you because you're so nice and—"

His expression softens with understanding, and he squeezes one of my hands in his. The sensation is so distracting that I completely forget what I was saying.

"Do you want to leave this place?" he asks.

"Yes," I say, so relieved that tears prick at my eyes. More than anything right now, I want to go home.

"Let's go, then." Holding my hand, he leads me through the people and out of the bar.

Outside, cool fresh air envelops me. It's less chaotic, and some of the tension leaks from me. I wouldn't say I'm relaxed, though. I'm still stressed halfway to death.

"I'm going to go," I say as I let go of his hand and edge away from him, itching to put everything here behind me. "I'm really sorry. I hope you have better luck with someone else."

He takes in the movement of my feet on the pavement and then searches my face intently. "We could try again. But only if you want."

"You'd do that?" I ask, unable to keep the incredulity from my voice. "I just had a panic attack and hid from you in the bathroom for half an hour. You should never want to see me again."

He stuffs his hands in his pockets and shrugs. "Just because something isn't perfect doesn't mean we need to throw it away. Plus, tonight's barely started."

His words catch me off guard, and I stare at him for a moment. I need to run, to escape, to crumple up tonight like a ruined sketch and start with a fresh sheet. And he's telling me not to. Worse than that, he makes perfect sense. And he's smiling again, taking my breath away and making me stupid.

Angry discomfort claws through me, and I hate his smile for how much I like it. I know it's illogical. I know it's cowardly. But I back away from him farther, shaking my head.

"I'm sorry, but I just . . . can't. I'm really so sorry," I say, and I hurry away so I don't have to see his disappointment.

The journey back to my place goes by in an anxious blur, and when I finally shut myself in my apartment, I take my high heels off and carelessly toss them aside on my way to the bathroom. I peel the red dress off and step into the shower, even though I showered a few hours ago. That's the routine after I've been out—unless I simply don't have the energy.

As I wash the makeup off my face and rinse the product out of my hair, I grimace at myself. What an abysmal waste. I should be at the bar right now drinking and flirting and being the most authentic version of myself—not to mention preparing to have life-altering adventure sex with an inappropriate yet exceedingly appealing man.

But I'm not. I'm home, where I'm safe. When I curl up on the couch in my pajamas and ugly fluffy bathrobe, I'm so relieved it's disgusting.

I'm also very much alone, and my apartment feels emptier and colder than it ever has before. Because I need a connection to others, no matter how slim, I get my phone. Surprisingly, I have two messages from Quan.

> *Hey, I hope you're ok.*
> *Did you make it back in one piece?*

Biting the inside of my cheek, I reply, *At home. I feel so horrible that I did this to you. Thank you for checking up on me.*

Don't feel bad. You looked like you were having a rough time. I don't really get it, but I get it, if you know what I mean, he says.

Against all odds, I find myself laughing. *I don't know what you mean.*

> *I mean I don't know exactly what you're going*
> *through, but I know there's something and I'm not*
> *taking it personal.*

Something about his words makes my eyes water with tears even as I smile down at my phone. I'm trying to figure out what to say in response when I get another message from him.

> *I'm grabbing Mexican for dinner. What are you*
> *having?*

The same, I say, but I'm not excited about it. It's the last quarter of a giant super burrito that I've been slowly consuming over the past week. I'd say there's a fifty-fifty chance it'll give me stomach cramps, but I hate to waste food and there's no way I'm leaving my apartment again today—unless there's a fire, or a puppy stranded in the middle of the street with a truck barreling toward it, or a family emergency, something like that.

I'll be home in about 30. Want to watch something with me tonight? he asks.

I cover my mouth as I process his unexpected invitation. It doesn't make sense to me. But I like it. A lot. I can't go out tonight, but I *can* do this.

I don't really understand why you want to stay in with me, I tell him.

Why do you say that? he asks.

> *Because you're . . . you. I saw you. You're extremely attractive and good with people. If you go to a club or somewhere like that, you'll have a date in minutes. Isn't that what you're looking for?*

I think I could say the same about you, he says with a winking emoji.

I'm NOT good with people, I reply, pressing the send button with an extra-hard jab of my thumb. After what happened at the bar, that's glaringly obvious. I don't think I'm "extremely attractive" either, but I know from past experience that pointing that out will just make him insist otherwise and I don't have the patience for that nonsense. Objectively speaking, I'm average in the looks department, and I dislike people lying to me about it. If someone's going to lie to make others feel good, it better be me.

Scratch that, I'm not supposed to do that anymore either.

You don't think it's possible that I get cold feet too? he asks.

I frown at the phone in my hands. I forgot about his health issues and surgery. He didn't look injured in any way at the bar. He looked like a man in his prime. It's difficult to wrap my mind around the idea that he might not be as confident as he seems.

I guess it IS hard for me to believe that you can be anything like me. We're so different, I say.

Not that different. We can watch that Our Planet documentary. It looks good, he suggests.

I liked that one a lot.

Lol, have you seen all the documentaries? he asks.

Yes, but I don't mind rewatching them. Then, after a short hesitation, I add, *We can watch something else if you want.*

Is this a yes to watching nerdy TV with me tonight?

Trying not to smile, and failing, I reply, *Yes*.

SEVEN

Quan

"WHOA, WHOA, WHOA," I SAY AS I JUMP IN BETWEEN THE TWO tinies whacking each other to death in the middle of the kendo studio and pull them apart, getting hit several times in the process myself. "Run after you strike. None of this standing and bashing. If these were real swords, you'd both be armless."

On the other side of the studio, Michael is supposed to be overseeing the other students, but he's watching me and laughing his ass off.

The bigger of the kids next to me, a seven-year-old, calls out, "Yes, sir," and backs away.

The smaller one, only five, totters around and tries to lunge at the big one, his sword poised to continue whacking. I can't help laughing as I yank him back and set him the required distance away from his opponent. He's got a lot of attitude, this dude, and it's stinking cute, especially because he's wearing his older brother's hand-me-down kendo gear and looks like Dark Helmet from *Spaceballs*.

I get their match started again, and they do make small improvements. It's still messy as hell, though—and bloodthirsty. But what can you expect when they're so small? Luckily, they wear enough armor that it's next to impossible to get hurt.

When it's time, I call an end to the sparring, and the kids back away from each other to form two neat rows, switch their wooden swords to their left hands in a resting position, bow, and shake hands like little warriors. We go through the closing rituals for class, and as the studio is emptying out, Michael punches me lightly on the arm.

"Good to see you here," he says. "It's been a while."

I unlace my helmet and pull it off. Then I untie the sweaty bandana from my head and stuff it inside my helmet. "It's good to be back. I didn't realize how much I missed this." And the kids specifically.

My family and friends all know about me being sick and everything, because I made the mistake of telling my sister, Vy, who told my mom, who then told literally everyone she knows. For the longest time, they treated me like I was two steps from dying. They still treat me different, like I'm made of glass or some shit—my mom is the worst. But these kids, they don't care. When I showed up this morning, they hog-piled me. I loved that.

This morning was good, and I know I'll be coming back to lead more Saturday classes. If I can wake up in time. I can't help cracking a big yawn as I untie the laces to my chest protector and shrug the heavy weight off my shoulders.

"You look tired. Up late last night?" Michael asks with careful casualness.

"Yeah. Didn't sleep until two something." The studio door shuts behind the last kids, so I take my uniform off and pull on a faded T-shirt and an old pair of jeans.

As Michael does the same, he arches his eyebrows at me. "Did you go out? With *someone*?"

I shake my head, not sure how to explain last night. "Not really. I was texting."

"Texting who?"

Busy packing my gear away, I say, "A girl. I met her on one of the apps."

He doesn't say anything right away, so I glance up at him and find him nodding with an impressed expression on his face. "Cool."

"It's not like that, so you can stop looking all pleased with yourself," I grumble.

"What's it like, then?" he asks.

"We tried to meet up for a one-night stand, but she panicked at the last second because she hasn't done it before. So we just ended up texting and watching TV together."

That same impressed look from before covers his face. "What did you talk about? And what did you watch?"

I duck my head as I admit, "She likes nature documentaries."

"*You* watched nature documentaries?" he asks with wide eyes.

I pick up one of his discarded gloves and throw it at him. "Yeah, I watched them. They were interesting. I'll probably watch more."

He catches the glove easily and laughs. "Especially if she watches with you."

"I don't even know if I'll see her again."

"You liked her, though?" he asks.

I shrug. "Yeah." I keep my tone light like it's not a big deal, because it's not. I know there's nothing going on between us. But I do really like her. Last night was a little awkward, especially the part where I waited for her at the bar for half an hour, but texting about random stuff and watching nerdy TV was good. There wasn't any pressure. Things flowed easily. I laughed a lot. It wasn't the reintroduction to dating that I was looking for, but truthfully, I think it's better.

Michael gives me a knowing look. "You guys are going to meet again. I bet you a hundred bucks."

I'm about to say something sarcastic when my phone starts buzzing repeatedly from inside my pocket. I dig it out, expecting it to be my mom, but the screen says *Anna*.

She's calling me. Not texting, but *calling*.

The knowledge that she felt comfortable enough to take this step makes my chest light up.

"Shit, is that her?" Michael asks, rushing over to peer at my phone over my shoulder. "Hurry up and answer."

I draw in a quick breath and exhale through my lips before accepting the call and bringing the phone to my ear. "Hey, Anna."

"Hi," she says, sounding shy and awkward and entirely like herself.

I shouldn't, but I break into a huge grin. "What's up?" Michael is watching me with pure delight, so I turn around to get some privacy from his nosy eyes.

"I was wondering if you wanted to try again tonight? Maybe at my place?" she asks.

"Yeah, that would be great. Should I bring anything? I can pick up takeout," I offer.

"Is that safe with your motorcycle?"

I laugh. "I have a car, too."

"Well, I was thinking we could cook something, so it's really not necessary. I'm usually better when I have something to do, and I'm okay in the kitchen as long as I don't have to touch raw meat. It's slimy." She sounds so tortured that I can't help laughing again.

"Are you a vegetarian, Anna?"

"No, but I don't eat a whole ton of meat."

"Because it's better for the planet," I guess.

"Because it's better for the planet," she confirms, and I can tell from her voice that she's smiling. "Are you okay with pasta? And mushrooms? And white wine sauce?"

Grinning, I say, "Yeah, I like pasta and mushrooms and white wine sauce."

"Does seven work for you tonight?"

"That's perfect."

"Great, I'll see you then," she says on a relieved breath. "I'll text you my address. When you get here, buzz me in apartment 3A, and I'll let you up."

"Got it, looking forward to it."

I expect her to say good-bye and hang up, but instead she says, "Me, too."

I smile so hard my face hurts. "Bye, Anna."

"Bye, Quan."

The line finally disconnects, and when I turn around, there's such glee on Michael's face that I pick up his second glove and chuck it at him. "Stop looking at me like that."

He's so busy smirking that the glove hits his chest and falls to the ground by his feet without getting his attention. "You *really* like her."

"We're just going to hook up and then we'll be done. This isn't a thing," I say reasonably.

"Okay," he says, but he's still smirking and I know he doesn't believe it for a second. He thinks I've met someone special, when I haven't.

I mean, she *is* special. But she's not *my* someone special.

I'm sure of this.

Mostly sure.

To change the subject, I open up an email that I've been debating sharing with him and hand him my phone. "Check this out. I got this email yesterday."

He reads out loud under his breath as his eyes dart across the screen, "Hi, Quan, congratulations on MLA's recent Jennifer Garner endorsement on social media! Her kids look adorably fabulous in your clothes. My wife ordered those same dresses for our twins. I asked around and was told you guys are looking for funding to take things to the next level. Let's set up a call. Angèlique Ikande, of LVMH Acquisitions." Frowning, he looks up from the phone and asks, "That's not the LV that I'm thinking, is it?"

"Pretty sure it is," I say.

"*Louis Vuitton*?" he asks, his eyes opened wider than I've ever seen.

"The one and only." I try to keep my smile from growing too big. This could be nothing. It could also be the break of a lifetime for a small company like ours. I've been trying my best not to get too excited. "The call is next Friday. I was going to wait until after the call to tell you—I'll know more then—but I figured if I were you, I'd want to know."

"I can't even . . ." Michael gives me back my phone and slumps against the wall, looking dazed. "But what does it mean if they acquire us? Will they change our name? Will they even keep you and me?"

"I can't imagine any scenario where they wouldn't keep you," I say, shaking my head at him in amusement. I'm not worried about myself, either. I'm no fashion designer, but Michael Larsen Apparel wouldn't be where it is today without me. I built the team at MLA from the ground up, formed the valuable connections with our suppliers, guided our marketing and PR efforts. When Michael lets me, I steer his designs in more profitable directions. We did this together. No matter how this goes, I'm fucking proud of us. "And I think our brand—MLA and your name—has value, so they wouldn't mess with it. What usually happens is they buy owners out for a certain amount, but we stay to lead the company under contract. The best thing is they're an enormous multinational company and they have the connections and resources to really get MLA out there. We could end up in malls and department stores worldwide, instead of selling mostly online and domestically like we do now."

Wide-eyed and slack-jawed, Michael rubs his face. After a moment, the first sign of a smile breaks through. "I can't wait to tell Stella. She's going to have a zillion questions. You should brace yourself."

I laugh, but I also make a mental note to be extra detail oriented and meticulous with everything LVMH related—*if* anything LVMH related happens. Because Stella *will* ask a ton of questions in that case, and as a genius numbers person, she tends to ask people things that make them squirm if they don't know their shit. "Well, all I know is what's in the email, so tell her to wait."

Michael gives me a thumbs-up and then focuses on packing up his gear, gloves inside the helmet, helmet inside the chest armor, everything wrapped up with the heavy fabric guard that ties around the waist. He makes sure the front flap, which is embroidered with the name of our school and his last name, is centered and facing outward.

When I'm done packing up my own stuff, I put my gear on the shelf in its assigned spot, and there our names are, side by side, LARSEN and DIEP, just like when our moms signed us up for lessons when we were in kindergarten. A lot has changed since then—I'm hardly the same person that I used to be, he isn't either—but it's still me and him. I think it's always going to be this way, and the knowledge is deeply, deeply comforting.

EIGHT

Anna

VIOLIN, PRACTICED (I PLAYED IN CIRCLES AGAIN). APARTMENT, cleaned (even my bathtub). Groceries, purchased. White wine, chilling in the freezer. Me, freshly showered and wearing a black wrap dress. Condoms, in my nightstand drawer.

Now I wait.

I'm too jittery to sit still, so I pace back and forth across my living room. Rock watches me quietly, and after several passes, I stop to pet him, hoping it'll calm me down.

"We're having a visitor tonight," I tell him.

He looks surprised by the news.

"We really are," I say. "Julian sent me a weird message today. What did it say?" I pull my phone out of my dress's pocket and find his message, so I can read it out loud: "Can't stop thinking about you. Last night was amazing. Same time, same place, next week?"

Rock's eyes bulge, and his smiling mouth looks more like a horrified grimace.

"That was my reaction, too. I told him that he probably messaged the wrong person, and he apologized right away, saying that it's not what it looks like—which I doubt. I'm not stupid. He said he misses me and asked if I want to meet up for lunch one of these days. I said I was busy and would catch up later. And then I called Quan and invited him over. It seemed like the perfect thing to do at the time, but now . . ." I sigh. "I'm so nervous."

Rock's smile turns apologetic, and I pat him on the head again before I hug my arms to my chest and get back to pacing. Fourteen strides there, fourteen strides back. Repeat.

When I notice I'm tapping my top teeth against my bottom teeth, I stretch out my jaw and then massage it. My dentist says if I don't stop, I'm going to wear down all the bone in my jaw and lose my teeth. There's a horrible irony there. During my childhood, I began tapping my teeth as an alternative to tapping my fingers, which is distracting and annoys people. Tapping my teeth, on the other hand, is silent and invisible. It can't harm anyone. Except for me, apparently.

I'm mid-step, halfway across the room, when the intercom buzzes. My heart squeezes painfully as adrenaline shoots through my body, and I race to the front door and hit the talk button on the intercom.

"Hello?" I say, wincing at how trembly and embarrassingly pathetic my voice sounds.

There's a short pause before he says, "Are you okay, Anna? We don't have to do this. We can rain-check or just watch TV again."

I worry my bottom lip as I internally debate this. I'm extremely tempted to take the out he's offered. But I need to do this.

It's time.

I hit the button that allows him to enter the building. "Come on up."

In the seconds that follow, disjointed thoughts flit through my head. I need to flirt. I need to have fun. I need to show Julian. I need to not care what people think. I need to overcome my insecurities. I want to be empowered, just like Rose described.

A knock sounds on my door. I'm expecting it, but I still flinch. My heart ramps up to warp speed, and my skin goes numb. I look through the peephole. Yes, it's him. One breath in. One breath out.

I open the door.

He's not wearing his motorcycle jacket tonight, just a graphic T-shirt, faded blue jeans, and tattoos. They're plain, unremarkable clothes, and I like that he didn't dress up. I don't want him trying to impress me. Even so, I can't help noticing how good he looks. I appreciate the way the fabric stretches over his chest and the swells of his biceps, the way his pants hang on his hips and fit his strong legs. There's a physicality to him that I'd find fascinating if I weren't panicked out of my wits.

Holding out a white cardboard box toward me, he starts to smile, but it fades into a frown as he gets a good look at me. "Are you sure you're okay? You're . . . greenish."

A slightly hysterical laugh bubbles out of me, and I cover my cheeks with my hands. "Sexy green, or scary green?"

He laughs, though his eyes are concerned. "Is 'sexy green' a thing?"

"I won't judge you if you think it is," I say, trying to laugh and failing. A wave of nausea has me breathing in through my nose and out through my mouth. Still, I put on a bright smile and step aside, opening the door invitingly. "Please, come in."

Once he comes inside, I accept the white box from him and, after hesitating a second, set it on the end table by the couch and welcome him with a hug. That seems like the right thing to do, given what we're planning to do later tonight. But then I'm in his arms, and it's not the casual greeting I meant it to be. I haven't been hugged, really hugged, in forever, and I can't help the broken sound that escapes my throat when he holds me.

"You're shaking," he whispers. "What's wrong?"

I don't have the faintest clue how to answer him, so I bury my face against his chest. I expect him to let me go, but his arms tighten around me instead, hard but not hurting. The embrace reaches deep into my bones, pure heaven, and I lean into him. Gradually, my muscles relax and my stomach unknots. My head spins in relief.

For long minutes, we stand there in each other's arms. He smells really good, like soap with the slightest hint of sandalwood. The steady beating of his heart comforts me.

"How are you doing?" he asks in a low voice.

"Better," I say, but I don't push away from him just yet. "This is nice."

His chest rumbles on a chuckle. "I'm an expert hugger."

I burrow closer, pressing my forehead to his neck. "You really are."

"My brother has Asperger's, and when we were little, he used to get overwhelmed from school and the bullies there. Hugging was the only thing that helped, so I got good at it," he says.

I peer up at him. "Kids can be the worst." I don't have a good understanding of what Asperger's is, but I do know what it's like to be teased. It's part of why I go to such great pains to fit in and earn people's approval.

"Those kids were," he agrees.

"Did you fight them?" I ask, though I suspect I already know.

His face darkens. "I did. It didn't always end well for me because there were a lot of them, and some were older. But you do what you gotta." He must see how sad that makes me because he smiles encouragingly and runs his hand up and down my back in a soothing motion. "Don't feel bad. I got better eventually. By the time my brother started high school, I was kind of a badass, and kids mostly knew to leave my family alone."

My mind opens as I put facts together and connect dots. Quan's kindness and rough exterior make perfect sense to me now. They're not contradictory.

I wish I'd had someone like him in my life when I was younger.

I'm about to say something to that effect when he presses his lips to my temple. It's not sexy, not demanding in any way. I know it's meant to be comforting.

But we're both aware it's a kiss.

He pulls back and shakes his head apologetically. "Sorry, you're vulnerable right now, and I got carried away and—"

I press my fingers to his mouth, silencing him. "It's okay. That's why I asked you to come. I want you to kiss me." It feels so brazen saying it that I avert my eyes and drop my hand away from him. I'm no longer touching his mouth, but my fingertips tingle from the memory of the softness of his lips.

"Are you sure you're ready?" he asks.

I honestly don't know if I am, so I turn the question around and ask, "Are *you*?"

He huffs out an amused breath, and after searching my face for a moment, he suggests, "How about we play this by ear and see what happens?"

"That works," I say.

A devastating smile breaks over his face, and my thoughts scatter. He separates from me, but he does it slowly, almost reluctantly, running his warm hand down my cold arm, leaving goose bumps in its wake. He squeezes my hand once before letting go.

Looking about curiously, he considers the books that overflow my bookshelves and spill onto the floor and tabletops, the mismatched throw blankets and decorative pillows on my old sofa, and the dozen or so candles placed in random locations. I'm struck by the odd realization that I have a man in my apartment, in my space. Julian preferred for me to go to his condo—his TV is a lot better than mine—so this is a rare occurrence, made even more extraordinary by the particular man involved. Quan seems to fill the space with his presence and vitality. The air around him is . . . charged.

He pads over the hardwood to stand by the French doors, and I can't help admiring him as he admires the view through the glass panes. There's a confidence and relaxed coordination in the way he moves that suggests he's been in a few fights—and won them. Have I lost my mind that this is intensely appealing to me, that hint of danger? And what does it mean that the designs on his skin no longer jar me like they did at first? They're just a part of him, and I accept them. I accept him.

"Nice place," he comments. "I love the balcony. That's one thing I wish my apartment had."

"I don't use it as much as I should, but I like it," I say.

His gaze touches upon my music stand and violin case, but after giving me an inquiring look, he doesn't ask the question that I always get: *Do you play?* It's a relief—I don't want to talk about my current difficulties—but it's also a disappointment. For some people, their work is just their work, a means of survival. It doesn't define them. But me, I'm a violinist. It's my identity, who I am, what I am. It's all that matters. Naturally, my favorite topic of discussion is music.

That reminds me why I invited him here in the first place, and steely determination floods my veins as I say, "Let's get started."

NINE

Quan

I HAVE TO GRIN WHEN I SEE THE PREPARATIONS ANNA'S MADE in her tiny kitchen. Everything is neatly laid out—a pot of water and a frying pan on the electric stove; garlic, parsley, and onion on the cutting board; lined up precisely on the countertop, wineglasses, a wine opener, a liquid measuring cup, olive oil, a block of cheese and a cheese shredder, a wooden spoon, tongs, the lid for the pot, salt, pepper, a box of fettuccini noodles. Over by the window, her kitchen table is set for two. She didn't forget a single thing.

I like knowing this thing about her. Some people collect stamps. I collect quirks, stowing away secret traits about people in my mind like treasure. It makes people real to me, special. My mom keeps two nail clippers attached to her key ring. It always makes me grin when I see that. Why *two*? How is she ever able to use them both? No one else I know does that. Khai has so many quirks that's a quirk in itself. Michael won't admit it, but I know he matches his outfit with his wife's every day. When he has kids, they're going to be *that* obnoxious family, and I can't wait for it. Now there's Anna, and I'm excited to learn everything there is to learn about her.

Talking so fast she's hardly breathing, she takes a wine bottle from the freezer and works on peeling the metal wrapping off the end. She tells me she's worried I won't like the white wine. She got a bottle of red just in case. It's in the pantry. Where is the appropriate place to put wine when people don't have wine cellars? She doesn't drink much. If she falls asleep on me, she's sorry in advance.

I've been worried about tonight. Am I really ready? What if she asks about my scar? What if she notices other stuff? What if I fuck up the fucking? But she's worse. She's a nervous wreck, and that makes this easier for me somehow. I've always been better at dealing with other people's problems. I even like it. It feels good to help people.

Acting on instinct, I step behind her and squeeze her shoulders before running my palms down her arms. She goes completely still.

I lean down and whisper in her ear, "Is this okay? Touching you like this?"

Her hair is up in a loose ponytail, so I can see the goose bumps standing up along the length of her neck. They're running down her arms as well. A good sign, I think.

She swallows and nods, so I let myself linger. I press my cheek to hers, enjoying the softness of her skin and drawing her scent into my lungs. It's clean, feminine, with something I can't quite name. Trying to figure out what it is, I nuzzle her neck. Pine. That's the scent. Because my lips are touching her, my touch naturally becomes a kiss, and I've never kissed a woman's neck without using my teeth at some point. When I scrape them along her smooth skin, tasting her at the same time, her breath breaks and the wine opener clatters from her fingers to the counter.

I manage to snatch the wine bottle before it falls, and she touches a flustered hand to the area beneath her jaw. Her cheeks are flushed, her eyes dazed, her breaths quick, and I try my best not to grin at what I've just learned.

Anna really, *really* likes having her neck kissed.

And bitten.

"M-maybe it's better if you open it," she says, handing the wine opener to me.

"Sure." I accidentally touch the backs of her fingers when I take the wine opener from her, and her entire hand jumps in reaction.

We separate so I can use both hands to uncork the bottle, and I feel the weight of her gaze on my hands and arms—she's looking at my tattoos, I realize. When I glance up at her, she quickly averts her eyes. But almost against her will, her gaze returns to me and drops to my mouth.

In this moment, I think that if there was ever a woman who *needed* to be kissed, it's her.

I lean toward her, completely focused on making it happen, when she turns away abruptly and cranks on the water in the sink.

As she washes her hands, she says in a brisk tone, "The pasta only takes about twenty minutes to make. If I get the timing right, the noodles are ready when the mushrooms are done."

"Sounds good." My voice is husky, and I clear my throat before I crank the corkscrew into the wine cork and pull it free with a pop.

After I fill the wineglasses, I hand one to her and watch with wide eyes as she finishes half in two large gulps and wipes her lips with the back of her hand.

"I'm trying to loosen my inhibitions," she explains self-consciously.

"You don't have to do that. We can just go slow," I say before taking a sip from my glass. It's crisp, not too sweet, pretty nice, but it's not like I know anything about wine. Mostly, I want to look relaxed so that she relaxes. That works sometimes.

"It's not that. Well, there is that." She looks like there's more to say, but she's not sure how.

"You'll tell me if I do something you don't like?" I ask, because from my perspective, that's all that matters.

Some of the tension leaks from her. She stands straighter and nods. "I can do that. Can you?"

That makes me smile. I'm an easygoing person, and there isn't much that bothers me. But I like that she cares, and not because I was sick and I'll never be the same but because I'm a person. "I can do that."

We start cooking then. I cut the ingredients. She adds them to the frying pan and stirs. We talk about everything and nothing, much like our text conversations. I learn that she's a violinist with the San Francisco Symphony, but she's taken a leave of absence. She doesn't explain why, and I don't press her. I tell her that I started a children's apparel company with my best friend, Michael, because we both love little kids. She asks if I want to have kids someday, and I change the subject. She notices, but she doesn't push me.

When the noodles are ready, she turns the stove off, and I drain the water from the pot using the lid and reach around her to pour them into the skillet with the mushrooms. I'm right behind her again, close enough to touch her, though I'm being careful not to. I think I went a little too fast earlier. But it's hard to resist the curve of her shoulder, the graceful arch of her neck, the fine line of her jaw. She even has pretty ears. I want to trace them with the tip of my tongue.

I try to keep my thoughts on neutral things as she scrapes the last noodles out of the pot with the wooden spoon. One is stuck to the bottom, and I lean close to get a better look at it—

And her lips press against mine.

My heart jumps. A current jolts through me. My blood rushes. I try to be gentle—she's so soft, so perfect—but I want to devour her. Barely restrained, I sweep my tongue into her mouth, and she tastes like wine, only sweeter. She gasps. I could get drunk off that sound; maybe I do. Leaning into the kiss, into me, she touches her tongue to mine. Everything in me tightens and clamors to be closer, and I pour that aching need into the kiss.

It goes on and on, kiss after kiss, for how long, I don't know. When we part, our breathing is ragged. Anna looks exactly like she's just been kissed long and hard. I'm not sure I've ever seen anything more beautiful than her. The pot is still in my hands, dinner is getting cold, and I don't care. All I want is more.

I take her lips in another greedy kiss, and she's there with me, kissing me back, letting me in. Until she turns away and presses clumsy fingers to her mouth.

"We should talk." Her voice is throaty, the goddamn sexiest thing I've ever heard.

I hear her, but my body sways toward her anyway, craving another taste. It takes effort to stop myself, but I manage. "Okay."

Her chin goes up a notch, and her expression turns stubborn. After a long pause, where she seems to struggle against herself, she finally says, "I don't want to give you a blow job."

My eyebrows shoot up on their own, and I stifle a surprised laugh—that's an immature response, especially when she looks so serious. "That's . . . perfectly fine." Maybe it's even a relief. Yes, on second thought, it's definitely a relief, and it's better that I didn't have to ask for it myself.

She gives me a skeptical look. "Are you sure?"

I can't help chuckling. "Yeah, it's just a blow job. If you don't want to do it, don't do it. It's not a big deal."

"You're wrong. It *is* a big deal. I'm supposed to like giving blow jobs. A partner's pleasure is supposed to give me pleasure, and if it doesn't, that means I'm selfish. In books I've read, women enjoy it so much sometimes they burst into spontaneous orgasm."

"Wait, what books are you reading?"

She ignores the question and says, "On the flip side, I don't need you to . . . you know." When I shake my head, clueless as to what she means, she blushes sunburn red and awkwardly clarifies, "I don't need you to give me oral sex. I don't want to feel obligated to reciprocate, and it never works for me anyway."

That almost seems like a challenge to me, and I ask, "What if I want to? Because I like it, not because I want you to do it back?" Because I do like it. It turns me on. I love the sounds women make when I go down on them, the way they move when they get close, their smell, their taste. It's fucking hot.

Looking pained and frustrated, she says, "It really won't work, and I'll still feel pressured to return the favor. Can you just please—"

"I don't need it," I say quickly. "I won't try to push it on you. I promise."

She searches my face. "You're really okay with this?"

"Yeah."

Her eyes narrow. "Are you secretly judging me?"

I smile and fondly trail my fingertips down the side of her face. "No, I'm not. I like having everything out in the open. It makes things a lot easier."

She releases a long shaky breath and relaxes against me.

For a while, we both stare at the pasta sitting in the skillet. When our gazes connect, we break into laughter.

"Let's eat," I say.

TEN

Anna

I'M NOT SURE I'M GOOD COMPANY AS WE EAT. THERE'S TOO much going on in my head for me to think of interesting things to say. I can barely taste the food and the wine. I can barely sit still. Every time our knees bump beneath my tiny kitchen table, my awareness of him escalates.

I'm really doing this. I'm going to have sex with a stranger.

I don't expect to enjoy it, but it means something to me that I'll be doing it on my terms, that I'm setting boundaries, even if it disappoints people—perhaps *especially* if it disappoints people. Telling Quan that I didn't want to give him a blow job might be the hardest thing I've ever done. But I did it. Part of me is still queasy from how unnatural it felt. Another part of me, however, is drunk with power.

That could just be the alcohol, though. Or his kisses.

I've never been kissed the way he kissed me. I've always loved kissing. It's the only part of sex that I wholeheartedly enjoy, but

Quan's kisses swept me away. I can't stop looking at his mouth, watching his jaw work as he chews, watching his throat bob as he swallows, fascinated by the way his tattoos shift. Is it normal to find a man's Adam's apple sexy?

This is physical attraction, I recognize. And I've never felt it before, not really. There are other things that I like about Julian—my parents hold his family in high esteem (his father is a urologist, and his mother is an obstetrician); he's extremely smart and talented (he went to Harvard and then Stanford for business school); he's hardworking (he's an investment banker at a leading bank); he has an even temperament and never yells at me, never scares me; I understand him; I know how to be what he wants. At least, I thought I did.

He doesn't know *me*, though. How can he, when even I don't?

Intuitively, I sense that if I stray from the version of myself that he's familiar with, he will no longer want me. That is, if he ever comes back to me.

Quan, on the other hand, has only known this chaotic, insecure, panic-attack-ridden side of me. He's seen me at my worst.

And he's still here.

For now. For tonight.

"You're doing the same thing my mom does," he observes.

I blink several times as I try to make sense of his words. "What does she do?"

"She watches people eat, like the food tastes better in someone else's mouth," he says with a grin.

I duck my head and tuck a loose tendril of hair behind my ear. "Sorry."

"I don't mind. She's a cook and loves feeding people, so I'm used to it. This pasta is good, too." He points at his empty plate.

I hate the thought of him being hungry—and I'm ridiculously pleased that he likes my cooking—so I push my half-full plate toward him. "Help me finish?"

After giving me an assessing look, he spins his fork in the noodles and takes a big bite. It's a bit unusual sharing a plate with him, but I like it. It feels intimate somehow. I prop my elbow on the table and rest my chin in my palm, watching him.

As he scoops up a second forkful, he asks, "Do you always keep it quiet like this? You don't like to play background music?"

"Do you want me to turn something on?"

"Not unless you want to. I'm just curious." He takes another big bite of pasta, and his gaze strays to my instrument case in the corner.

"I like having music on while I cook and things," I say, but then I frown down at the dwindling noodles on my plate. "Well, I used to. Lately, I can't listen to music without picking it apart and overanalyzing everything until my head hurts. I haven't listened to music for my own enjoyment in . . . a long time. I think I've forgotten how. Ironic, I know."

When his expression turns thoughtful and he looks like he wants to delve deeper into the topic, I quickly steer the conversation away from me by asking, "What kind of music do you like?"

After a short hesitation, he says, "Most kinds, I guess. I'm not picky. To be honest, I'm really tone-deaf."

"Tone-deaf as in . . . you can't differentiate notes?" As a professional musician, one with perfect pitch no less, I can't fathom what that must be like.

"As in my brother and sister can't sing 'Rock-a-bye Baby' correctly because I taught it to them when we were little." His smile looks slightly embarrassed, and he concentrates on scooping up the last forkful of noodles and eating them.

I think some people would laugh upon hearing this confession, but I don't. Imagining a small Quan singing out of tune to his siblings as he tucks them in at night spills warmth into my chest.

"Did you take care of them a lot?" I ask.

"My dad left when we were really small, and my mom told me it was my job to be man of the house," he says in a matter-of-fact manner as he idly spins his wineglass. "But"—he glances at me, his eyes dancing and a mischievous smile hinting at the corners of his mouth—"I was no angel. I got into *a lot* of trouble."

"Somehow that doesn't surprise me," I say, and I can't keep the amusement from my voice. "What kind of trouble was it?"

"The regular stuff, skipping class, practical jokes on the principal. The agriculture teacher was a racist, and we thought it would be a good idea to salt the fields. Looking back, I regret it. There was the fighting, too. There was *always* fighting. I almost got expelled for punching this kid in the face after he tripped my brother in the cafeteria. His dad was going to press charges but dropped it when my mom made me apologize." He shrugs, and down on the table, I see him fist his right hand, making the letters inked onto his knuckles stand out in sharp relief. "I don't regret punching him."

Acting on a desire I've been fighting since we sat down, I settle my hand over his and bump my fingertips along his knuckles. His skin is warm, slightly rough. "What do these letters mean? MVKM?"

He smiles slightly, though his gaze is intense—I can only take it in split-second doses. I look away, only to return, and then look away again.

"Are you sure you want to know? They don't represent my fallen enemies or anything," he says.

"Do they correspond with people?" I ask.

"Yeah. My family, minus my dad. *M* is for Mom, *V* is my sister, *K* for my brother, Khai, and the last *M* is for Michael, my cousin and best friend." He opens his hand and turns it so he can interlace his fingers with mine, a movement that makes my heart knock around my chest like a Ping-Pong ball. "I wanted them on my right hand because they're important to me."

"I like that," I say, and I feel a sharp stab of envy for these people whom I've never met. No one has ever wanted to carry a reminder of me on their skin.

His smile widens in response. His gaze drops to my mouth, intensifies, and I stop breathing. Moving slowly, like he's giving me time to back away, he leans toward me and cups my jaw with his free hand. His thumb brushes over my bottom lip, and the breath seeps from my lungs as I touch the tip of my tongue to his skin and scrape him with my teeth.

I'm worrying that was too weird, I've never done something like that before, when he closes the distance between us and crushes our lips together. His tongue strokes into my mouth, taking, claiming, like he wants to consume me whole, and weakness shoots through my body. I *love* the way he kisses me.

He pulls back, his lungs heaving, his lips red, one hand bracing the table. I guess I almost knocked it over. "We should take this somewhere else," he says in a low rasp, urging me to my feet.

"Couch is right there. Bedroom around the corner," I say, and my voice doesn't sound like me. It's husky, breathy, completely unfamiliar.

"Couch is closer." He guides us a few steps in that direction but stops to kiss me again, like he can't help himself, licking my bottom lip before sucking it into his mouth.

To keep from melting to the floor, I wrap my arms around his neck and press my body to his. He's deliciously solid, thick and strong where I'm not.

His arms close around me, and I feel his hands smooth up and down my back, before gripping my hips and pulling me close, onto my tiptoes. I gasp into his kiss as his hardness settles into the cradle of my thighs. Inside, I clench with a pure wanting. I've had sex hundreds of times, more probably, but I've never *ached* for it like this. I can't quite grasp why everything is different now.

My back meets the cushions of the couch, and Quan settles against me, kissing my mouth, my jaw. "You still with me?" he asks against my neck, and shivers race down my spine.

I can't talk, so I run my hands down his chest until I find the hem of his shirt and pull it up. His eyes meet mine for a burning second before he pulls his shirt over his head and tosses it to the ground.

Thought fails me as I touch shaking fingers to the lean muscles of his abdomen, push my palms up to his wide chest. He's scalding hot, but smooth, starkly masculine. I can feel his heart beating, his lungs rising and falling. The sight of my unmarked skin against the dense designs inked onto him mesmerizes me. There are crashing black waves with intricate detail like in a Japanese watercolor painting, a water dragon, wide-sailed ships. I trace my fingertips along the calligraphy that continues from his neck down one side of his chest, ending beneath his ribs. I want to know the story written in his skin, but I suspect it's too personal to be shared with me.

Hidden in the waves by his right hip, my fingers find . . . a small octopus, and I draw in a sharp breath and gaze at him in wonder. "You have . . ."

He grins. "That's the tattoo you want to talk about? Out of all of them?"

"Is it the one from the documentary?"

"Nah," he says, smiling wider before he kisses my neck. "I got that one a long time ago. I like the ocean and sea creatures and things."

"Are octo—" His lips part, and the wet heat of his mouth sears my skin. I forget what I was talking about. All I know is the feel of his lips, his tongue, his teeth. I arch closer to him, unable to control the sounds coming from my throat.

The front of my dress falls open as he kisses his way to my collarbones and down to the edge of my bra. Instead of going through the work of undoing the clasps in back, he yanks it down, baring my breasts to the cool air for an instant before he sucks my nipple into his mouth. My entire being tightens in response, my stomach, my core, between my thighs.

"You're really good at that," I hear myself say, my surprise evident in the wondering tone of my voice.

He releases my nipple from his mouth, and a knowing smile touches his lips. Watching me, he licks the hardened tip, nuzzles the underside of my breast, and takes a tiny bite, sending a starburst of sensation washing over me in a red haze before he soothes me with his warm palm. He kisses his way to my other breast and teases me. He blows on my nipple, licks it lightly, pinches it with his fingertips, and then he takes me into his mouth and draws with exquisite pressure.

I cling to him, alternately gasping and hissing through my teeth as he caresses me with his hands and mouth. It turns out I am absolutely crazy about breast play. I had no clue.

When our lips meet again, I kiss him with abandon, tangling my tongue with his as I touch him everywhere my hands can reach. His chest, his shoulders, the broad expanse of his back, his head. His closely buzzed hair scrapes against my palms in the most interesting way.

He shifts against me, pulling my thigh up along his side, and rolls his hips. I feel him, hard where I'm soft, and I know what's coming. The good part of sex is ending, and the not-so-good part is starting. I don't mind, though. This has been the best sex of my life.

I expect him to sit back and remove our underwear so we can get things moving, but he doesn't. He continues kissing me, touching me. One hand cups my face, tilting my head back so he can kiss me deeper. With his other hand, he strokes my thigh, my butt, squeezes it.

"What do you like, Anna?" he whispers.

When I stare at him, completely stunned by the question, he works his hand between us and eases his fingers beneath the waistband of my underwear. I catch my breath when his fingertips slip through my folds and explore me with languid strokes. I'm wet, extremely so, and that's unusual for me. When Julian and I have sex, it's uncomfortable for both of us until my body eventually warms up and self-lubricates, but even then, I'm not like this.

He trails his mouth to my ear and asks, "How about this?"

I don't know what he means until he begins circling my clitoris in slow, gentle circles. It feels . . . *almost* good. So *close* to good. If he would just—

His slippery fingertips shift and rub directly over me as he nips my ear. A moan escapes my throat—that bite, I don't know why I like it so much, but I do—and he continues the same motion with his fingers, which, again, is *almost* good. I hide my face against his neck as he strokes me. It's arousing. I get wetter. But it's not what I need.

"Anna," he asks, teasing a finger into me just the barest bit. "How do you like to be touched?"

I press my face tighter to his neck. I want to be the kind of woman who can boldly tell a man how she likes to have her sex touched. But I can't answer him. Someone could threaten to kill me right now, and I still couldn't answer. I wish he just knew. Why don't men just *know*?

His finger pushes deeper into me, and I arch into the penetration, surprised when he slides in with little resistance.

"More?" he asks, and a second finger works into me gradually.

I love the sensation as my body stretches to accept him. It's decadent and unbearably sexy, but it isn't long before the pleasure ebbs. When he strokes his fingers in and out and curls them, touching me deep inside, it's nice. But that's it. Just nice.

Clinging to him tightly, unable to look at him, I whisper, "I'm ready now."

"Ready for what?" he asks.

"Ready for you."

ELEVEN

Quan

IF THERE WAS ANY QUESTION WHETHER OR NOT THINGS WERE in working condition, it's definitely answered now. My cock is so hard I hurt. She's soft and tight against my fingers, drenching me, and I want inside her.

"Is that what it takes for you to come?" I ask, breathing kisses into her hair because her face is hidden from me.

Instead of answering, she hugs me tighter and burrows closer, and feelings of tenderness nearly overwhelm me.

"Anna?"

Silence. At this point, the first shreds of worry creep into my mind.

"Can you talk to me? Did I do something wrong? If I did, just tell me, and I'll fix it. I want this to be good for you." That's important to me, maybe more important now than it's ever been in the past.

"Can't we just . . . keep going?" she asks without looking at me. She runs her hand down my arm and then presses on my hand that's between her thighs, undulates against it, so my fingers push deeper into her. Fuck, that's hot. "This is fine."

Fine? I don't want sex with me to be *fine*. I try to ease her away from my neck, so I can see her face. "Will that be—"

She presses her mouth to mine before I can finish the question, and hell if I don't respond. I could kiss her for hours, just kissing, nothing else. Her mouth is perfect, her tongue, those breathless sounds she makes.

"Don't worry about me," she whispers between kisses. "This is enough for me, kissing you."

She palms my cock through my pants, scrapes her nails over the denim, and my blood rushes, everything tightens, every hair on my body stands on end, I almost come. Damn if that isn't the sexiest thing.

But then her words sink into my brain.

Kissing is enough? She doesn't expect to get anything out of sex with me? She's okay if I nut on her like she's a blow-up doll or some shit?

Like I'm some kind of charity sex case because I'm not whole anymore.

My fly comes undone, and she reaches inside, and I can't help it, I stiffen, I jerk away, I put distance between myself and the couch and her.

She stares at me, her eyes wide and startled. Her hair is disheveled, her dress open, showing off her gorgeous tits and thighs. The sight is almost enough to bring me to my knees. I take deep breaths and run my hands over my face, only to smell her on my slick fingers. I stifle a groan and drop my hands to my sides.

"Anna, I'm sorry. I just . . ." I shake my head. Honestly, I don't know what to say.

She pulls the folds of her dress together and seems to shrink in upon herself. With her face turned away from me, she asks, "Is this it? Are we done?"

"Can we talk through this?"

She grimaces and opens her mouth like she wants to speak, but words don't come. She takes a breath and tries again to speak, but, again, words don't come.

I take a step toward her. She's so clearly struggling, and I hate seeing that. I want to make things better. My fly is hanging open, and I zip and button everything before sitting in the armchair adjacent to the couch.

"Remember when I told you it's been a while for me?" I ask softly. It doesn't feel good sharing about myself, but I can't stand the idea of her misunderstanding the situation.

"Your surgery," she says.

"Yeah." I exhale tightly. "I often feel like . . . my body isn't right anymore. Tonight, I was hoping to, I guess, prove that I'm still—I don't know. If you're not with me, if you're not feeling it, I can't—" I make a frustrated sound. It would help if I gave her specific details, but I can't bring myself to do it. I don't want her to look at me differently. I don't want her to think I'm *less*. "Do you know what I'm saying? I need you to be just as into it as I am."

She frowns at me for a long moment before she says, "Maybe?"

"Is there anything that I could have—"

She covers her face with her hands. "Can you not, please? People don't talk about this stuff."

"They do. *I* do."

"They really don't," she says.

I tilt my head to the side as I try to figure this out. "How does a guy know how to touch you, then? I tried the regular stuff, and it didn't seem to do it for you."

She makes a miserable sound and shrinks deeper into herself.

A suspicion rises, and I ask, "Are you a virgin? Have you never . . ."

She drops her hands from her face and gives me an impatient look. "I'm not a virgin. I've had sex many, many, *many* times."

"Have you ever come before, like, had an orgasm? That's, uh, when your body—"

She claps her hands to her face again. "I know what an orgasm is."

"Have you had one?"

She draws her knees to her chest, and after a while I hear a muffled, "Yes."

"Do they happen on accident? Or . . . can you make them happen?" I feel like I'm playing a guessing game, but I keep going.

"They do happen on accident sometimes, during sex, a few times when I was sleeping," she confesses, and I arch my eyebrows. From my perspective, that's a clear sign that a girl isn't getting the proper loving. "But I also"—she clears her throat—"by myself, I can—" She drops her fingers to her mouth, and her face is red, her expression painfully embarrassed.

Because I can't stand her discomfort, I move to the couch, next to her, and she immediately curls up against me, pressing her face to my neck. I wrap my arms around her, and those same feelings from before swamp me: tenderness, protectiveness.

"I don't really see why that's so embarrassing. I do it all the time," I say, and her body shakes as she laughs. "Like every day, sometimes more than once a day."

"It's different for guys," she says, hitting me lightly on the chest with a small fist.

I pick up her fist and kiss her knuckles. "It shouldn't be."

"It still is, though."

"I think it's hot as fuck when chicks do it," I tell her.

She laughs again, and I gently pull on her until she looks at me.

"I mean it," I say, completely serious. "If you can't tell me what you like, you could show me."

Her lungs expand on a sharp inhalation, and her face flushes an even deeper shade of red. "I could never, ever, ever . . ."

"Why?"

"*Quan*," she says, her tone accusing, like I should know why.

"It's just you and me here. It's not like anyone is watching."

She shakes her head quickly and looks away from me.

"You're okay with never having good sex, then?" The idea is horrifying to me. "And what about all those times you've had sex in the past? They were all shitty?"

She says nothing.

"Anna, it would have been so easy just to—"

Her body tenses, and she sit upright, shooting daggers at me with her eyes. "It's not 'easy.' Not for me. If it was, I would have done it."

"I'm sorry. I just think—"

"I think this is as far as we're going to get," she says, and there's a finality in her voice that tells me she's done. Her dating profile was clear that she only wanted one night, and this was our one night—since the first night didn't count.

A sense of loss threads through me. I don't want this to be how we part. I didn't accomplish what I wanted, and I don't think she did either, not if she wanted to get over her ex—whoever that dickhole is—by having rebound sex. But we really are at a standstill. We both want things the other won't give.

I stand and pick my shirt up off the ground. As I pull it on, I'm aware of her eyes on me. She likes what she sees. That's something, even if it's only skin-deep. With the right person, I think she'll open up, and it'll be fucking glorious. But that person isn't me.

"Thank you for tonight," I say when I'm standing in front of her door. "I know it was rocky in the end, but I had a great time."

She joins me in the entryway. "It was the same for me. Thank you—for being you."

It seems like the right thing to hug her good-bye. When I have her in my arms, it *feels* like the right thing. She fits against me like she belongs here. I don't mean to kiss her. It just happens. And she kisses me back. There's a moment when we hesitate, both unsure of what we're doing, but our lips come together again. I don't know who initiates it, her or me, maybe it's both of us, but I kiss her like it's our last kiss. Because that's what this is.

When we finally separate, her eyes are dreamy, her lips red. I run my thumb over her swollen bottom lip, unable to stand the fact that this is the last time I'll be able to do this.

Without stopping to think, I say, "What if we tried again?"

She blinks several times, her brow wrinkling. "You think we can finally have a proper one-night stand if we try one more time?"

I huff out a soundless laugh. "Third time's a charm."

"But you—I—we . . ."

"I think there are things we both could work on. Why not try it together?" I hold my breath and wait for her to answer.

She concentrates on tracing the MLA graphic on my T-shirt with her fingertip as she says, "I don't think I can do . . . the things you wanted."

"Maybe we can figure out another way, meet in the middle somehow."

"Do you have any ideas?" she asks.

"Not yet," I admit. The thought of fucking her while she lies there, wishing for it to be over, puts a bitter taste in my mouth, but there has to be another way, something else we can do. We can't be the first people in history to have this kind of problem.

"Okay," she says, squaring her shoulders as a determined glint enters her eyes. "Let's try it one more time."

I don't attempt to stop myself from smiling. "Okay."

"Next weekend?" she asks.

"That works."

"Are we completely ridiculous?"

"Maybe," I say with a laugh.

She laughs along with me, and for a moment, we stand there in each other's arms, just looking at one another.

Eventually, I pull away. "I'm going to head out, but we should text and decide on next weekend."

"Sure." She flashes a smile at me. "Bye, Quan."

Giving her one last, quick kiss on the lips, I say, "Bye, Anna."

Then I leave, and she shuts the door behind me. As I walk to my car, I brainstorm different ways we can approach our intimacy problems. Nothing seems quite right, but I think we'll get there.

TWELVE

Anna

"HOW HAVE YOU BEEN, ANNA?" JENNIFER ANISTON ASKS. TO-day, she's wearing a loose dress with Aztec designs and leather sandals that loop around her big toes and ankles.

The usual answer slips from my lips. "The same." But then I hesitate. "Well, not entirely." A lot has happened in the weeks since our last appointment.

Her eyes spark with interest. "How so?"

"My boyfriend decided he wanted to have an open relationship."

She opens her mouth to reply, but it takes a second before she actually speaks. "There's a lot to unpack there."

"Yeah." I smile awkwardly and look down at my hands, which are clasped together in my lap as usual.

"How do you feel about it?" she asks.

I hesitate to answer, examining her face as I try to determine what her opinion is on the matter.

"How do *you* feel, Anna," she says softly. "Not me. What I think isn't important."

I push a long breath out through my mouth. "You say that, but you're not a stranger I'm meeting for a one-night stand. You're someone I'll be seeing on a regular basis for the foreseeable future. If you don't like me, that makes things difficult for me."

"Well, I do like you," she says with a kind yet amused smile, "and I have no interest in judging you, only helping you. So tell me what happened. Are you in an open relationship now? Since you mentioned it, do you want to tell me if you had a one-night stand?"

"We *are* in an open relationship now," I say. "I'm certain he's seeing other people."

The corners of her mouth droop downward, and her eyes darken with understanding. "That's got to be hard to accept."

"It was. I cried when I found out. But then I immediately arranged to have a one-night stand with someone from a dating app." I sit straighter, trying to make myself look bold and indifferent, but my muscles tighten as I brace myself for her condemnation.

"I might have done the same thing, in your shoes," she says. "How did it go?"

At her casual acceptance of my attempt at revenge sex, my stomach muscles loosen a notch. Still, I struggle to describe my time with Quan. He's been on my mind nonstop, what we did—and didn't do—and I've been restless and extra absentminded all week. This morning, I forgot I'd left my contacts in last night, and I stuck in another pair. I thought I was going blind for an entire hour before I realized what I'd done.

"It wasn't a success," I say finally. "We didn't . . . you know."

Jennifer gives me a commiserating look. "That happens. But

that's the nice thing about one-night stands. If they don't go well, you just brush them off and keep on with your life."

I nod in agreement. "That's what I had in mind. I thought a lot about what you said last time about masking, people pleasing, and worrying too much about what others think. I hoped that I could use the time during a one-night stand to experiment."

"That's such an interesting approach. Did it work?" Jennifer asks.

"A little, but I was so nervous for most of the time that I couldn't think clearly. And then in the end, it was just . . ." I shake my head. "People are—they're *so confusing*. Sometimes, if I think about things long enough and hard enough, I can understand them. But other times, no matter how hard I try, it's impossible."

"I wanted to talk to you about that, actually," Jennifer says, and there's an expression on her face that I haven't seen before. I can't read it.

She gets up and goes to the desk on the other side of the room to sift through one of the big drawers. She extracts a thick manila folder, which she hands to me before sitting back down in the chair across from me.

"This is for you," she says. "Go on and take a look."

Feeling strange, I open the folder. There's a paperback on top of a stack of printouts held together with various staples and a large paper clip. I run my fingertips over the book's title, *Aspergirls: Empowering Females with Asperger Syndrome*, and give her a questioning look.

"I recommend you read that book in your free time," she says. "It's not a comprehensive source by any means, but I do think parts of it will speak to you."

"Okay. I'll read it," I say, though I'm still not sure *why* she wants me to read it. I mean, there's one obvious reason, but I discount that immediately. There has to be another reason.

Because I'm curious, I set the book aside and inspect the printouts. In bold print, the top sheet reads "Understanding Your Autism." Various sentences and bullet points have been highlighted in yellow, but when I read them, I don't understand their meaning. All I can think about is the title.

"Based on what you've told me about your current issues and childhood, and what I've personally seen over the past months with you, it's my opinion that you're on the autism spectrum, Anna," Jennifer says.

In a flash, it's like the air is sucked from the room. A loud ringing fills my ears. My thoughts narrow to those words—*autism spectrum*. She continues speaking, but my brain is too shaken to pick up everything. I catch only bits and pieces.

Difficulty socializing.
Need for routine.
Repetitive motions.
Sensory issues.
Consuming interests.
Meltdowns.

She's describing autism, I realize. It also sounds eerily like she's describing *me*, but that's simply not possible.

"I can't be autistic," I say, interrupting her. "I hate math. I don't have a photographic memory. I fit in. I have friends, a boyfriend, even my mom's friends like me. I'm nothing like Sheldon from *The Big Bang Theory* or—or—or the brother in *Rain Man*."

"None of those things are diagnostic criteria. They're stereotypes and misperceptions. And I believe your fitting in is a result of a great deal of masking on your part. It's common for high-functioning autistic women like you to acquire late diagnoses because they 'pass,' but it's not healthy. I'm concerned you're on your way to autistic burnout—if you're not already there," Jennifer says with a worried frown.

I have no response. Her observation has literally made me speechless.

We get through the rest of the session, but when I step outside the building, I don't remember much. I squint up at the blinding brightness of the sky. It's the same sky that's always been above me, but it feels different now. Everything feels different. The sun, the wind in the trees, the pavement beneath my shoes.

There's a green bench to the side. I've walked by it for months without once sitting on it. I sit on it now, open the book Jennifer gave me, and read. Hours pass. Clouds race over the sun, momentarily shrouding me in darkness before passing on. In these pages, I read about other women, their experiences, their difficulties, their strengths. But it feels exactly like I'm reading about myself—the way I copy my peers so I fit in; the way I don't understand them but I pretend; the way I used to hide under the table at parties to avoid the noise and the chaos and the stressful social interactions, much to my parents' embarrassment; the way I need rigid structure in my day or I can't function; the way I can't stand to focus on something unless it's interesting to me and then I get tunnel vision; even the way I'm tapping my teeth right now. I'm stimming. In secret. In broad daylight. I've been doing it my entire life.

Just like the women in the book, there's always been a lot "off" about me, so much to change, to suppress, to hide—to mask. It was painstaking, often exhausting, work, but my efforts were rewarded with my family's approval and the acquisition of friends and a boyfriend. By changing myself, I earned a sense of belonging.

But maybe I belonged all along. Just with a different group of people.

I did all that work. I experienced all that confusion and pain. And maybe I didn't need to. Maybe with the proper insight, I could have been accepted the way I was.

When I'm done reading pertinent sections of the book and everything in the manila folder, it's the golden hour. This used to be my favorite time of day to play the violin because it feels like there's magic in the air. Logically, I know it's not magic, it's light falling at an angle as the sun descends toward the horizon, but it adds something indefinable to the gravity of now.

I walk home in a sort of trance. It's not until passing pedestrians give me double takes and odd looks that I realize I'm crying.

I don't try to stop.

I let the tears fall.

I cry for the girl I used to be.

I cry for me.

It's a foreign experience. Self-pity is not an indulgence that I allow myself. This doesn't feel like pity, though. It feels like self-*compassion*, and the realization makes me cry harder.

No one should need a diagnosis in order to be compassionate to themself.

But I did. Tough love doesn't allow room for weakness, and tough love is all I've known. Maybe for now, just this once, I can experiment with a different kind of love. Something kinder.

I cry until my muscles ache, and then I cry more, like I'm letting out tears for a future sadness. People watch, and they whisper among themselves. A little girl points at me and asks her mommy what's wrong with me, and the woman picks her child up and hurries away.

I see, and for the first time in my adult life, I don't care that I'm making a scene. I haven't hurt anyone. I shouldn't be ashamed. I shouldn't need to apologize.

This is me.

THIRTEEN

Quan

WHEN I HANG UP FROM THE CALL WITH LVMH ACQUISITIONS, I sit back in my chair and stare at Michael, who's seated across my desk from me. Neither of us speaks for a full minute. The stunned expression on his face says it all. I'm pretty sure I look the same.

"Did that just happen?" he asks, breaking the silence.

I open up my email program on my laptop, and when I see what I was looking for, I turn it around so the screen faces Michael. "I think it did. Look, her lawyers are already contacting our lawyers to move acquisition talks forward. Prepare to be cc'd on everything."

"There's a real chance we're going to be a household name?" he asks.

An amazed kind of laugh breaks out of me. "I guess so? We might hate their offer and conditions, though. They could also change their minds for no reason. These things go nowhere all the time."

He nods, but he also sags into his chair and rubs his face like he can't quite believe this is real life. After a moment, he blinks and declares, "We need to celebrate."

I grin. "I'm down with that."

"Tomorrow night," he adds.

"I have something then," I say, but before he can suggest another time, I continue, "but I'll reschedule. I want to reschedule, actually."

He gives me a curious look. "It's something . . . with *her*?"

"Yeah." I keep my tone casual as I straighten up my desk, gathering financial printouts into a neat pile. "Things didn't go too perfectly last time, so we decided to try hooking up one more time."

Michael props an elbow on his chair's armrest and rests his chin on his fist as he looks at me. "What do you mean by 'not too perfectly'?"

"I didn't sleep with her. We did some stuff, and it was really good. But we both have issues, and we're working on it," I say lightly, like I haven't been thinking about her all week and jerking off to fantasies of her every chance I get.

Michael arches his eyebrows, asking, "You guys have tried to hook up how many times?"

"Only two," I say.

"At what point is it dating? Three times? Four?"

"It's dating when we *say* it's dating. And we're not," I say.

He sits forward in his chair like he's a bloodhound who's caught a scent. "Why do you want to reschedule?"

I shrug and put the printouts in the proper file in my desk drawer. Generally, I'm kind of messy—when I got around to cleaning my apartment the other week, I saw that my dishes really were growing mold; that's a new level of nasty, even for me—but when it comes to this business, I'm super organized. I keep things alphabetized and color coordinated. My email inbox drops to zero unread at the end of every day. Everything's paid exactly on time.

"Is it because you don't want it to be over?" Michael asks. "You're dragging it out?"

I don't answer. Because it's complicated. It's true that Anna and I have been texting all week, making random observations, sharing funny news articles and cute animal videos and stuff like that. Talking to her fills a space in my life that I didn't realize was empty, and I'll be sad to see that end.

But I'm also nervous. I think I know what I need to do the next time we're together, and I break into a sweat every time I think about it.

"I'm going to ask her about rescheduling while I'm thinking about it," I say, picking up my phone and texting her the message *Hey, can we meet on Sunday night instead of tomorrow?*

"So let's say you guys meet one more time and you finally hook up. What then? It's over? You never talk to each other again?" he asks.

"That's what usually happens after a hookup," I say, but I don't feel good about it.

Michael starts to comment, but my phone buzzes with a message from Anna. *That's fine.*

That's all she says. There aren't any emojis, no funny comments. Something's off.

Are you ok? We can stick to the original time if it's a problem for you, I tell her.

I'm ok, she replies, and again, that's it. This isn't like her.

"I have to call her real quick," I say out loud, and Michael frowns slightly as he watches me dial her number and put the phone to my ear.

The phone rings so many times that I'm sure it's going to voice mail, but she finally answers, "Hello?" Her voice has a strange quality to it that puts me on edge.

"Are you really okay? If you want to stick to tomorrow, that's fine. Or we can cancel or rain-check. Whatever you're—"

"No, Sunday is fine. I'm fine," she says, but her voice breaks half-way through the last word.

She's crying.

The sound stabs straight at my chest, and before I'm completely aware of it, I'm opening my desk drawer and putting my wallet and keys and things in my pockets.

"Where are you?" I ask. There's noise in the background. Pretty sure she's outside.

"On my way home," she says.

"Cross streets?"

"Why do you ... Oh. You don't need to come see me. That's really nice of you, but I'm okay." She releases a shaky breath that's like a mile long. "I see my apartment building. I'll be home in two minutes."

"Be right there."

"Quan—"

I hang up before I can hear the rest of what she says.

Getting up from his chair, Michael asks, "What's going on?"

"She's crying. I need to check up on her."

He nods seriously. On things like this, we get each other one hundred percent.

On my way out, I pause to say, "I'll let you know about plans for tomorrow. We might need to celebrate later."

"Don't worry about it. Go see your woman." He squeezes my shoulder, and I nod at him once before leaving.

As I'm getting onto my Ducati, however, the significance of what he said hits me. *Your woman.*

Anna isn't mine.

But I have to admit I like the sound of that. A lot.

———————

WHEN I GET TO ANNA'S BUILDING, I MANAGE TO CATCH THE door while someone is leaving and run up the three sets of stairs to her apartment. I don't stop to catch my breath before knocking.

She opens the door, and things move uncomfortably inside me. Her eyes are puffy and red. Her face is blotchy. She looks horrible. But at least she's in one piece.

"You got here so fast," she says, looking down the hall behind me with wide eyes like she's searching for a teleportation device or something. "You didn't need—"

I take her in my arms and hold her tight, whispering, "I *did* need to."

She's stiff at first, but slowly relaxes against me with a long, shuddering sigh. When she presses her forehead to my neck, everything that shifted out of place upon seeing her settles back into place.

"What's wrong? What happened?" I ask.

She's unresponsive for a long moment before she shakes her head, saying nothing, and my stomach sinks with disappointment. It's obvious there's *something*. It's also obvious she doesn't trust me enough to tell me, and that sucks. I tell myself it's okay. The thing between us isn't a *thing*. But my disappointment remains. I want to be someone she can tell things to. With other people, I'm that person—or I used to be, back before I became fragile in their eyes.

After standing with her by the front door for several minutes, I guide her to the couch and sit with her. I don't know what to do, so I just hold her, sweeping my hand up and down her back.

I'm pretty sure she's fallen asleep when she murmurs, "I don't have energy for our third try tonight."

"I didn't come here to have sex with you," I say firmly. What kind of dick does she think I am?

She turns her face to the side and looks up at me. "So today doesn't count?"

"No."

A faint smile touches her mouth. "Thank you. For coming."

"I was worried."

Sighing, she shuts her eyes. "I had therapy today."

"Did it help?" I ask, hoping she'll elaborate.

Her chest expands with a long, deep breath and falls. "I don't know. It's complicated and . . ." Her forehead wrinkles slightly. "It's hard to talk when I'm so tired. Just saying the words . . ." She lifts her hand, and it falls limply to her lap, making the point for her.

"You can tell me later. If you want."

She nods, and I hold her tighter as the sky turns to night, shrouding her living room in darkness. It's not exactly comfortable. I'm still wearing my motorcycle jacket, and while the synthetic fabric is great if you wipe out during a ride, it's definitely not lounging attire. But I like the way she's resting on me. It satisfies needs that I wasn't aware I had. I soak up the moment until my muscles go stiff from inaction. When I can't take it anymore and stretch out one of my arms, her head slides a fraction down my chest.

She's fallen asleep.

I'd bet my Ducati that she doesn't fall asleep with just anybody. But she did with me. That means something.

FOURTEEN

Anna

THE FIRST THING I SEE WHEN I OPEN MY EYES IS QUAN—HE'S on his side, facing me, deep asleep. The sight is so unexpected that my heart starts racing, and I look around in a panic, trying to make sense of things. This is my bed, my room. I didn't draw the blinds shut last night, and everything is tinted gray and hushed, the way it is right before dawn. I don't usually wake up at this time. Only when I'm traveling or accidentally go to sleep super early.

Memories of yesterday flit though my mind. My regular (failed) practice, seeing Jennifer, *the news*, the book, crying in public, Quan worrying about me . . .

I vaguely remember him moving me from the couch last night and then—I slap a hand over my mouth. *I asked him to stay.* That's why he's here, sleeping on top of my covers and looking cold. I sit up and carefully fold my blankets over him.

For a while, I sit there, scared to move for fear of waking him. What do women do when they have strangers in their beds? As soon as the thought crosses my mind, I frown. *Stranger* doesn't feel like quite the right word for Quan. But he's not my *one-night stand*—not yet. He's definitely not my *lover*. *Acquaintance* seems too distant. He's talked to me a reasonable amount, listened to me, laughed with me, seen me at my worst, held me while I cried. And he stayed because I asked him to.

I think . . . he might be my friend.

That's an uncomfortable realization and too much for me to handle this early in the morning, so I grab my phone from where it's charging on my nightstand—Quan must have done that for me—and sneak away from him.

As I brush my teeth as quietly as possible, I scroll through the hundred-plus text messages on my phone. Most of them are from Rose and Suzie. They were discussing the new twelve-year-old violin prodigy who's recently hit the classical music scene. For a while after I accidentally went Internet famous, *I* was the one everyone was talking about. But it's not me anymore.

My time has passed.

I never yearned to be spotlighted in that way, but I suppose I do feel a sense of loss now. It's nice to be wanted. And sad to be discarded. But I know that's the nature of shiny new things. I need to move forward with my life like all the other people who are no longer shiny and new and find meaning where I can.

After catching up on Rose and Suzie's group chat, I see I missed a text from my sister, Priscilla. It says only *How are you?* She checks up on me about once a month. If she didn't, we'd never talk because I get too enmeshed in my day-to-day grind.

I type in my response (it's always the same) with my left hand: *Fine, and you?*

She's on the East Coast, so the chances of her being up are pretty high. I'm not surprised when my phone starts vibrating with an in-coming call.

I hurry to rinse my mouth and find a place in my apartment where I can talk. Nowhere seems suitable, so I pull on my ugly bathrobe and step onto my rarely used balcony. It's freezing out here, especially be-cause I'm barefoot and there's condensation on the ground, and I hold the folds of my robe shut with a hand.

After taking a quick second to collect myself, I answer, "Hi, Pris-cilla je." I have to add the *je* for "older sister." When I was little, I called her just "Priscilla" once and she made me kneel in the bath-room with my arms crossed for two hours. She's older than me by fifteen years, so she got to do things like that. Because my parents were always busy working, she was also the one who came to pick me up from the principal's office when I started sobbing uncontrollably and refused to get on the school bus to go home on the first day of kindergarten. If I went trick-or-treating, she took me. If I had a birthday party, she organized it.

"Hey, Mui mui. You're up early," she says. From the rhythm of her words, I'm certain she's speed-walking somewhere. (She doesn't walk at regular human speed. I don't think she knows how.) "It's what, six A.M. your time?"

"I fell asleep early last night. I think I slept for almost twelve hours," I say as I do the math in my head.

She laughs, and the sound is rich and smooth, almost musical. "I want your life."

"No, you don't."

"Whatever. You're not pulling eighty-hour weeks. I'm getting too old for this," she says.

"You're not old, and I thought you loved your job." Year after year, she earns humongous bonuses from her consulting company that my mom delights in humble-bragging about to her friends.

She makes a scoffing sound. "Everything gets old after a while, but enough about me. How's Julian? What have you two been up to?"

"He seems to be doing pretty well," I say. "But we haven't been up to much, not together."

"What's that mean?" she asks suspiciously.

I consider lying but decide there's no point. "He wanted to see other people for a while."

"He *what*?"

"He's dating other women," I explain, since she didn't seem to understand the way I said it before. "He's seeing what else is out there before he makes a commitment because he doesn't want to have regrets."

"Oh my God, I can't even . . ." There's a long pause before she says, "When did this start?"

"About a month ago."

"An entire month? And you didn't think to *tell me*?" she nearly shouts.

Someone is out walking their dog on the sidewalk below, so I angle myself toward my doors and mumble, "Sorry."

"Before this happened, did you . . . do anything weird?" she asks.

My shoulders slump, and I stare up at the brightening sky. This is why I didn't tell her earlier. I knew she'd think it was my fault somehow.

Was it my fault?

"Not that I know of," I say.

"Have you been in another of your lazy phases?" she asks.

I grimace at her choice of words. "No, I haven't. I've . . ." But my voice trails off as I remember the weeks after I returned from the tour. I barely got out of bed during those days—but not because I was "lazy." My brain simply quit functioning. After being so busy for months, performing for enormous audiences, interacting with countless conductors, musicians, and people from the press, being *on* for so long, I shut down. I remember looking in my fridge, seeing food, and being completely overwhelmed, bewildered even, by all the steps that it took to get it into my stomach. For several days, I only ate Cheetos. I didn't have the mental capacity for cooking, let alone going out with Julian, contorting my face into the proper expressions, saying all the right things to his friends, and giving him the blow jobs he loves. For weeks, when Julian wanted to hang out, I made excuses.

Maybe I really did drive him away after all.

Priscilla sighs loudly. "Oh, Anna, what am I going to do with you?"

I know it's a rhetorical question, but I'm tempted to answer, *Nothing*, anyway. I don't want or expect her to solve my problems. I don't say anything, however. She gets mad at me when I have an "attitude," which is what she calls it when I disagree with her or express frustration or anger or any emotion contrary to what she wants.

"Everyone really liked him for you," she says with another sigh.

"I'm sorry. I know you got along really well with him." She was the one who introduced us—he was an intern at her company. At family get-togethers and things, Julian and Priscilla usually sat next to each other, immersed in stock market talk, and I loved knowing that my boyfriend and sister were on good terms.

"Don't make it sound like you dated him for *me*," she says stiffly.

I almost laugh. That's exactly why I dated him. Priscilla is my smart, beautiful, extremely successful big sister, the person I respect most in the entire world. In lots of ways, she's more of a mom to me than my actual mom. For as far back as I can remember, I've been striving to earn her approval, and Julian is most definitely Priscilla approved—as well as parent approved.

I don't know how to respond, so I just say, "Okay."

"Don't have an attitude, Anna," she snaps. "He got you to come out and do things, be social, not just hole up in your apartment with your music. You were smiling and laughing more. You were *happy*."

"Smiling and laughing doesn't always mean happy."

"I can tell when you're happy," she says confidently.

I shake my head quietly. There's no way she knows when I'm happy, not when the things I say and do around her are specifically designed to make *her* happy.

"I've started seeing a therapist," I blurt out, surprising myself with the confession. It's something I've been intentionally holding back out of fear, but so much has happened. I guess I want her to know now.

"Oh. Wow. Okay," she says. I've stunned her into inarticulation—a rare occurrence for socially savvy Priscilla.

I press a hand to my chest and hold my breath as I wait for her to say more.

"Do Mom and Dad know?" she asks.

A short laugh bubbles out of me. "No."

"That's probably for the best." She clears her throat before asking, "How did you even find this therapist?"

"I searched for 'therapist' plus 'local' and picked the one that sounded the best."

She makes a sound in her throat—just a sound, it's not even a word, but I know she disapproves. After a moment, she asks, "Was it because of Julian?"

"No, it wasn't because of Julian. It was before he—we—it was just before that," I say awkwardly. "I've been having trouble with my music. Ever since the tour and that YouTube video and everything."

"You could have talked to *me* about this instead of some random person you found on the Internet," Priscilla says in a frustrated voice. "We're *family*. I'm always here for you. It's the pressure, right? Pressure is my life. I can talk you through it."

I squeeze my eyes shut and refrain from groaning. I know what's coming.

"Prioritize, break things into small achievable tasks, and make a to-do list. I do that every day," she says.

I zone out as she tells me how satisfying it is to check things off her list and gives her TED Talk on how to present to CEOs and big bosses. I've heard all this stuff before. It doesn't help. My compulsions are too strong.

The door to my balcony opens a crack, and Quan holds up my electric toothbrush, a silent question on his face.

I cover the bottom of my phone and say, "I have extra toothbrush heads. Feel free to take one. Also, feel free to sleep longer. You look really tired."

He smiles and self-consciously rubs a hand over his head. "Thanks, but I have something this morning. I'm just going to . . ." He points over his shoulder, back toward the bathroom, and heads away.

Guilt spills through me. I don't like that he's sleep-deprived because of me.

"I thought you said you hadn't seen Julian in a while," Priscilla says, interrupting my thoughts. "But he's at your place right now? How does that work?"

She's not here to see, but I duck my head anyway. "That, uh, wasn't Julian."

"No way," she says. "You're seeing someone else?"

It takes me a while to respond. Things between me and Quan aren't easy to explain when I hardly understand them myself. "I figured if he could see other people, I could, too."

"I mean, yeah. Of course you can," Priscilla says, but she still sounds stunned. "How did you meet him?"

I narrow my eyes. "Are you sure you want to know?"

"The Internet again?" she replies, sounding like I'm physically hurting her. "And you spent the night with him? Who are you and what have you done with my baby sister? Is he shady? Are you okay? Do you need help getting him to leave? Or are you at his place?"

"He's not shady, and I'm fine. We didn't even—" I release a frustrated breath. Priscilla doesn't need to hear about my sex life. I certainly don't want to hear about hers. I'd rather jump off my balcony. "He's at my place, but he's leaving soon. Don't worry about it, okay?"

There's noise on Priscilla's end, like she's entered a busy restaurant, and she says, "I have to go, but I'll call you later, all right?"

"That's fine. Bye, Je je," I say.

"Bye, Mui mui."

The call disconnects, and I slowly lower the phone from my ear, my thoughts heavy from what I told her and even more so from what I *didn't* tell her. My diagnosis is looming over me, and I want to talk about it. Maybe I *need* to talk about it in order to really understand and accept it. But I'm also afraid.

If she's suddenly ashamed of me, it'll break my heart.

Back inside my apartment, Quan is crouched by the front door, tying his shoelaces. When he sees me, he asks, "Je? That's Chinese, right?"

"Yeah, Cantonese. That's almost all I can say, though."

The corner of his mouth lifts. "My brother is like that with Vietnamese. He understands it pretty well, though."

"Oh, I don't understand it either," I say lightly.

I expect him to laugh like other people do when I say things like this, but he doesn't. Instead, he asks, "Is that hard for you sometimes? One of my cousins only speaks English, and he gets teased a lot by family for it. They give his parents crap for it, too, and then his parents blame him."

"Actually, yeah," I admit. "My big sister is almost quadrilingual—she speaks Cantonese, Mandarin, and a bit of a rare dialect from the south, in addition to English, of course—and me . . ." I lift a shoulder. "When I was little, they couldn't get me to talk at all, and the doctor suspected all the languages were too much for me. Apparently, as soon as they only spoke one language with me, things started to click. I never picked up anything else after that. It embarrasses my mom."

"Well, I don't speak *any* Chinese," he says as he finishes tying his laces and stands up. When he gets a good look at my ugly bathrobe, he grins.

My face heats instantly. I didn't think ahead when I put this on earlier, and I should have. With Julian, I was always alert and careful, so he never saw me like this. But it's too late now. "I know it's ugly, but it's really soft."

"It's really . . . bright. Is it salmon color?" Still grinning, he approaches me and pulls the front together tighter, like he's trying to keep me warm. He doesn't seem disgusted or derisive, and it's making me feel off-balance.

"It's coral," I say. "I don't wear this and imagine I'm a tropical fish in the ocean, if that's what you're thinking. When I'm home, where people can't see me, I like to wear bright colors and rainbows and things. It makes me happy. A little."

His brow creases. "Why does it have to be where people can't see you?"

"Because people are mean. They say things like 'Did you see her?' 'I can't believe she's wearing that' or they just look at each other and laugh—at me. I hate being laughed at. It used to happen a lot, but I've gotten better at preventing it."

"I'll wear rainbows out with you. I don't give a shit," he nearly growls as he pulls me close unexpectedly and hugs me.

I'm not used to affectionate acts like this—my family definitely isn't touchy-feely, and neither was Julian—so it takes me a second or two to relax and rest my cheek on his chest. When I imagine badass Quan decked out in rainbows and people's confused reactions, I smile and say, "That would be something."

"Something awesome, yeah."

He hugs me tighter, and happiness expands in my chest. I love this, being held by him, feeling safe.

"It was thoughtless of me to ask, but thank you for staying," I say.

"It was no problem," he says. "Are you feeling better now?"

"I am."

"Do you want to talk about it?" he asks.

A barrage of emotions wells up at his suggestion—fear, excitement, anxiety, uncertainty, and, greatest of all, hope—and I swallow it down. "You have somewhere you need to be, remember?"

"I can be late. It's just kendo practice with my cousin and brother. Then teaching kids' class later."

"You're the only Asian I know who actually does martial arts," I comment, intentionally skirting around the issue.

He laughs. "I guess I'm a walking stereotype, then. Guess who my childhood idol was? Hint: There weren't a ton of options."

I gasp. "*No.*"

"Bruce Lee, yeah," he says with another laugh. "My calligraphy is that quote of his translated into Vietnamese. You know the one."

"Be water, my friend," I say in a deep voice that is my approximation of Bruce Lee.

"Yeah, but the whole quote, starting with 'Empty your mind,'" he says.

As the realization hits me, I pull away and look at the tattoos on his arms like I'm seeing them for the first time—the waves, the sea creatures. It appears he tried to take Bruce Lee's advice literally. "I can't believe it. You're *dorky*."

A huge grin covers his face, though he looks almost shy. "A little, yeah."

I touch my fingers to the fish that's inked onto his forearm and trace the scales on his smooth skin. I can't stop smiling. His dorkiness *delights* me. This shy side of him, too. "This looks like a sea carp."

"It's a koi fish, and don't go accusing me of putting freshwater fish in the ocean. My arms are different bodies of water from the rest of me."

I laugh helplessly. "That's such a dorky thing to say, Quan."

"You like it."

"I do. You might even be more—"

He cuts me off with a deep kiss that makes me cling to him. He tastes clean, faintly of my toothpaste, but salty, mysterious. When he pulls away, I bite back a protest. I could kiss him forever.

"Tomorrow night, right?" he asks, watching me carefully.

I put on a smile and nod, but I feel slightly panicked. Tomorrow is the last time I'll see him. Ever. That's been the biggest benefit to our interactions since this started, but it doesn't feel that way now. Something's changed.

Even so, it's a reminder of why I've been seeing him in the first place. I can tell him things that I can't tell other people. Because he doesn't matter.

Except he does.

But I really won't be seeing him after tomorrow. That's what we both want. Well, I used to. I don't know what I want anymore.

"You asked about yesterday." I can't bring myself to look him in the face, so I focus on his T-shirt as I say, "My therapist told me something." My heart beats so hard I can feel it in my throat. This moment is loud, weighted.

He takes my hands in his and holds on. "What did she say?"

"She said I'm—" Something occurs to me, and I gaze up at him curiously. "Do you think I'm anything like your brother?"

He lifts his eyebrows. "I . . . don't know? I haven't thought about it before. Why?"

"We're not similar at all?"

"You're *a lot* prettier than he is," he says with a twinkle in his eyes.

I shake my head, though I smile, too. "That's not what I mean, but thank you."

"Then what do you mean? I won't be a dick, I promise."

That's when I realize that I trust him. Over the past weeks, he's proven time and again that he respects me, that he won't hurt me. I can tell him things. Not because he doesn't matter. But because he is kind.

"She told me I'm on the autism spectrum," I say. And there it is. The words are out. It feels real now.

"Is that it?" he asks, like he's still waiting for me to share the big news.

A disbelieving laugh spills out of me. "That's it."

He tilts his head to the side and looks at me in a considering way.

When he doesn't speak for the longest time, my insecurities catch up with me, and I say, "If this changes things and you don't want to meet tomorrow, I completely understand and—"

"I want to meet tomorrow," he says quickly. "I was trying to think of similarities between you and my brother."

"And?"

"Honestly, you're both really different, and I don't even know what to look for. I'm not a therapist or anything. What do you think? Does it feel right to you?" he asks, and I can tell that's what matters to him. He trusts me to know myself. I didn't know how important that was to me until now.

I get to be the expert on me.

I touch the center of my chest and nod slowly as my eyes sting. "It fits. When my therapist described autism to me, when I read about it, I felt understood in a way I've never been before. I felt *seen*, the real me, and *accepted*. All my life, I've been told that I need to change and be . . . something else, something more, and I try. Sometimes I try so hard it feels like I'm breaking. Like my music right now, no matter what I do I can't get it to be *more*. Being told that it's okay to be me, it's . . ." I shake my head as words fail me.

He touches his thumb to the corner of my eye, wiping a tear away. "Then why are you so sad?"

"I don't know." I laugh, but a knot is forming in my throat. I swipe at my eyes with my sleeves. "I can't seem to stop crying."

He gathers me closer and holds me tight, pressing his cheek to my forehead, his skin to my skin. His calmness spreads to me, the steady beating of his heart, the even rhythm of his breathing.

When his pocket buzzes, we're both startled.

"It's just my phone," he says. "Ignore it." But it keeps buzzing.

"You should answer. It might be important."

With a sigh, he breaks away from me and lifts his phone to his ear. "Hey . . . No, sorry, I just got held up with something . . . I probably won't make it today—"

"No, no, please," I hurry to say. "You should go. I'm okay, really." I don't want him canceling his plans on my behalf, especially when I'm not having any sort of emergency.

"Hold on a sec," he says into the phone before putting it on mute and focusing on me. "Are you sure? I can stay, and we can get breakfast or something. Whatever you want."

"That's super nice of you, but . . ." A series of excuses and tiny lies pile up in my mouth, but I decide to be honest and say, "I need to be alone and process things. Plus, I have to practice soon, and I can't do that with you here. It's better if you go."

He smiles in understanding and unmutes the phone to say, "Actually, I'll head down. See you guys in a bit." After hanging up, he clasps one of my hands. "Sure you're okay?"

"Yes. You should go. You're already late."

He leans in and kisses me softly on the lips. It's the briefest kiss, but shivers ripple over me. "Tomorrow night."

I nod. "Tomorrow night."

He squeezes my hand once before he leaves. As I shut the door behind him, I hesitate. Neither of us said good-bye.

But tomorrow we will.

FIFTEEN

Quan

AFTER PRACTICE, WE DECIDE TO HANG OUT IN KHAI'S BACK-yard and have drinks to celebrate the LVMH news instead of going out. He's remodeling and just had a fire pit installed. There's nice outdoor furniture and blooming whatever-the-fuck trees (the flowers are purple, that's all I know), and the fire keeps people from getting cold at night. It's a sweet arrangement.

"What are we celebrating again?" Khai asks as he hands margaritas to me and Michael. He makes the best margaritas. They're strong, and he lines the rim with salt—my favorite part.

"Good news with LVMH," I say.

"Have you guys signed anything?" he asks.

I take a sip of my drink, and yeah, it's really good. "Nah, it's too early for that."

"So we're celebrating a phone call?" he asks with a skeptical frown.

Michael laughs. "Yeah, we're celebrating a phone call. It was a good one. Cheers." He holds out his drink, and we all clink our glasses together. As I'm swallowing a mouthful of tequila and lime juice, he adds, "We're also celebrating Quan's new girlfriend."

I choke and alcohol burns down my windpipe, making me wheeze and cough while Khai pounds not so helpfully on my back. When I can finally breathe, I rasp out, "What the fuck? She's not my girl-friend."

Khai perks up and looks to Michael for confirmation. "He's see-ing someone?"

Over the rim of his margarita glass, Michael grins like that cat from *Alice in Wonderland*. "He *is*."

"We're *hooking up*. That hardly counts as 'seeing someone,'" I say, and I don't like that I'm right.

Michael rolls his eyes. "Did you guys finally get it on last night?"

"No, she was crying and upset about stuff and I'm not an ass-hole," I say.

"He heard she was crying and ran over to see her so fast," Michael says to Khai in a loud fake whisper. "Our man Quan has himself a girlfriend."

Khai nods tentatively. "If I was only hooking up with someone, I'd stay away from them when they were crying."

"She's *not* my girlfriend," I say firmly.

"Do you want her to be?" Michael asks.

I look down into my margarita and shake the glass so the liquid swirls. "Maybe." I sigh and admit the truth, "Okay, yeah. I like Anna a lot, but she specifically wanted something simple. She's coming out of a relationship and going through some life stuff. Plus, I'm not sure I'm ready."

Khai frowns, but he nods, accepting what I've said. He's never pushy or nosy. He's the best listener.

Michael, on the other hand, makes a scoffing sound. "Bullshit you're not ready. It's been over a year since your surgery. And what happened when you came over? Was she uncomfortable about it? Did she send you away?"

"She asked me to stay the night," I reveal, and the resulting look on Michael's face is so delighted that I kind of want to punch him. "You're so annoying, you know that?"

He tries to look innocent. "So you spent the night, and you didn't get it on. That's definitely hookup territory."

Khai grins, though he doesn't say anything.

"The plan is to finally get our one-night stand right tomorrow," I say.

"That'll be their fourth try at hooking up," Michael explains to Khai, who looks confused.

I stiffen in my seat. "No, last night doesn't count. And why are you counting, anyway?"

Michael ignores me and aims a smart-aleck smile at Khai, waggling his eyebrows. What a dick.

"Let me get this straight," Khai says as he rubs his chin. "As soon as you guys sleep together, it's over?"

I take a large drink from my glass and swallow, noting that it suddenly tastes bitter. "Yeah."

"That means you've been seeing each other without sleeping together," he says in an academic manner.

"Yeah."

"And they text and talk and watch nature documentaries together," Michael adds, pretending he doesn't see when I glare at him.

"How long has this been going on?" Khai asks.

"Only a couple weeks," I say.

"I'm no expert, but that sounds a lot like you have a girlfriend," Khai says. "Especially the part where you spent the night."

I make a sound in my throat and toss back the rest of my drink. "It's wasn't like that. She was in a vulnerable place emotionally, and I was there for her. As a friend. Nothing more."

"What's she like?" Michael asks.

I set my glass down on a side table and turn it in circles as I say, "She's . . . quirky, funny, really nice."

"You do like quirky," Michael says. To Khai, he says, "Remember that chick he dated who couldn't stand it when people saw her eating so she doggy-bagged everything?"

"Don't judge. Everyone's got their own issues," I point out.

"There was also the one who made him brush his teeth before kissing," Khai adds.

"That's just good hygiene, especially in the morning," I say.

Michael points his glass at me. "She also made you use hand sanitizer before holding hands and shower before sex."

I shrug. "That wasn't a big deal."

"There was also the one who liked to lick him in public," Khai says.

"Okay, I didn't love that." I rub my eye as I remember how it stung when her spit got in there.

Michael takes a sip of his margarita and casually asks, "So when are we going to meet her?"

"That's not going to happen."

"Why not, though? Why don't you just tell her how you feel?" Khai asks.

"It's not that easy—"

"Yeah, it is," Michael interjects. "It's exactly that easy."

"It's not," I say, and my certainty is conveyed in the tone of my voice.

Khai starts to speak, but Michael shakes his head at him so he falls silent.

I spin my glass several more times, around and around. "I don't know how to tell her about what happened."

"Then don't," Khai says. "It's not information that she needs to know."

Michael nods in agreement. "He's got a point. You can tell her later if things progress."

I just shake my head. Parts of me don't look quite right anymore. That's the simple truth and something that I feel I need to explain. There's also the other thing, the thing that I haven't told anyone yet, because it's awkward and it sucks and sometimes it still makes me cry. But I'd have to tell Anna. It's relevant when it comes to relationships.

"You know, I can tell based purely off text messages if a girl is into someone," Michael says.

"Yeah, like if the message says 'I'm into you,' that's a pretty sure sign," I say dryly.

"No, get your phone out and text her. I'll show you what I'm talking about. I can tell within three lines," he insists. "Plus, don't you want to know how she's doing? You guys were originally going to meet up tonight."

Grumbling, I take my phone out of my pocket and text her, *How you doing?*

"I'm not going to show you if she says something personal. Also, what if she doesn't respond right a—"

Dots start jumping on the screen, and I get a new message with a smiley face. *I'm okay. You?*

I show Michael so he can analyze the exchange like it's tea leaves or some shit, and he grins right away. "A smiley emoji straight off. That's a really good sign."

I narrow my eyes at him before typing, *Me too. Was thinking about you.*

Before I hit the send button, Michael looks over my shoulder at my phone and says, "What, no emoji? That's so impersonal. Add a heart."

I give him a disgusted look. "Marriage has warped your brain if you think—"

He snatches the phone from me, body checks me when I lunge at him, and dances away, typing on my phone screen with his thumbs. When he tosses the phone back to me, the damage has been done. He sent my original message. Except there's a big red heart after it.

I'm going to kill him.

With my bare hands.

As painfully as possible.

But then my phone buzzes with a new message from Anna. *I was thinking about you too.* And there, at the end, is a red heart, just like mine.

I stare at her message for the longest time, completely stunned out of my rage. "Do you think she . . . does she . . . maybe she . . ."

Michael wraps an arm around my shoulders. "That, my friend, means she likes you. I read about this in *Cosmo*."

"I don't know how you can stand reading those magazines," Khai says as he gets up and collects our glasses. "I have a bunch of limes, so I'm going to make another round. I think Quan needs it."

"Yeah, thanks," I say as I drop back into my chair, still staring at her message and that red heart.

This changes things. I need to completely scrap my plans for tomorrow. It's not just about sex anymore. If it ever was.

SIXTEEN

Anna

THIS WEEKEND, WHEN I'M NOT PRACTICING, I'M FEVERISHLY researching autism, consuming information in all possible manners—books, articles online, videos on YouTube, podcasts, postings in autistic people groups on Facebook, even a made-for-TV film about Temple Grandin starring Claire Danes. The more I learn, the more certain I am that this is me. This is where I belong.

I want to tell people, my family, my friends, my fellow musicians at the symphony. I want them to understand me at last. The key to me is right here, in these books and media.

It's early evening, and I'm nervously waiting for Quan to arrive for our last date and reading an autistic woman's personal blog entry about proper terminology. Apparently, *Asperger's syndrome* is no longer used diagnostically in the United States. In 2013, it was grouped, along with other former neurological conditions, under the broad umbrella of *autism spectrum disorder*. Many in the autistic community prefer the use of descriptors like *with low support needs* as opposed to *high-functioning*, which was how Jennifer described me. I'm mouthing the words *autistic with low support needs* and getting used to the feel of them when my phone rings. It's Priscilla, so I pick up immediately.

"Hi, Je je."

There's noise in the background, like she's at a restaurant or a party. She's perpetually "networking" and doing social things. I could never live her life, not happily anyway. "Hey, I had a free minute, so I thought I'd call you. What's up?"

"Not much, just reading," I say as I scroll past the terminology blog entry to one about poor spatial awareness. There's a picture of the blogger's bruised legs, and I compare them to mine. Aside from our skin tone, we look the same. Just like her, I'm constantly running into table corners and chairs and door handles and things, but the worst for me is glass cases in department stores. I get distracted by the shiny things inside, and seven times out of ten, I bang my face on the glass as I lean close to get a better look—one of the many reasons why I hate shopping.

"I spoke to Mom earlier. She said Dad's not feeling great. You might want to check up on them one of these days," Priscilla says, and there's censure in her voice, as there always is when it comes to this topic.

"What's wrong?" My dad is on the older side—sixteen years older than my mom—but I never noticed until recent years, when congestive heart failure forced him into retirement against his will.

"He's just really tired. Mom says he's napping today, and you know how he feels about naps," she says with a subdued laugh.

"I'll try to make it home next weekend."

"You'll *try*?" she asks, and I look up at the ceiling as my fingers flex into claws. I loathe being told what to do like this, absolutely loathe it, and it's worse when it involves doing things with or for my parents. They're close to Priscilla. They *wanted* Priscilla. Me, I'm their accidental second child, the result of a Mexico vacation and too many piña coladas. Worse than that, I'm overly sensitive, difficult, "lazy," and, quite frankly, a bit of a disappointment—except for my relationship with Julian, the son-in-law of their dreams, and my accidental Internet fame.

Things with Julian aren't looking great, however, and the fame isn't lasting. I'm getting upstaged by a twelve-year-old. I admit I watched videos of her playing with trepidation. I didn't want to be impressed, but she's genuinely amazing. I've never seen bow work that fluid. She deserves the accolades. Still, now I don't have anything to show my parents, no great news, no fresh accomplishments, nothing my mom can humble-brag about to her friends, and I know she craves it. I don't know if it's better never to be successful at all, or to have success for a short while, only to lose it.

"I *will* visit next weekend." I sound peppy and excited as I say it. I even smile. Because that's how she wants me to be—easygoing and eager to please. Like a golden retriever.

"Good. They'll be happy to see you," she says.

I almost laugh at that—a bitter, disrespectful kind of laugh—but I manage to hold it in. If they find out about the shambles I've made of my life, they most certainly *won't* be happy. There's no more Julian. No more publicity. The tour is over. My career is circling the toilet drain because I can't get my act together. I'm in therapy. There's this *thing*, whatever it is, with Quan. (What's worse? Trying to have casual sex with a stranger or failing at having casual sex with a stranger?) And then the latest development . . .

An odd impulse grabs hold of me, and without actively deciding to do anything, I hear myself saying, "My therapist told me something the other day."

"Yeah, what did they say?"

"She said I have autism spectrum disorder. I'm autistic with low support needs." The words sound strange falling off my tongue. They're too new. But they're mine, and I want her to know. They explain so much about me—the trouble I had when I was little, the things I'm going through now, everything.

Even so, I hold my breath as I wait for her to respond. It feels like my heart pauses its beating. Will she be ashamed? Will she walk on eggshells around me now?

Will she still love me?

"No, you're not," she says with conviction.

For a moment, I'm too flustered to speak. Disbelief wasn't a reaction I'd foreseen. "My *therapist* told me this. One of her specializations is—"

She makes an impatient sound. "None of that means anything. People get diagnosed with all kinds of stuff nowadays. It's a scam to get your money. Don't let them take advantage of you, Anna."

My jaw drops as her words seep into my brain. How she can so easily disregard a professional opinion just because she doesn't like it? How can she be so certain?

"Autism often looks different in women," I try to explain. "It's due to a phenomenon called masking, which is when—"

"Trust me, you're *not* autistic," Priscilla says.

"I think I am."

"Don't use this as an excuse for your shortcomings, Anna. You're minimizing the struggles that real autistic people face when you do this."

"I'm not trying to minimize anything for anyone," I say, horrified by the accusation. "Autism can be different from what you've seen. They call it a spectrum for a reason. There are people who have more obvious impairments, but there are also people like me. Just because I look like I'm doing okay doesn't mean it's always true."

"Oh my God, I can't believe we're even discussing this. You're *not* disabled," she says in an exasperated tone.

"I didn't say I was. I don't think I qualify, personally. But it's true that there are certain things that are harder for me to—"

"I have to go. Let's talk about this later." The line disconnects.

I lower my phone from my ear and stare ahead without seeing anything. That didn't go at all how I thought it would, and a deep sense of disappointment and frustration grips me. I told her because I yearned for her to understand me. But it's never been more clear how much she doesn't.

Self-doubt takes control of me. I must be wrong. Jennifer must be wrong. Those epiphanies that I had were fake. That sense of identification was misguided. It is human to struggle. If there was a diagnosis for every difficulty, they wouldn't mean anything.

My intercom buzzes, and I scramble to my feet and run to the front door to hit the button. "Hello?"

"It's me," Quan says. "Ready?"

"Yes," I say, but I don't really know if it's true. I've done a lot of thinking tonight, and I haven't found a way around my issues. I can't do the things he wants. I *can't*. But we put this thing in motion, and I want to see it through. I finish what I begin. If I don't . . . it fills me with suffering. "Come on up."

When a knock sounds a short while later, I take a second to collect myself, paste a smile on my face, and open the door.

He's dressed similar to the first night we met—motorcycle jacket, dark pants, boots. His helmet is tucked under his arm, and he's smiling at me, that smile that makes it hard for me to think. Once he gets a good look at me, however, his smile fades.

"What's wrong?" he asks.

"Nothing." I shake my head and shrug my shoulders.

He gives me a skeptical look, so I explain, "I was just on the phone with my sister. I told her about . . . you know."

"She didn't take it well?" he asks, his brow wrinkled with concern.

"I'm not sure how to answer that question. She thinks my therapist is wrong, that *I'm* wrong. And maybe I am. I don't know anymore." I hold my palms out and drop them to my sides as a sense of heaviness weighs me down.

He frowns at me for a second before looking at my living room over my shoulder. "Do you want to get out for a bit? Take a walk or something? Fresh air usually helps me feel better."

"Okay, sure," I say. Aside from what I have to do for transportation purposes, I'm not much of a walker. Or jogger. Or any kind of exerciser. But it's been days since I've been out, and I don't mind the idea.

I step into my ballet slippers, which are neatly arranged in the entryway, lock the door, and follow him out of my building. The sky is darkening and it's a bit chilly, but I don't go back for a sweater or coat. I don't expect us to be out long.

When we walk past a black motorcycle parked next to the curb, I ask, "Yours?"

The corner of his mouth lifts. "Want to go for a ride? I promise to be careful."

I fumble with a response. I've never ridden a motorcycle before. I've never *wanted* to because Priscilla thinks it's a foolish thing to do. According to her, anyone who gets injured while riding was basically asking for it and shouldn't be surprised when they get brain damage.

Before I can answer, he aims a carefree smile at me and says, "I was just asking. Don't feel pressured."

He walks past the motorcycle, but I grab his arm to stop him and quickly say, "No, I want to. I'm just a little nervous."

"You sure? I won't be sad if we don't. Really."

"I'm sure," I say. Priscilla isn't here to judge me. More important, I'm tired of the never-ending and fruitless battle to earn her approval. It's brought me misery more than anything else, and right now, I want to give in and see what it's like not to fight so hard. On my last night with this wonderful, completely wrong-for-me man, I want to do something memorable.

"Okay, but just tell me if you want us to stop, and I will," he says.

As he settles the extra helmet he brought onto my head and clips it under my chin, I smile up at him—a real smile. I *am* nervous, but I'm also strangely energized. He said he'd be careful, and I trust him. Before climbing onto the bike, he hesitates, takes his jacket off, and settles it over my shoulders.

"Just in case," he says.

I'm about to protest, but the jacket is deliciously warm and it smells like him. I thread my arms into the sleeves and pull the front portion over my nose, so I can breathe in his scent. "Are you sure you don't need it?"

"Nah, my temperature runs hot. I'm good." He zips me up and nods with satisfaction, and I laugh awkwardly as I wiggle my arms, making the too-big sleeves flap like wings.

"I must look pretty funny like this."

"You look perfect." To prove it, he leans in and kisses me on the lips. It's a short kiss, but it goes to my head anyway. His lips are cool, his breath warm. When he pulls away, it takes me a moment to reorient myself, and he grins as he rolls one of his jacket sleeves up to my wrist.

"I can do this myself," I say, not used to people helping me with something like this—or anything, really.

He simply shakes his head and continues working on the other sleeve. "I like to."

That's a novel concept to me. In the world unique to my worka-holic, success-driven family, self-sufficiency is key. I vividly remember a time when I was sick during grade school. My dad handed me a Tylenol bottle and instructed me to read the directions as he rushed out the door to catch a flight for a business trip, leaving me to manage my fever on my own. I was old enough that it wasn't illegal to be home alone (I think), and clearly, I managed just fine. But I lost something that day. Or maybe I just grew up. I don't know.

What I *do* know is that right now, as Quan does this trivial thing for me, I feel downright spoiled. And I love it.

He puts his own helmet on, climbs onto the motorcycle, and motions for me to join him. "Put your feet here and wrap your arms around my waist."

Once I'm behind him, holding on tightly, excitement, both good and bad, rushes through my veins. It's like I have carbonation in my blood.

"Ready?" he asks, looking back at me over his shoulder.

I nod, and he smiles at me and revs the engine.

My stomach dips as we pull away from the curb, and every muscle in my body tenses. There's nothing between me and the giant metal vehicles hurtling down the street. I can feel the wind on my legs, on my hands, on my face, and I squeeze my eyes shut as terror seizes me. If the end is coming, I don't want to see it.

The end doesn't come, though. Not in a minute. Not in two, three, four, or five. The thing with feelings is they pass. Hearts aren't designed to feel anything too intensely for too long, be it joy, sorrow, or anger. Everything passes in time. All colors fade.

Even though I understand I could still get in an accident at any moment, my fear recedes, and I open my eyes. It's too much to take in at first. We're going fast, and the world around me is a blur. But eventually, I catch my breath, and my heartbeat slows a notch.

The city is alive. Streetlights shine, taillights blink, a cloud of exhaust from a passing truck washes over my face. Somehow everything is sharper, brighter.

I get my bearings. I've walked these streets. I know where I am. Especially when he turns onto Franklin Street. The modern geometric design of the Davies Symphony Hall comes into view. It's the back of the building so it's not as impressive, but it feels like home to me. I've missed it.

Next, we pass the War Memorial Opera House and the San Francisco Ballet, glimpse the back of the grand rounded dome of city hall, and continue north. I assume we're heading to the ocean, somewhere I never go unless I'm introducing the city to someone from out of town, but he turns before we get there. We head down quiet side streets lined with trees, upscale apartments, and parks, and I realize he's steering clear of the busy parts of town. He's being careful, just as he promised. He's keeping me safe.

Gratitude and something else swell in my chest, and I hug him tighter. This is when I become aware of our physical proximity. Our bodies are pressed against each other, his back to my chest, my thighs to his, my arms around his waist. He's solid against me, a steady anchor in this whirlwind chaos. My focus narrows to him. I watch, captivated, as he competently steers us through the traffic. He doesn't speed. He signals when he turns. He doesn't run the yellow lights. He's not trying to show off—he's confident enough that he doesn't need to—and I really, really like that.

He stops across the street from a park and helps me climb off the motorcycle and remove my helmet, asking, "How was that? How are you doing?"

"That was . . . I don't have words," I say. I'm trembling slightly, but I can't stop smiling.

"Good, then?" he asks just to be sure.

"Yes." I smile wider. "Thank you."

He nods, pleased by my response, before looking at the park across the way. "Have you ever been here? It's best at night."

"No. I mean, I've gone past it a bunch of times, I knew it was here, but I never stopped to walk around and explore," I say.

"Come on. I think you'll like it," he says.

As he takes my hand and crosses the street with me, I take in the view, seeing the Palace of Fine Arts with new eyes. A fountain sprays within a lagoon surrounded by drowsy weeping willows, and beyond it, Roman colonnades rise, leading to a soaring rotunda that glows golden beneath clever nighttime illumination. It looks, I decide, like a fairy-tale setting.

There's a large stretch of open grass before the water, dotted here and there with blooming trees. I can't see the color of the flowers in the dark, but when the breeze picks up, petals fall like snowflakes, lending a honey scent to the air. Couples amble along the pathways. A stranger takes a group photo for a family of six (two parents and four little girls of varying ages with matching dresses and pigtails) and hands the phone back to them. A shaggy dog barks enthusiastically as it hurtles by, its leash dragging on the grass. Several yards behind, a harried man races after the dog, yelling, "Bad boy! No chasing!"

A laugh bubbles out of me, and Quan squeezes my hand. "Feeling better?"

"Yes," I say automatically. The ride was such a good distraction that it takes me a few seconds to remember why I was unhappy before, but as soon as I recall my recent discussion with Priscilla, heaviness settles on my shoulders. "My sister thinks I'm trying to use the diagnosis as an excuse for my failures."

He grimaces. "What the fff—heck?"

I shake my head at him, smiling despite the tightness in my chest. "You can swear around me, you know. I'm a grown-up."

"You never do," he says.

"I would if I was better at it, but the words sound wrong when I say them. Also, why are they so bad anyway? One is just . . . feces, which every healthy person makes. The other is sex, and most people really like sex, so . . ."

"Says the person who can't tell me what she likes in bed," he whispers in my ear, sending a shiver down my neck.

"Okay, you have a point." I squirm internally as my face heats to a thousand degrees.

He gives me a good-natured yet knowing kind of look before switching back to the original topic. "What did you say to your sister after she said that? Did you get mad?"

"No, mad is never okay. It's disrespectful, you know? I tried to explain, but she wouldn't really listen. I don't know what to do now. And maybe she's right. Maybe I *am* just looking for excuses."

"Fuck that," he says abruptly. "You're not like that."

"Is autism right for me, though? She said I'm hurting real autistic people when I claim it for myself."

"*What?*" he says in disgust. "You're not hurting anyone. If a diagnosis can help improve your life, it's the right one for you, and only *you* can know that. What do you think? Does it help you or not?"

"I think . . . it helps."

"Then your therapist is right," he says simply, like it's all settled.

"But what do I do when my family doesn't believe me?" I ask.

His mouth twists like there's a bad taste on his tongue. "Ignore what they say, and live your life the way you need to."

I release a heavy sigh. "That's not easy to do."

"I know," he says, and there's a weariness in his expression that implies he really does understand. "*I* believe you, though. That's something, right?"

"Yes," I whisper. That *is* something. Right now, it feels like everything.

SEVENTEEN

Quan

IT'S KIND OF CORNY, BUT THE PALACE OF FINE ARTS IS ONE OF my favorite places in the city. I love the columns and the lights and the water. It's romantic. Lots of people do their weddings here, and yeah, I like weddings. Sometimes I get teary when people say their vows—if they're good vows or they're said with feeling. It gets me every time when old dads cry, maybe because I wish my dad cared about me that way.

"This place doesn't look real," Anna says as she looks around with wonder, reverently touching her fingertips to the reddish stone on one of the columns while we walk through the gardens.

"It gets better this way," I say, and lead her down the colonnade to the rotunda.

Inside, she tilts her head back and gazes at the intricate geometric patterns on the ceiling. Light reflects off the surface of the water outside, and waves ripple over the hexagonal shapes overhead. It's a work of architectural genius, but what captivates me is Anna's profile, the way her lips are parted ever so slightly, how much I like seeing her in my jacket.

"I've always wanted to kiss a girl in the middle of this room," I confess, feeling determined and a little bit queasy at what I'm planning to do.

She grins at me, and light dances in her eyes. "I bet you've taken lots of girls here."

"I have." I stride to the exact center of the echoing space.

"Do you kiss them all right there?" she asks, hanging close to the walls, away from me.

"Nah," I say.

"Why?"

"It never felt right before."

She tries to smile, but her lips won't quite cooperate. "Maybe with the right person."

I hold my hand out toward her, inviting her to join me here in the center. "The view is best right here. It's perfectly symmetrical." I have a feeling she loves symmetry like cats love catnip.

She takes a few steps toward me but stops out of my reach. Looking up at the ceiling, she smiles and says, "You're right. The view *is* better here. I love this."

"You're not in the middle, Anna."

She bites her lip and takes one more step toward me.

I capture one of her hands and gently pull her to the middle with me. "You don't want to stand next to me?"

She meets my eyes for the barest fraction of a second before glancing away. "I don't want you to feel pressured to . . . do things with me."

"I don't."

A smile flashes on her mouth as she nods. "Okay, good."

Courage, I tell myself. She sent me a heart emoji. I can do this.

Steeling myself, I tuck a tendril of her hair behind her ear. When her cheek twitches, I ask, "Do you mind when I do that?"

She starts to shake her head, but stops. "I like the sentiment."

"But?" I ask.

With her gaze trained up at the ceiling, she adds, "But . . . it bothers me when people touch my hair."

I store that information away and run the backs of my fingers along her cheek and cup her jaw in my hand, bringing her attention back to me. "What about when I touch you like this?"

She takes a shaky breath and exhales. "It's okay."

"Okay good, or okay bad?"

Her lips curve. "Okay good."

"Good to know." I lean down, aching to press my mouth to hers, but I only allow my nose to graze against the bridge of hers, a caress that makes her eyes drift shut.

I brush my lips over hers, and when she moves as if to prolong contact, my control snaps and I take her mouth the way I've been craving to. She makes a tiny sound in her throat, and I'm lost. I kiss her like I'm drowning.

I wanted to memorize everything about this moment, kissing her in this place, but her mouth is all I can think about. Her intoxicating softness, her taste, the way she seems to draw me deeper. I can't get enough. I can't stop.

She's the one who pulls away, her hands gripping my shoulders tightly. "Can we get arrested for lewd kissing in public?"

A gruff laugh comes out of me. "I don't think so? And you think this is lewd? You haven't seen anything yet." I slide my palms down her back, grip her hips, and arch against her, so she can feel what she does to me.

She gasps and hides her face against my neck, saying my name like it's a protest, and I chuckle.

This is the right time, so I say it.

"I really like you, Anna."

"I like you, too," she says, and there's a weight to her words that tells me she means it.

"I don't want this to be our last night together," I confess. "I want to keep seeing you after this. Instead of trying to have a one-night stand . . . why don't we just date and see where things go?" I ask, having difficulty hearing my voice over the loud crashing of my heart.

She draws in a sharp breath and steps away from me. "Does that mean you want to be my boyfriend?"

"We don't need to put labels on things if it makes you uncomfortable." But I'm not sure if I'm saying that for me or for her. If we're in a committed relationship, I have to be up front with her about things, and that isn't easy, even though she's been open with me about her own issues. I want to be her rock, someone she's not afraid to depend on. I *need* her to see me as whole.

"My boyfriend and I . . ." She frowns and brushes the hair away from her face with an impatient swipe of her hand. "He wanted us to be in an open relationship. I should have told you earlier, but I didn't know that we would—that you would—that I—" She gives up trying to explain.

It takes me a moment to understand what she's saying, but then a weird mixture of feelings boils inside me. I was wrong. She wasn't trying to get over someone. She just wanted to try something new. Because her shitty boyfriend was. It stings that she didn't tell me, but I get why she didn't. We were never supposed to be anything.

"Are you angry?" she asks.

Hell if I know the answer to that, so I ask the only question that really matters right now: "Do you still want to be with him?"

She worries her bottom lip and then shakes her head slowly but decisively. "I don't."

My heart jumps. My hands ache to touch her, but I keep them down at my sides. "Do you want—"

"I want to be with *you*," she says, holding my gaze in a way she rarely has before.

I take a step toward her. "How long have you guys been . . . doing this?"

"Basically since you and I met. It's surprisingly easy to be apart," she says. "For the record, there's only been you."

I have to smile at that. I'm the only one she hid from in the bathroom.

"Since we're being honest with each other . . ." Nausea washes over me, and I exhale through my mouth, trying to breathe it away.

She watches me with a frown, waiting for me to speak.

"I didn't have some kind of injury before. I was sick." My nausea increases until I'm almost dizzy, and I force the ugly words out. "I had testicular cancer, and they had to remove one. Some people would say I'm only half the—"

She presses her fingers to my lips to silence the rest of my words. "Don't say that."

I'm not done. There's more to drag into the open. But my eyes are watery, and there's a fist lodged in my throat. No matter how many times I swallow, it refuses to go away. I don't want to be like this in front of her. I want to be the person she thought I was, a confident motherfucker who wouldn't give a shit about any of this. But I do give a shit. I want to be enough—for her, for me, for the people in my life.

She touches my face like I did to her earlier, her eyes creased with concern. "Does it hurt?"

"Not at all. I've been healed and cancer-free for a while now."

A brilliant smile stretches across her face. "That's the best news."

"Not quite the best news. I don't look the way I should down there. It's not—"

She breaks into laughter, surprising me. Honestly, it burns a little.

"Sorry, I'm not laughing at you," she says. "But really, I don't care what you look like down there. I've read books where women are obsessed with how a guy's balls look, and I never understood it. 'Nice' ones, 'not nice' ones, they're all the same to me. I don't, uh, know how to appreciate them."

I could get angry, I realize. Her words are insensitive in a way. But I know she doesn't mean them to be. She wants me to know that she doesn't care if I'm more lopsided than I should be, that it really doesn't matter to her.

So I let it go.

I choose to be angry at the situation, at cancer, and *not* at her.

I imagine her puzzling over elaborate descriptions of hairy balls, maybe looking at a mosaic of scrotums as she tries to understand their appeal, and I can't help being amused. She has a point. Before I had the surgery, my doctor encouraged me to get a silicone prosthesis to replace what they were removing, and I said no. After having cancer, I didn't want fake junk in my junk. I told myself that I could handle looking different and no one cared anyway. But that was *before*, when I hadn't lost anything yet. After the surgery, I felt vulnerable in a way I'd never experienced. I still haven't gotten over it.

But I want to. Maybe I'm finally on my way.

"You keep talking about these books that you're reading," I say. "What kind of books are they?"

She purses her lips, stubbornly silent, though a smile hints at the corners of her mouth, and I sigh and touch my forehead to hers.

"Let's do this—you and me, together—and see what happens," I say.

"Okay." That's all she says, but that's more than enough.

Now that we're not talking, the roar of the fountain in the lagoon fills my ears. I'm aware of Anna, the building around us, the rippling light above us, and the night beyond.

Everything, every single thing, is absolutely perfect.

EIGHTEEN

Anna

WE GRAB FALAFEL AND PITA SANDWICHES FROM A FOOD truck and eat them as we walk by the marina, where the sail-less masts of the boats point toward the sky like upside-down lollipops. We talk about octopi and joke about the possible places where we might find one hiding along the shore. Like usual for us, we end up kissing, but when Quan touches me, his hands feel like ice on my skin. I don't want him to die of hypothermia, so I insist we call it a night.

Outside my apartment building, I debate things for a second before asking, "Do you want to come up?"

"Do you want me to?" he asks instead.

"I asked first."

He laughs as he fiddles with my helmet. It seems to take him a long time to lock it to the back of his bike before he says, "Yeah, I want to."

"Then come up with me," I say.

After attaching his own helmet to his bike, he follows me into the building and up three sets of musty old stairs to my apartment. Inside, I step out of my shoes, remove his jacket, and drape it over the back of my armchair, suddenly ill at ease. I know what comes next, but I don't know how to get us there.

"A-are you thirsty?" I ask.

"No, thanks," he says.

"Do you want to watch TV?"

His lips quirk in amusement. "It would be different to finally watch something with you in person, but no, I don't feel like TV right now."

He advances toward me, and my breath catches. The way he walks, like he's going somewhere important, appeals to me. Because he's coming to me.

"I figured out how we need to do this the first time," he says.

"How?"

He leans down and presses his lips to my temple, my cheek, the soft spot behind my ear. "In the dark."

I immediately think of his self-consciousness with regard to his surgery and nod. "I'm okay with that."

We head down the hall to my bedroom, and in the doorway, I automatically fumble around for the light switch until Quan whispers, "Let's keep the lights off. Unless you changed your mind?"

"No, I just forgot." I wander through the darkness, eventually bumping my knees against the cushioned side of my mattress.

I turn around to find him, and smack straight into his chest with an *ooof*.

"Okay?" he asks.

"Yes, but this is a little awkward."

"A little," he agrees. "But I kind of like it, too. I get to learn a whole new side of you."

"The clumsy side of me?"

"I'm so used to seeing you. Now I get to focus on feeling you." His lips land on my forehead, on an eyebrow, eliciting a laugh from me, on the tip of my nose, my mouth. He sucks on my bottom lip, licks, and then claims my mouth with bold strokes of his tongue as his hands sweep over my body.

When he palms my behind and squeezes, my inner muscles clench tight, and moisture floods between my thighs. Logically, I know he won't ease the ache in my body—there's no way he could know how—but I want him anyway. I want his kisses, his caresses. I want him close. Most of all, I want him to want me.

My kisses acquire a wild edge. I slip my hands under his shirt and test the firmness of his stomach, his chest, his back. Even without the light, I can sense how strong he is, how fast. I am neither of those things, and I delight in our differences. When I register the hardness pressing against my lower belly, I rise instinctively onto the tips of my toes until we line up . . . just right.

He makes a hoarse sound and rocks against me, slowly. Sensation arrows straight to my core, and my knees buckle. He doesn't let me fall. He holds me up, pulls one of my thighs over his hip, and rubs sinuously between my legs as he kisses me deeper. The rawness of the action, the friction, his mouth, it all overwhelms me.

I hardly notice when he settles me on the bed. I just know that our bodies are closer now. Closer is better. I push his shirt up, impatient with the layers of fabric between us, and he breaks the kiss to yank it off. Our mouths come back together like we can't stand to be separated. I suppose that's true, for now. I'm addicted to his kisses. And his taste, his scent, his skin. I slide my hands down his back, trailing my fingertips along his spine, luxuriating in the feel of him. When I encounter the waistband of his pants, I slip my fingers underneath and venture down, so I can fill my hands with the perfectly rounded globes of his ass. Instantly, I'm obsessed.

"You're in trouble," I say between kisses.

"Why?"

"Now that I know what you feel like, I won't be able to stop touching you here. I'm going to do it all the time." I'm being completely honest, so I don't understand at first when he breaks out laughing, but I decide it *is* a little funny.

"I'm glad you like it," he says, and even though I can't see him, I can tell he's smiling from the timbre of his voice. "Touch me as much as you like."

"Anywhere?" I ask, because I remember what happened last time.

He pauses for a moment, and then the bed shifts as he moves. I hear the zip as he undoes his pants and the thud when they hit the floor. It doesn't make sense, but I feel intensely self-conscious as I pull my dress over my head, toss it aside, and remove my underclothes.

I shouldn't feel this way. He can't see me. *I* can't even see me. But it's like my mind still hasn't accepted that the darkness is real. I'm waiting for someone to judge me, my body, my actions.

He stretches out next to me and pulls me toward him so our bodies are flush together, front to front, skin to skin. The rigid length of his sex burns against my pelvis, but I ignore it.

"You feel so good," he whispers, running his hand up my leg and over my hip.

"So do you." I touch his face, his neck, and rest my palm against the center of his chest. "I can feel your heart beating. It's fast. Are you nervous?"

"A little," he admits.

"Me, too."

"Do you want to stop?" he asks.

"No."

Brushing his lips softly against mine, he whispers, "Should I stop talking and get back to kissing you then?"

"Yes, pl—"

His tongue strokes between my lips, and he kisses me with so much feeling that my toes curl. For ages, that's all we do. We kiss until we can barely breathe. We touch each other, but our hands remain in safe places—arms, legs, stomachs, backs. Yes, I grab his butt because I'm an indecent woman, but I don't have the nerve to do more than that after last time.

When I shift restlessly, his length slides between my thighs and rubs over my sex, and he groans against my neck as his body stiffens.

"I'm sorry."

"Don't be sorry." Breathing roughly, he nuzzles my neck and sucks on my earlobe before saying, "If I show you how I like to be touched, will you do the same?"

"Can't I just touch you?"

He makes a frustrated growling sound and presses a hard kiss to my mouth. "I want us both to enjoy this."

"I am." Sex with Julian was work—physically, mentally, and emotionally. Because I was always trying to be something other than what I was. *This* is . . . something else.

"You know what I mean," Quan says. "Talk to me, or show me, anything."

"I can't. I *want* to. For you. But I can't. It's embarrassing, and if anyone—"

"Anyone what? It's just the two of us here, Anna."

"I know, but . . ." I don't finish. I don't know how to explain.

"You want me. Unless I'm imagining things."

"I do." I turn my burning face away from him, but then I remember he can't see and I feel silly.

He gathers me closer and kisses my temple. "I can't leave you with lady blue balls. That's shit-boyfriend territory."

"That's not a thing," I say, unable to contain my amusement.

"It's totally a thing. You just don't notice because you have them constantly."

"I really don't."

"How often do you touch yourself?" he whispers.

My face burns hotter, but I make myself answer, "I don't know. I haven't tracked it."

"Once a day?"

"No."

"Once a week?"

It takes me two tries before I manage to say, "Maybe."

"When you do, do you touch here?" His fingers trail from my collarbones down to my breast, and he teases the nipple until it hardens into a tight peak.

My throat locks, taking away my ability to speak. Before I met him, I never touched my own breasts that way. But after he kissed me there, I did try to replicate the way he made me feel. I wasn't successful.

"I guess I don't need to ask. I already know you liked what I did last time." He adjusts his body position slightly, and in the next instant, the heat of his mouth closes around my nipple. He sucks and strokes with his tongue, and I feel the draw deep inside. I can't help the sound I make—half gasp, half moan. "You made that same sound. I fucking love that sound." He switches to my other breast and mirrors his actions there. I try not to, but I make that sound again. I grasp at the bedsheets, clenching them tightly as I writhe beneath his mouth.

"I wish I knew how to get that sound when I touch you here."

With that, he smooths a hand over my stomach, down to the curls between my legs. A finger eases between slick folds and circles my clitoris with languid motions. My breath tears, and my hips rise sharply against his hand. It's so close to being what I need. So close. But still so far.

"Faster?" he asks in a low voice.

I can't answer.

"Harder?"

I stare into the darkness, quietly raging against . . . everything. But mostly myself. Why am I like this? Why can't I change? Why can't I speak up?

"Should we stop, Anna?" he whispers.

My eyes flood with tears that slowly spill down my face and soak into the blankets. "I don't want to stop."

He's silent for a long span of time before he captures one of my hands and kisses the knuckles, sucks on the tip of a finger before nipping at it, and then guides my hand between my thighs to my sex. "Let's try this, then," he whispers, maneuvering my fingers so they're pressed against my most sensitive place. "I can't see you. I won't know what you're doing. You don't have to say a single thing."

"Quan, I can't—"

He silences me with an openmouthed kiss as his fingers sneak between mine and stroke my clitoris, trapping my hand beneath his as he touches me. Just like before, it's so close to being what I need. But still so far.

Only this time, my fingers are right there, and the temptation to do as he suggested is nearly unbearable. I fight it. I try to do the good thing. I succeed.

For a while.

But the longer he kisses me, the greater the temptation grows. My hips push against his fingers, seeking the kind of caress that's eluding me. He doesn't give it to me. He can't. He doesn't know how. But *my* fingers are right there, and they're impossibly slippery from the force of my need. Every muscle in my body draws tight as an A string.

One of my fingers twitches, betraying my control, and I rub myself the way I like. Just a little, I tell myself. Just a little. I cry out against Quan's mouth as my arousal sharpens almost painfully.

"That's it," he whispers as he pulls his hand away, leaving me to touch myself freely.

I shouldn't, but I do it again. And then again, moaning his name. My sex clenches hard, and my hips jerk.

"Don't stop," he says, kissing my temple, my cheek, my mouth, my jaw.

I do it again, and the sound of my fingers fluttering over my slick flesh is loud in the dark of the room. Loud, and starkly erotic.

"So fucking hot," he whispers in my ear, and I glow inside at his praise.

Driven by the desire to hear more, I cave in, and I touch myself with abandon as I lick his lips and spear my tongue into his mouth, bite his bottom lip, his chin, suck on the strong cords of his neck. I rise quickly toward orgasm, but then I hover at the edge, unable to go over, as insidious thoughts invade my head.

I must look so funny right now, touching myself when I have this beautiful man here. I should have sex the right way, let him do the touching. I should be easy to pleasure. I should orgasm for him instantly, multiple times, every time, *any* time he wants me to. People would laugh at me if they saw.

He kisses me and whispers encouragement as I tremble in his arms. But he doesn't quite drown out the voices in my head. They have gotten too loud. My hips twitch as I undulate against my hand, chasing a release that remains out of reach until sweat covers my body.

His hand strokes my inner thigh, and my heart lurches. I freeze, afraid he'll investigate what I'm doing and find out how I need to touch myself, how strange I am. I don't want him to know. He can't know.

"I can't—it's not—we need to stop," I say, and it sounds like pleading.

"Okay. We'll stop." His words are husky, rough, but he does as I ask. He stops. He rolls onto his back and pulls me partially onto his chest, where I hear the wild beating of his heart, feel the deep billowing of his breaths. Farther below, his sex is like a brand against my leg, stiff and hot.

A sense of failure makes me want to cry. "I'm sorry."

"Don't be," he says.

"But I didn't. And you didn't." I can't bring myself to say *what* we didn't.

"We did *a lot*."

"You're not angry?" I ask.

"No, I'm not *angry*," he all but growls as he hugs me tighter. "I'm fucking proud of you. I'm honored that you trusted me. I'm not angry, not even a little."

"You're still . . ." I shift my leg and move my hand from his chest downward. He stops me, pinning my hand against his stomach.

"Next time maybe," he rasps.

"You want there to be a next time?"

"Yes, I want there to be a next time. I want there to be lots of times."

"You might get really . . ." I'm not sure how to phrase it in a way that sounds good and settle on . . . "sexually frustrated. If you keep waiting for me."

"Then I'll get sexually frustrated," he says.

I almost tell him that by choosing to wait, he's putting pressure on me, but I don't. This isn't just about me. It's about both of us. He has his own reasons for needing things to be a certain way, and I respect that.

Feeling wrung out and exhausted, I ask, "Do we sleep now?"

"Are you inviting me to stay?"

I'm tired, but I smile. "Yes."

"Then yeah, let's sleep now."

THE INSISTENT RINGING OF A PHONE DRAGS ME BACK INTO consciousness. I must not have been asleep for long. My hair is still damp with sweat, and I feel uncomfortably messy between my legs. Groaning, I push myself into a sitting position.

"Let them leave a message," Quan murmurs sleepily.

"I can't. That's my mom's ringtone." I slip out of bed to grope around the floor blindly for my dress.

I find something that feels dress-like and pull it over my head, only to have it fall just below my butt. It must be Quan's shirt, but it'll have to do. I find my way to the door and go to my living room to hunt for my phone, turning on the lamp on the end table as I go. My phone's stopped ringing, and I can't remember where in the world I stuck it (a common problem for me). I look all over—on my coffee table and bookshelves, under my couch pillows. I even check inside my shoes and get down on all fours to peer under my couch.

"It's in my jacket pocket."

I glance over my shoulder, and the sight of Quan makes my heart sigh. He's leaning casually against the wall, shirtless, wearing only his jeans, which ride low on his hips. I touched all of that, that skin, that ink, without seeing any of it. It's a shame that we did everything in the dark.

Except if it wasn't dark, I never could have done what I did.

Was that why he suggested it? Not for himself, but for me?

His gaze sweeps over me, dark, intense, possessive even, and I become aware of my bent-over, kneeling position and the fact that I'm not wearing any underwear. He must have quite the view. I straighten and yank on the hem of his T-shirt, embarrassed and self-conscious. But I also feel immensely desired and sexy, things I'm not sure I've ever truly felt before.

My phone starts ringing again from within his pocket, and I hurry to fish it out. It's almost midnight. This can't be good.

"Hi, Ma. Is everything okay?"

"You finally picked up." There's an odd muffled sound followed by a long, high-pitched keening. I'm so unfamiliar with it that it takes me a moment to fully comprehend what it is. It's crying. My mom is crying.

I have never, not once in my entire life, heard my mom cry like this.

"What's going on? Where are you?" I ask.

"The hospital. It's your ba. I thought he was sleeping," she says before she breaks into heartrending sobs.

"W-what happened?" Possibilities flicker through my mind, each one worse than the one before it. Pressure builds in my head, so great that my scalp pricks and tingles.

"He had a stroke, a big one. Come see him, Anna. Come right away."

Part Two

During

NINETEEN

Anna

I'M NUMB DURING THE HOUR-LONG TRIP TO THE HOSPITAL, barely noticing when Quan stops at the parking garage beneath his apartment building to swap his motorcycle for a black Audi SUV. It has that new-car smell, which I find nauseating, but I like that he cares about my safety. I don't own a car, so I really appreciate that he's driving me. I would have arranged an Uber otherwise—was in the process of doing it when he asked me what in the world I was doing.

So this is what it's like to have a boyfriend who isn't gone all the time. When this numbness is gone, I'm sure I'll have feelings about this.

For now, I need facts, information. I don't cry, I don't grieve, I will hold this ice in place until I know more.

I'd ask Priscilla—she always knows everything—but according to the text messages I missed while Quan and I were fooling around, she jumped on a red-eye to California and will be unavailable until morning.

At the hospital, the front desk gives us visitor badges and complicated directions to my dad's room. I'm on the verge of panic as I struggle to remember all the turns, but Quan takes my hand and shows me the way, like he's been here before. Maybe he has.

The hallways are bright and busy. It could be daytime. Sickness doesn't keep normal hours.

When we reach my dad's room, I release Quan's hand and take a moment to gather myself. I shut my eyes and automatically reach for the appropriate persona. My posture changes. I change.

I knock once to announce my presence and open the door to step inside while Quan hangs behind. It's a big double room, but the second bed is empty. There's a blue curtain around the occupied half of the room, and I pull it aside. My dad's asleep in the bed, connected to various tubes and wires, and seated next to him, holding his hand, is my mom. Her face is unnaturally pale, but as always, she's impeccably dressed in a black cashmere sweater with decorative gold and pearl beading and black slacks.

"Ma," I say, careful not to be too loud. "How is he?"

She covers her mouth and shakes her head.

Swallowing, I approach the bed slowly. My dad has always been on the tall, sturdy side, but he looks small now. Thin. Fragile. His hair wasn't this gray before. I didn't notice all these sunspots on his face before. His vitality dimmed them into irrelevance. When I saw him a few months ago, I couldn't understand why my mom bothered him so relentlessly about applying sunscreen. It's like he's aged ten years since then. He doesn't look like the man who used to buy me candy while he was away and hide it in the trunk of his car so I'd find it when I went to bring his luggage into the house, a ritual solely between the two of us, kept secret from my mom, who would have disapproved.

I reach out to rest my hand on top of my dad's free one. He's cool to the touch and unresponsive, and I glance at the screen next to him where the numbers and lines move, reassuring myself that he's alive.

"Ba, it's me, Anna. I came to see you," I say.

His eyes drift open, and he blinks sleepily at the room for a while before focusing on me. I expect to see recognition light up his eyes. I expect him to smile, just a small one, and say my name.

But his eyes don't light up. He doesn't smile. When he speaks, the words seem to take a massive effort and come out slurred and garbled. I can't make sense of them. I'm not even sure what language he's trying to speak.

"What was that?" I ask, urging him to repeat himself.

His eyelids droop shut, and his forehead creases as more garbled sounds fall painstakingly from his lips. Eventually, his face relaxes, and his breathing evens out. He's gone back to sleep.

I look up at my mom, at a complete loss.

Shaking with quiet sobs, she buries her face in her hands. In a tormented whisper, she says, "I told him to take a nap. I thought he'd feel better tomorrow."

A doctor enters the room, a tall woman with the regular white lab coat, long braids pulled back in a thick ponytail, and red glasses. In a low voice, she says, "I just wanted to check up on him before my shift ends." She acknowledges my mom with a compassionate nod. "Mrs. Sun." To me, she says, "I'm Dr. Robinson," and shakes my hand in a firm grip.

"I'm Anna, his daughter," I manage to reply. I realize I forgot to smile, and I do it belatedly, though my lips feel like plastic.

As she examines my dad, scrutinizing his vitals, making sure the IV and medications look right, she explains, "As I already told your mom . . ."

I feel like I step outside myself as she goes into detail regarding my dad's condition. I hear her talking. I hear myself asking questions from a distance, like it's someone else. I see her, my dad, my mom. I feel like I see myself, too, that clueless, ineffectual woman, even though it's impossible. Quan is somewhere on the other side of the blue curtain. Dr. Robinson uses medical terminology that I'm not familiar with, but I come to understand that my dad suffered significant brain damage because he didn't receive medical treatment soon enough after his stroke. The doctor doesn't recommend surgery because of my dad's age, and there's little they can do anyway. He might not make it through the week. If he does, half of his body is paralyzed. His cognitive ability may be impaired. With the proper therapies, he *might* someday be able to talk, sit up on his own, and eat solids.

Does he have an advance directive?

My mom tells her no.

When the doctor leaves, a heavy silence descends upon us. I'm so overwhelmed I don't know what to think or do. I think my mom feels the same. She must be waiting for Priscilla to come and take charge. We just have to wait until morning.

Fifteen minutes pass while we sit there, wooden and speechless, and finally I say, "Ma, you look tired. You should go home and get some rest."

"I can't. What if he . . ." Her face crumples, and she doesn't finish her sentence.

"I'll stay. If something happens, I'll call you right away. You need to take it easy. You'll get sick otherwise." Adrenaline is running through my body, giving me energy that my mom has clearly run out of.

She thinks it over a moment, and I can see that she's torn. She wants to stay, but today must have been horrible. She doesn't look like she can take much more, let alone handle an all-nighter.

"Please, Ma. Home isn't far from here. If you come right when I call, it shouldn't take more than fifteen minutes to get here."

She finally nods and gets slowly to her feet. "Okay, this way I can clean the mess at home. People will come to visit, and they need somewhere to stay."

As she loops her Louis Vuitton purse over her arm, Quan steps around the curtain, and she physically recoils at the sight of him.

"I can drive you home if you need. I'm Quan, Anna's . . . friend. Nice to meet you." He holds his hand out to shake my mom's, smiling in his disarming way.

It doesn't work on her like it does on me. She just stares at him with unnaturally wide eyes, like she's being held up at gunpoint. I know what she's seeing—his tattoos, his buzzed head, his motorcycle jacket. I know what she's thinking. And I start sweating uncontrollably.

"Your friend?" she asks me in a stunned voice.

"Yes," I say. I'm so anxious it feels like cold needles are pricking my lips. "D-do you want a ride? Quan drove me here."

"No, thank you," she says with extreme politeness and the world's fakest smile. "I drove here. I'll drive home. Good night." She hurries past Quan, giving me a horrified look over her shoulder, and leaves.

Quan watches her go with an unreadable expression on his face and then looks downward. He seems so alone, so sad, like a dog who's tied to a tree outside his owner's house, and I feel awful.

"I'm sorry," I say. I desperately want to take away the cold reception my mom gave him. He didn't deserve that, not at all. "I should have—"

"Hey," he whispers, hugging me and kissing my forehead. "It's okay. It's not a big deal."

"It *is* a big deal."

"Your dad is not doing great. No one's expected to be at their best right now. Don't worry about me, okay?" he says.

"But—"

"I mean it. I'll work on your mom, figure out how to get her to like me. It doesn't have to be right away."

I'm too tired to argue, so I tell myself I'll figure everything out later. For now, I just nod and let myself relax in his arms. I let him hold me up. I'm so grateful he's not making this harder.

"Do you have everything you need? Want me to get you anything?" he asks.

"I think I have everything."

"I can ask the nurses if they can bring in a cot or something."

That suggestion reminds me of the long night ahead, and I sigh. "It's probably better if I don't sleep. But you should. You have work tomorrow. You should go home, actually."

"I don't mind staying," he says, and I can see from the look on his face that he's worried about me. "I can take tomorrow off."

"You don't need to, and maybe . . . I want to have some time alone with my dad."

He searches my face before saying, "Okay, but you can call me whenever and I'll come right away."

I touch his cheek and scrape my fingertips over the buzzed hair on his scalp. "Thank you."

He kisses me on the lips once and pulls away. "Text me if you need someone to talk to, okay?"

"Okay."

With one last smile at me and a silent glance at my dad, he leaves, and I'm alone with my dad. It feels like good-bye as I sit there with him. I hold his hand. I look at his sleeping face, which looks like him, but *not* him. I remember our times together. He used to be an engineer at an international semiconductor company and was out of the country for most of my childhood, but he always tried to be there for the big moments in my life—opening concerts, graduation, et cetera. He made an effort to be there for small moments, too, even though he was gone so often, and looking back, those were more important. He wanted to know what I was interested in. He always wanted to see me when he came home. He quietly checked up on me when I got in trouble with my mom and often defended me, even though he was scared of her, too.

I miss his full-bodied laugh. I miss his dry humor. I miss his crotchety stubbornness. I am afraid, very afraid, that those parts of him, the parts that differentiate him from everyone else, the *essential* parts of him, are gone forever.

TWENTY

Quan

MONDAY MORNING, MY ALARM WAKES ME UP AT THE REGULAR time. After shutting it off, I immediately check for text messages. I don't have any. I rub my face and sigh. Knowing Anna, she didn't want to bother me.

She doesn't understand yet that I *want* her to bother me.

But I'll do my best to help her understand. Toward that end, I quickly type out a message: *Hey, just woke up. How are you? How's your dad?*

She doesn't respond right away—I don't expect her to—but my bed, my whole goddamn apartment, feels enormous and sterile. I want to wake up with her next to me. I want to continue where we left off yesterday.

Thinking about what we did, the sounds she made, the way she called my name when she got close, makes me instantly hard, and it feels completely normal when I lower my boxers and grip myself in my hand as thoughts of Anna fill my head. Just remembering the way she looked as she searched under the couch for her phone, wearing nothing but my T-shirt, makes me groan out loud. I fantasize about what I would have done if circumstances were different, things like putting my mouth on her and making her come on my tongue, then pulling her hips back and pushing myself deep into—

My phone dings loudly, and I yank my hand away, pressing my palm against the cool sheets as my lungs heave. When I can string two thoughts together, I pick up my phone and read her message: *I'm okay. My dad is the same as yesterday. My sister just got here from NYC, and things are really hectic.*

I throw my head back and stare up at the ceiling, all sexy thoughts banished from my mind. *Is there anything I can do?*

Not really, but thank you for asking, she says, and her next message is a red heart.

It's super pathetic of me, but I fucking love getting hearts from Anna.

Because I'm crazy about her, I send her a heart of my own, followed by *Do you want me to come see you?*

It's probably better if you don't for now, she replies.

Okay. Just let me know, I say.

I will. Thank you. I have to go, she texts, and I know that's the last that I'll hear from her in a while.

It doesn't feel right to me that she's going through hard times and I can't be there with her, but I get it. This is a family time, and I'm not part of her family. Based on the way her mom looked at me, I have a long road ahead of me if I want to be accepted by the people in her life. I've always had a take-it-or-leave-it attitude when it comes to people, meaning if they don't like what they see, they can fuck off. But this is Anna's mom. I have to make an effort and figure this out, even if it's uncomfortable and frustrating and goes against who I am.

Anna cares, so I care.

In good news, I have an inbox full of emails relating to the possible acquisition by LVMH and a meeting today with all the lawyers. I've been trying to keep my head cool, but things are getting real. My gut tells me this is going to happen. It'll be the culmination of years of hard work and the start of a new phase of my partnership with Michael. We're going to take over the world together. And I'm going to make a shitload of money in the process.

That won't hurt when it comes to Anna's mom. If I'm rich enough, I know that woman will respect me. It won't matter what I look like or where I went to school or how I sound when I talk or what's left of my body.

I'm going to be good enough for her daughter.

TWENTY-ONE

Anna

AS WE ALL KNEW WOULD HAPPEN, PRISCILLA TAKES CHARGE as soon as she arrives at the hospital. She arranges for second opinions and third opinions on our dad's condition. She scrutinizes all the records she can get her hands on, she gets copies of his brain scans, she dogs the nurses and doctors with so many questions and directions that I feel sorry for them. They look positively harassed, and her lack of confidence in their competence must be hard for them to swallow. They don't understand that this is just her way, it's not personal, but she's already put one of the nurses in tears. To make up for it, I try to be as nice to everyone as humanly possible. I am kind, I am sweet, I am considerate, I buy the hospital staff pastries.

I appreciate you. Please don't hate my family. Please care about my dad.

Priscilla sends word out through the family grapevine that our dad is possibly on his deathbed, and it works like a homing signal, summoning everyone near and far to come. Within the next few days, the hospital is inundated with a conspicuously large number of Asians. We're packed into my dad's room. We've moved into the visiting room on my dad's floor and stocked it with beverages and seafood-flavored snacks. We're occupying all the chairs in the lobby. There's a long bench in the hallway by the elevators, and we've claimed that for ourselves, too. I'm bracing myself for the moment when the hospital administrators ask us to dial it down. I honestly don't know how we'll do that. My dad is the oldest in the Sun clan, the patriarch, and everyone wants to pay their respects and say their good-byes.

The problem—that's not the right word, but I can't think of a better one—is that every time we believe it's the end, he miraculously pulls through. We cry, we say good-bye, we let him go. And then he opens his eyes the next day, not recovered, not remotely improved, but definitely still here, still alive. We rejoice and cry happy tears. But as time stretches on, something new happens; he appears to have an episode of some kind or his heart rate fluctuates dangerously, the doctor says he won't make it through the night, and everyone rushes back to his room. We cry, we say good-bye, we let him go. And then he opens his eyes the next day again, and we rejoice again. This happens three times before his condition seems to stabilize. It's an emotional roller coaster unlike anything I've ever experienced.

Tonight, the elders (that means my mom and all four of my dad's siblings and their respective spouses), Priscilla, and I are in the visiting room with the door shut. It smells like the eggrolls that my cousin brought back after lunch, and the air is stale, overwarm. There aren't enough chairs, so as the youngest and least important, I'm standing with my back against the wall, hugging my arms to my chest and trying to blend in with the wallpaper. I'm so tired that I've been seeing double, but I do my best to focus. This is important.

I watch as Priscilla explains the situation and guides the discussion. Her Cantonese is excellent (I've been told) for someone born and raised in the States, but she still has to use English when things get technical. Words like *paralyzed* and *feeding tube* and *hospice care* stand out, and my aunts and uncles look stricken as they absorb the news. In an unusual physical display of affection, Aunt Linda rubs my mom's back as she cries into her palms. She's repeating the same sentence over and over, and even though it's not English, I can guess what she's saying: *I thought he was sleeping*.

There's some back-and-forth, but it's not heated. Everyone is sad and exhausted, not angry. However, when it looks like a consensus has been reached, Priscilla leaves the room without telling me anything. I have to race after her to find out.

Behind her in the hall, I ask, "What did everyone decide?"

Her no-nonsense, barracuda-in-the-boardroom stride halts as she turns around. "There wasn't much of a choice. Everyone's on the same page. We're not putting Dad in hospice. They'll just kill him with morphine. And he has to get the feeding tube."

"They think that's what Dad wants?" I ask hesitantly.

"He'll die otherwise," Priscilla states. "Do *you* want to be responsible for killing him?"

I shake my head quickly and regret that I said anything.

Priscilla sighs, looking more tired and stressed than I've ever seen her. "I need to go fill out the paperwork to get the procedure done and then look into transitioning Dad home, where we can take better care of him and help him get stronger."

I nod dazedly, but I'm terrified. Priscilla seems to think our dad can get better, but based on what I've seen and heard from the doctors, I think it's unlikely he's going to get stronger or regain any quality of life. I'm just one opinion, though, and I'm youngest so I don't count.

But she said "we." That means her and *me*, taking care of our bedridden dad, seeing to literally all his needs.

What do I know about caring for anyone? I've never babysat or even kept a pet (other than Rock, who, despite his undeniable charisma, isn't actually alive). I'm woefully unprepared for what lies ahead.

"You can take some time off from the symphony, right? You're not a key player, so they should be able to fill your chair pretty easily," Priscilla says, her tone all business. Her dismissive words sting, but I'm used to this. It's tough love, meant to help me overcome my extreme sensitivity and be realistic about myself. "As for your record deal, I'm sure you can push that out. They should be understanding."

"Yes," I reply unsteadily. She doesn't know that the symphony filled my chair months ago or that I've already pushed out my recording deadline because I just can't play anymore. If I did it once, however, I can probably do it again, so I say, "I can make the time."

Priscilla gives me a proud smile, and even though I'm emotionally overwhelmed, her approval fills me with warmth. "I have a ton of vacation time saved up, and if it comes down to it, I'll just quit. We're in this together, Mui mui. In the meantime, try to get some sleep if you can. I took a nap in Dad's car earlier, and that was pretty nice. Just remember to open all the windows."

She hands me the keys to our dad's Mercedes and continues down the hall, her eyes focused like she's on a mission, and I suppose she is. She's trying, very valiantly, to save our dad's life. That's what you do when you love someone. You fight, no matter the cost. You fight even when it's hopeless.

Right?

I wander down the hall, waving at my cousins seated on the benches, take the elevator to the ground floor, go through the lobby, where I wave at yet more cousins and second cousins and my cousins' cousins who aren't even related to me, and exit the building. The car is parked under a tree on the far side of the parking lot, its windshield matted with tree sap and white squirts of bird poop. I make a note to get it a car wash one of these days. My dad loves this car even though it's older than I am—a tan 1980s convertible that he *never* lets anyone take the top down on.

The passenger seat is already reclined all the way back, so I get in on that side and roll the windows down—they're manual, so I don't have to start the engine. Shutting my eyes, I enjoy the feel of sunlight dancing on my face and will myself to fall asleep.

No matter how hard I try to clear my mind, however, my head keeps buzzing. Disjointed snapshots flicker behind my eyes. The doctor recommending hospice and pain medication to make my dad comfortable in his last days. My cousin, an exercise and health food professional, saying we should only give him natural products like marijuana extracts because when he gets better, we don't want him to be addicted to painkillers. My mom repeating that same sentence over and over, seeking forgiveness from everyone around her because she can't forgive herself. Priscilla, filled with determination to do the right thing. And my dad, moaning and flailing, trapped in his bed, trapped in his own body.

While I was watching him last night, he began thrashing about. His movements continued for several heart-stopping minutes, and when the nurse finally came after I paged her, she checked his vitals and inspected him only to determine he had to relieve himself. She kindly explained to him that he couldn't get up to use the toilet and encouraged him to go in his bed, but he fought and he fought. He fought until his body finally won, and then he cried like he was broken, turning his face into his pillow.

I want a reprieve from these thoughts so badly that I consider turning music on, but the radio's been broken since forever, just like the air-conditioning, and the same tape has been stuck in the cassette player for decades—*Teresa Cheung's Greatest Hits*. When I was a kid, I asked my dad why he didn't get it fixed, and he said why waste money on repairs when it was playing exactly what he wanted to listen to.

If I listen to that tape right now, it'll destroy me, so I resort to the distraction provided by my phone. I'm pleasantly surprised to see messages from Quan:

> *Accidentally stepped on a snail while running today and I thought of you*
>
> *Not because you're slow and slimy*
>
> *(you're not)*
>
> *It reminded me of octopuses*
>
> *Anyway, I know there's a lot going on, but I just wanted you to know I was thinking of you*

His messages make me smile for the first time today, but before I reply to him, I need to text Jennifer first.

My dad is in the hospital, so I won't be able to make it to therapy anytime soon, I tell her. It's a relief—I can't say I enjoy therapy—

but I also recognize that canceling our sessions might not be the healthiest thing for me, especially now.

She responds right away, leading me to think she's put someone's therapy session on hold just for me. *I'm so sorry to hear this. I'm here if you need me, and please check in when you can so I know you're okay.*

Thank you. I'll try, I say, and she "likes" the message so I know she's seen it.

As I'm switching back to Quan's message screen, I get a new text message, but it's not from him or Jennifer. It's from Julian.

Hey, my mom heard about your dad and told me. Is it okay if we come visit tomorrow?

My heart jerks and starts thumping painfully. I don't want to see Julian, and I definitely don't want to deal with his mom. I'm barely keeping it together as it is.

Thank you, but can you tell your mom that tomorrow's not a good time? My dad's going to have a procedure done soon, and we're looking into moving him home. If she really wants to visit, a couple weeks later is better, I say.

That's great that he's coming home! I'll tell my mom, he says.

Yes, we're all very relieved, I reply.

Dots dance on the screen, stop, like he deleted what he typed, and start dancing again. A minute later, I get a new text from him. *I've missed you, Anna.*

I roll my eyes. Sure he has.

I mean it, he insists.

I can't bring myself to say I've missed him as well (that would be a lie), so I reply, *Thanks*. As soon as the message is marked as read, I grimace. That wasn't the nicest response I could have given, but I just don't have the energy to be what he wants right now.

Let's talk more, okay? I'm here for you, he says.

I exit the text window without replying and put my phone on the center console. I don't want him to be here for me.

Someone else is much better at it than he is.

TWENTY-TWO

Quan

ANNA'S PARENTS' HOUSE IS SMACK IN THE MIDDLE OF PALO
Alto, not too far from my mom's place in EPA (East Palo Alto), fifteen minutes tops, but it's a world away from the place where I grew
up. The front yards are well lit and don't double as junkyards. There
are no chain-link fences. The landscaping is immaculately mani-
cured. Everyone has solar panels. As for the homes themselves, each
one could grace the cover of *Better Homes and Gardens* magazine,
especially Anna's parents'. There's a two-story main house up front
and a separate guest house in back. They're Mediterranean style with
cream stucco and orange tiled roofs, very California.

The driveway is empty, but I pull up next to the curb. The driveway doesn't feel like it's for me.

Just parked outside, I tell Anna in a text message.

It's stupid, but I'm nervous. It's been forever since I last saw her
(two whole weeks), and I have this irrational worry that things be-

tween us have changed for the worse during that time, even though we've been texting and talking.

I don't get a reply from her, and I drum my fingers on the steering wheel as I debate walking up to the front door and ringing the doorbell. That might wake someone up, though. They've broken her dad's care into eight-hour shifts so there's always someone watching him throughout the day, but that means there's always someone sleeping, too.

Before I can text her again, the front door opens and Anna races out in bare feet. Her hair's up in a messy ponytail and she's wearing the ugliest sweat suit, but she's the best thing I've seen in a long time.

I get out of my car just in time for her to crash into my arms, and I hold her close and breathe her in.

"Hey," I say in a gruff voice.

Instead of speaking, she hugs me tighter.

"Is everything okay? Your dad's okay?" I ask.

"He's the same," she murmurs without opening her eyes.

"Are you—"

"I'm fine," she says. "It's just really, really, really nice to have you here."

That makes me smile. "I would have come earlier."

"I know. Things were just so hectic and—"

"You don't have to explain. I get it," I reassure her.

She sighs, and I feel her tensed-up muscles relax.

"Are you hungry? I told my mom about you and your family, and she gave me three boxes of food for you, not exaggerating," I say.

She straightens and looks at my car curiously. "From her restaurant?"

"Yeah, spring rolls and noodle soup and stuff." I open the trunk so she can see all the plastic soup cartons and foam containers, and her jaw drops.

"I don't know if we have enough room in our fridge . . ."

I rub my neck as my skin flushes. "It freezes really well. I can bring some home with me, too." But I'd have to try to eat it on my own, because sure as hell, I can't tell my mom Anna didn't take it all.

"Let's, uh, bring it in and see if it fits," she says dazedly, and we pick up the boxes and cart them inside.

The entryway of her parents' house is the showstopper kind. There's a long marble hallway lined with paintings and a grandfather clock. To the side, there's a sitting room with a grand fireplace, exposed wooden ceiling beams, elegant furniture, and the most expensive-looking drapes I've ever seen. They look like they're made of gold, but I'm pretty sure it's just silk—really nice silk. A ways down, I can see a formal dining room with an antique dining table that seats ten and a crystal chandelier.

This place is nothing like my mom's house, where aesthetics take a back seat to utility and cost but the food is always good. The only thing that's familiar to me here is the rug by the front door with all the shoes lined up in neat rows. I think my mom owns that same pair of orange plastic sandals, actually.

I toe my shoes off and follow Anna down the hall, feeling the coldness of the marble seeping through my socks to the soles of my feet. I make a discovery that should have been obvious, but wasn't, because I never walked on so much marble without shoes before now: Marble is *hard*. Anna is going to get plantar fasciitis walking on this shit all day.

At the end of the hall, she veers left and enters a humongous kitchen / great room area with a twenty-foot-tall ceiling and more of those gold drapes. Anna sets her box of food on one of the granite islands (there are two) and opens one of the Sub-Zero refrigerators (there are also two) with custom wood paneling to match the cabinetry.

As we're shuffling stuff around, trying to make room for all my mom's food, a third person joins us.

"Hey, can you get the heat packs from the microwave for—" It's a woman, older than Anna, more compact, a little shorter, but clearly related to her. They part their hair in exactly the same place, too.

I smile and wipe my hand on my jeans in case there's fish sauce on it or something before holding it out toward her. "Hey, I'm Quan. Nice to meet you."

For a split second, she stares at me just like their mom did a week ago—wide-eyed, slack-jawed, amazed in a horrified way—but then she sees the boxes of food. She can probably smell it, too. There's fried chicken, and fried chicken smells fucking delicious. My mom's is the absolute best, too, with crispy salty skin that crunches on your teeth and then melts on your tongue. She recovers, and a grateful smile warms her face as she shakes my hand.

"I'm Priscilla, Anna's sister. This is so nice of you. Thank you." Everything about her, from her posture, to the direct way she makes eye contact, to the confident sound of her voice, tells me she's in charge of this place. If I need to work on impressing someone, it's her.

"Don't mention it. My mom likes to feed people," I say.

Anna scratches her head as she frowns at the inside of the fridge, looking slightly panicked. "You might have to take a box back with you, Quan. I don't think we have room for all of this—"

"What?" Priscilla interjects. "We have room. There's also the extra fridge in the garage and that big freezer."

"Oh right. I forgot," Anna says, and her voice sounds so different that the hairs on the back of my neck stand up. It's high-pitched and hesitant, extremely soft. Not herself. "Should I put most of this out there, then?"

"No," Priscilla decides. "Put as much as you can in here. I think Mom will like it."

"Okay," Anna says in that same unnaturally young voice, smiling like the idea of refrigerating things is really exciting.

I glance back and forth between the sisters to see if Priscilla notices Anna's dramatic change. She doesn't seem to.

"You should freeze some of the wontons. There are a lot. The chicken is best if you eat it today with noodles," I suggest, acting like my girlfriend didn't just age back twenty years. "Did you eat yet? I can show you how to put it all together."

Priscilla's face brightens with something that looks like glee. "I would *love* some—" She stiffens and glances over her shoulder toward a part of the house I haven't seen, like she's heard something no one else detected. "I worry when he coughs like that after we feed him. We have to space things out more." She grabs a bundle of fabric from the microwave, slams it shut, and races away.

"She has superhuman hearing now, like moms do. My dad is basically her baby," Anna says, and her voice and demeanor are completely returned to normal. She's the Anna I know again as she takes cartons out of the boxes and lines them up on the table with geometrical precision.

I give her a questioning look, and her expression turns confused.

"What? Do I have something on my face?" she asks, touching her cheek.

"No, I was just—did you . . ." I'm not sure what I'd achieve by pointing things out—she's got enough on her plate—so I ask, "Should we heat up something for your sister and bring it in to her? Also, should I say hi to your dad?"

Anna shakes her head. "We don't eat in there. That would be wrong, you know? Because he can't. But if we get a bowl ready for her, she'll come out and eat it real fast. That's why we have that baby monitor." She points to a small screen on one of the counters. The volume is off, but a grainy video feed shows Priscilla hovering over their dad, adjusting his pillows and things while he sleeps.

"I guess I shouldn't say hi while he's sleeping."

"Yeah, when he's awake is better," she agrees. "But don't be offended when he doesn't respond. I'm not sure he's aware of what's happening most of the time. I've tried talking to him, showing him movies on YouTube, playing music. Nothing reaches him. Nothing that I do, anyway." She lifts a shoulder and touches the bent corner of a foam container.

For a long moment, she seems lost in her thoughts, but she eventually blinks out of it, focuses on me, and smiles. "Let's eat. I'm hungry, and this smells so good."

I show her how to reheat things for maximal deliciousness. My mom gave me specific instructions: broil the fried chicken in the oven for five minutes so it stays crispy, reboil soup broth in a pot over the gas range, and microwave the egg noodles, wontons, and barbecue pork. When everything is hot, I put it together, fried chicken on top, and sprinkle chives and pickled jalapeños over each bowl. Anna runs to get her sister, and the three of us seat ourselves on the leather barstools at the outer granite island and eat while the baby monitor crackles, the volume now turned up to the max.

"This might be the best wonton noodle soup I've ever had," Priscilla says as she somehow, astonishingly, empties her entire bowl. Even her chicken bones are picked clean.

"Thanks. I'll tell my mom you said so," I say. "She loves to cook and is constantly working on improving her recipes. You should see when she tries out a new restaurant. She orders one of everything and analyzes each bite."

"An artist, then, like Anna," Priscilla says, elbowing Anna in the side teasingly.

"I guess you could say that, but she doesn't make anything fancy. If my mom's cooking was music, it would be . . . folk music or, I don't know, country music. Not like the stuff Anna plays. I could be wrong, though. I've never heard Anna play. I just assumed it was classical music."

Instead of commenting, Anna shrugs and stuffs more noodles into her mouth. Little wisps of hair are hanging in front of her face, but I don't tuck them behind her ear. She doesn't like that.

"Really? Never?" Priscilla asks in disbelief. When I shake my head, she continues, "Not even her YouTube video?"

"There's a YouTube video?" That's the first I've heard of it, and now I'm kicking myself that I never searched her name on the Internet.

"You didn't *show* him?" Priscilla asks Anna.

"No, it's not like that's an accurate representation of how I play," Anna says in that same careful soft voice from before. I didn't make it up. She changes into someone else around her sister. "It's just a trick of clever editing and—"

"Oh my God, we have to show him." Priscilla pulls her phone from the pocket of her tight jeans and opens YouTube, where she searches for "anna sun vivaldi" before saying, "You can't just search her name because this pop song comes up."

"Your name is a song?" I ask.

Anna grins at me, and in a voice that's closer to regular—but not quite there—she says, "That sounds like a line from a poem. You must like me a lot."

Priscilla rolls her eyes. "You guys are too cute. Okay, here it is." She holds her phone out for me to take.

As I accept it, I see a thumbnail picture of Anna on a stage with her violin. It has more than a hundred million views.

"Holy shit," I say.

Priscilla smiles at me. "Impressive, right?" She elbows Anna again, affectionately this time.

Anna makes a point of stuffing her mouth with the biggest wonton in her bowl, but even as she acts like she's ignoring us, I can tell she's paying close attention.

I start the video and watch as a woman in a black dress, unmistakably Anna, carries her violin across the stage. And trips on a cellist's music stand, almost falling over. Flustered, she rights the music stand, picks up all the sheet music that fell to the floor, and stuffs it back where it was.

"So, so sorry, Mr. Music Stand. I didn't mean to hurt you," Video Anna says, patting the music stand while the offended cello player stares at her with his mouth hanging open and the crowd breaks into laughter.

Next to me, Real Anna presses a hand over her eyes. "I have a bad habit of talking to inanimate objects."

That's so like her that I have to bite my lip to keep from grinning. It only gets harder when Video Anna reaches center stage and self-consciously addresses the audience. "Hi, thank you, everyone, for, um, coming here tonight. I regret to inform you that world-renowned violinist Daniel Hope and several of our finest San Francisco Symphony violinists were in a car accident earlier today. Rest assured, the doctors say that while there are some broken bones, Daniel, along with everyone else, is expected to make a full recovery and play again in the near future. Anyway, because of this, I'll be, um, soloing for you tonight. My sincerest apologies to those who came here to listen to Daniel. I'm disappointed, too."

There's a long pause, and the camera zooms in on faces in the audience, showing their grimaces and expressions of regret. Then Anna nods at the musicians behind her on the stage and lifts her violin to her chin. Her posture straightens. Her eyes focus. Her awkwardness falls away.

She plays.

And she defies every single expectation that the first part of the clip could have led someone to have. She's not the Asian equivalent of a dumb blonde. She's not a second-rate backup player.

Anna is *talented*.

The music builds like a storm and pours from her violin with a violence that's all the more impressive for how controlled it is. Her fingers are precise. They don't slip. Her movements are perfectly fluid. But more than that, what I hear and see, what draws me to her more than anything else, is passion. She's lost to the music. The look on her face, it's pain, it's pleasure, joy, sorrow, everything all at once.

She's beautiful.

When the video finishes, I can't speak.

"Amazing, right?" Priscilla says.

I clear my throat and swallow before I say, "Yeah." I look at Anna, and it's like I'm seeing her for the first time all over again. "I had no idea . . ."

She meets my eyes for the barest second before she glances away. "Don't look at me like that. After that beginning, I only needed to be passable to impress people. I'm just a regular violinist."

"I don't think you'd have gotten a hundred million views if you were just passable," I say with a laugh.

"It's the story that people like. Airhead girl exceeds expectations." She grimaces and carries everyone's bowls to the sink.

"It's more than that. You—"

Priscilla grabs my arm and shakes her head at me. "Just leave it."

I'm not sure why I should leave it, but I figure she knows Anna better than I do. Switching topics, I ask, "Do you want me to get your violin for you? You usually practice every day, right?"

She turns the water on and washes the dishes by hand, keeping her head bent over the sink. "That's really nice of you, but no, thanks. I can't practice here."

Priscilla aims an impatient look at her sister. "Oh, come on, that's an excuse if I ever heard one."

"The piece isn't coming along well. I don't want anyone to hear me," Anna says.

Priscilla makes a scoffing sound. "I've heard you play a million times."

"I know. I just . . ." Anna doesn't finish. She focuses on stacking the dishes on the dishrack and wiping down the stove and counter.

"You should play for Dad. He'd love that," Priscilla says. "Actually, his birthday is coming soon. We should throw him a party, and *you* should play his favorite song. I'm going to tell him and see what he thinks. I know Mom will be excited. We can put him in his wheelchair and take him outside, too."

Priscilla hops down from her barstool and disappears only to reappear on the baby monitor's screen.

"What do you think about having a birthday party, Ba?" she asks, her words gentle, like she's speaking to a baby. She sits next to him on the bed, picks up his hand, which is curled up in an uncomfortable-looking way, and massages it. "We'll invite everyone over and cook—okay, probably cater—and Anna will play the violin for you. You'd like that, wouldn't you?"

Their dad doesn't respond.

"Wouldn't you, Ba?" she presses him. "You'd like that, right? Ba? A birthday party? We'll put you in your chair, and you can get around?"

Without opening his eyes, he makes the barest moan, and she beams.

"We'll do it!" she says. "Did you guys hear that? Dad wants a party."

Anna turns the baby monitor off and looks out at the nighttime darkness beyond the window, a deep frown on her face.

"You okay?" I ask, walking to her side.

"I don't think I can play if there's a party," she says.

"You don't want to?"

She flattens her hands against the granite counter and then fists them. "It's not that. I *do* want to. It would be a good thing to do. I just don't think I *can*."

"Why not?"

"It's complicated," she says with a tight sigh.

"Complicated how?"

She glances at me for an instant before she looks down at her hands. "Over the past six months, I haven't been able to make it all the way through a single piece. I play in circles, starting, making mistakes, returning to the beginning, making new mistakes, over and over. I can't finish anything I start. Something in my brain isn't right."

"You can't mess up . . . and just keep going?" I ask, reminded of that first night when she couldn't finish the date with me because it started off wrong.

She shakes her head slowly. "I can't."

"Why, though?"

"People have expectations now. Because of that video. They think I'm a big deal," she says.

"You are."

Her eyes turn glassy, and her mouth turns down at the corners. "I'm not. But I keep trying to earn things for real this time." Her tears spill over, and I pull her into my arms and hold her, wishing I knew how to make things better.

"Why do you think you didn't earn it before?"

"I got that solo spot because Daniel Hope got *hit by a car*, and all the violinists who would have been next in line, too. And then after that, the composer, Max Richter, invited me to tour in Daniel's place because his ribs were broken and my video went viral, which was only because I tripped and talked to the music stand. That's some horrible kind of luck, not hard work, and definitely not talent," she says.

"Okay, yeah, I get what you're saying. Luck had a lot to do with it, but you had to be a strong violinist in order to make success out of the opportunity. Not everyone could have done that," I say, hoping cool logic will help her feel better. "And I don't know anyone else who would have spoken to that music stand. That's all you."

She makes a half-laughing, half-sobbing sound. "That's my true claim to fame—talking to things that aren't alive." Pushing away from me, she wipes a sleeve across her face. "I'm sorry I'm such a mess. This can't be fun for you." She takes a breath and puts on a smile that's bright and happy. It's so convincing that I can't tell it's fake, and that's kind of terrifying.

"I didn't come here to have fun. I just wanted to be with you," I tell her. "I don't need you to pretend to be anything other than what you are, even if you're sad."

Her smile immediately fades, but she takes my hand in hers and holds it to her chest, over her heart, as fresh tears track down her face and her chin wobbles. She doesn't say anything, but I understand what she means.

I kiss her temple and her cheek, wipe her tears away with my fingers, trying to comfort her, trying to let her know that I care. She turns toward me so our lips meet, and the kiss is slow and aches with feeling. It says the things I didn't say earlier.

You're a big deal—to me. You're amazing—to me.

This yearning for her, this craving, it's sunk so deep into me that it's part of me now. This is how Quan is now. He's crazy about this one girl.

There's a loud clanging as something hits the floor, and we both turn toward the sound. Anna's mom stares at us in her floral-print old-lady pajamas, her short hair standing up all over like she just rolled out of bed. On the floor, sitting on its side in a small pool of water, is a large metal cup, the insulated kind that keeps things hot or cold for hours.

"Hi, Ma," Anna says before she rushes to get a towel and clean up the mess while her mom watches without moving. "You're up early."

I smile at Anna's mom like I wasn't just caught kissing her daughter and kind of bow my head without saying anything. I don't know how to address her. "Mrs. Sun" feels too formal, but even if I knew her name—which I don't—I wouldn't feel comfortable using it. She's at the same level as my mom, and calling my mom by her name is the kind of disrespectful thing that would get me smacked in the mouth.

"Are you hungry? Quan brought food from his mom's restaurant. I'll heat it up for you," Anna says quickly.

"Not yet." Her mom finally moves and walks over to the island by the fridges and peeks inside the boxes. "From your mom?" she asks me in surprise.

"Yeah, the wontons freeze really well," I say. "When you want to eat them, you just boil them until they float."

"Tell her thank you for us, please," Anna's mom says, looking genuinely touched.

"Sure, she'll—"

A shout from the other side of the house interrupts me. "Anna, I need help pulling Dad up."

Anna sets her mom's freshly washed metal cup on the table and hurries off. "Be right back."

I can't stand around doing nothing, so I start sorting through the food that didn't make it into the fridges. "Priscilla said there's another fridge in the garage. I'll take this out there if you show me the way."

"No, no, leave it there. I'll take care of it." Anna's mom shoos me away from the boxes with her hands. Giving me a considering look, she asks, "Quan. How do you spell that?"

Immediately, I know she's not asking because she wants to write me a letter someday. She wants to know where my parents came from and thinks she can guess it from the spelling of my name.

"Q-U-A-N. It's Vietnamese," I say, making it easy for her, and though she nods and smiles, I can tell that wasn't the answer she wanted to hear. I'm the wrong variety of Asian for her daughter. We're really not all the same.

Anna returns to the kitchen. "Priscilla wants to give my dad a bath, and I should help."

"I'll get going, then," I say. I've only been here about an hour and it took just as long to get here, but I know when I shouldn't hang around.

Her forehead wrinkles with worry. "Are you sure—"

"It's no problem." I squeeze her hand once so she knows I mean it, but when I sense her mom is watching us closely, and disapproving, I let her go.

"It was good to see you," I tell her mom before Anna walks me back to the front door, where we stand in the doorway, not ready to part yet.

"Text me when you get home?" she says.

That makes me smile. "Yeah, okay."

"Is that a clingy-girlfriend kind of thing to ask?"

"I don't think so, but maybe I like clingy girlfriends," I say. Whatever kind of girlfriend Anna is, that's the kind I like. "Good night." I kiss her mouth once, just once, and words—I don't know where they came from—catch in my mouth, wanting to be freed. I don't let them go, though. They're scary.

"Drive safe." She touches my face wistfully, and I leave the house and return to my car.

Once I start the engine, I sit there a moment, thinking about the words that I almost said. I'm glad I held them back, but not because I don't feel them. I *do* feel them. I just don't think Anna is ready to hear them.

I need to win her family over first.

TWENTY-THREE

Anna

AS PRISCILLA SCRUBS OUR DAD'S FEET WITH A SOAPY WASH-cloth, I shave the shady-looking mustache and beard from his face with an electric razor. I'm *not* good at this. I keep worrying he'll breathe in his shavings, so I wipe his mouth repeatedly. I can tell he doesn't like it. He keeps grimacing and trying to turn away from me, and it feels like I'm torturing him.

"Are you sure we need to do this?" I ask.

"Yes," Priscilla says in the brusque, annoyed tone that she often uses with me. "Stop being a baby and get it done. He hates it because you take too long."

"Sorry, Daddy," I whisper as I shave the last bit of hair from his upper lip and then wipe it away.

Our mom enters the room, her favorite cup in hand, steam rising from the hot tea, and sits on the sofa close to our dad's bed.

"What happened to Julian?" she asks.

Before I can answer, Priscilla does—in Cantonese, so I have no idea what she's saying. Judging by our mom's face as she absorbs the information and the tone of her voice as she replies, she doesn't like what she heard.

"It's an open relationship, Ma. People are doing it these days," Priscilla says, switching to English for my benefit.

"Julian wanted this? An . . . open relationship?" our mom asks in disbelief.

I nod and quietly finish shaving our dad's chin.

"And what does this Quan do for work?" she asks.

"He started an apparel company with his cousin."

Priscilla glances up from our dad's feet, arching her eyebrows at me. "You mean he sells T-shirts out of his trunk?"

"I don't know, actually. He doesn't talk about his work very much." I try to sound matter-of-fact about it, but I'm squirming inside. Selling T-shirts from a trunk is a very far drop from investment banking for Goldman Sachs.

"Yeah, I'm pretty sure I know what you guys spend your time doing, and it's not talking about work," Priscilla says with a smirk.

"We still haven't done that," I reply, perversely happy that my sexual hang-ups—and Quan's—led to me getting one over on my sister. I squirt shampoo into my hand and carefully work it into our dad's hair.

"And what did I see in the kitchen?" our mom asks indignantly.

"Skank," Priscilla says, but she looks envious. "I hope I don't need to remind you that what you two are doing is just for fun. Don't go getting attached."

It's too late for that, but I keep that to myself.

"Just for fun." Our mom shakes her head, looking like she can barely understand the concept.

"Oh, come on, Ma," Priscilla says. "You never dated before Ba?"

Our mom gives a tired sigh. "No, Ba was my first and only." She reaches past me and touches our dad's hand, a soft remembering smile on her face, before she focuses on me. "I thought Julian would be your first and only, Anna."

"I thought so, too, but . . ." I shrug because I honestly don't care anymore. I soak a towel in warm water, ring it out, and then use it to get the soap out of our dad's hair. He likes this, I think. His facial muscles are relaxed, and his breathing is slow and calm. Bath time is the only time he looks this way.

"Are you guys still talking at all?" Priscilla asks.

"He's been texting recently." The reminder has my mouth flattening. I have a bunch of texts from him to reply to, but I've been putting it off because it's so exhausting.

"Anna, that's a good sign," Priscilla says. "He might be getting ready to settle down."

That thought had crossed my mind, but unlike Priscilla, it doesn't make me happy. If Julian is back in the picture, I'll have to tell someone no, and that is really hard for me.

"Though maybe . . ." Priscilla looks at me in a considering way. "Maybe *you're* not ready to settle down yet."

Our mom makes this horrified sound, like demons are chasing her. "She's ready. She's had enough fun."

Priscilla doubles over and laughs like our mom's reaction is hilarious.

"You kids these days. *Fun.*" Our mom shakes her head like her dignity's been wounded, and that makes Priscilla laugh harder.

"It's only fair. If he's seeing people, I can, too," I say in my defense, but I feel like I'm being dishonest somehow. That was what Quan was to me in the beginning—an adventure, revenge, a means to an end—but he's more now.

Our mom's jaw stiffens, but she nods. "His mom is visiting soon. I'm going to have a talk with her."

"Ma, no, you don't need to do that," I say.

"I agree, Ma. Don't do it," Priscilla adds.

Our mom waves our words away. "I know how to say things."

"Not always," Priscilla says, holding our mom accountable in a way I could never get away with. "That reminds me, Ba's birthday is coming up. We should throw him a party. We could put him in his chair and have everyone over. I think he'd like that." She smiles down at our dad and pets his shin as she speaks to him like he's a baby: "Wouldn't you, Ba?"

Our mom nods in approval. "Anna could play his song."

I bite the inside of my cheek to prevent myself from commenting on how both of them volunteered me for the night's entertainment without bothering to ask me first. My compliance is and has always been a foregone conclusion with them.

In these modern times, people are told that they have the right to say no anytime they want, for whatever reason they wish. We can let nos rain from our lips like confetti.

But when it comes to my family, that word is not mine. I'm female. I'm youngest. I'm unremarkable. My opinion, my voice, has little to no value, and because of that, my place is to listen. My place is to respect.

I say *yes*.

And I look happy when I do it. Service with a smile.

"I'll start organizing it, then," Priscilla says.

As we finish our dad's bath, carefully turning him to his side so we can wash his back and change his diaper, she rambles on about who she'll invite and what we'll eat, how much fun it'll be for everyone. Except for me. She knows parties are challenging for me, though clearly she's not interested in *why*, and fully expects me to attend and be at my absolute best anyway. I'm not allowed to protest or complain or have an "attitude." That's unacceptable.

For the rest of the night, I don't speak. I keep my anger and frustration and hurt inside where it belongs.

No one notices. That's how it's supposed to be.

TWENTY-FOUR

Anna

THE FOLLOWING DAYS PASS IN A SLOW CRAWL, AND YET, WHEN I look back, I'm amazed that an entire week has passed. Time seems to flow at a different speed here. The leathery pads on the tips of my fingers on my left hand have begun to wear away because it's been so long since I've practiced. Quan brought me my violin, but it's remained in its case, untouched, as I've focused on caring for my dad.

That's all we do here. Our lives revolve around the intricate schedule Priscilla created to ensure he's getting the best care possible. We rotate him every two hours so he doesn't get bedsores, surrounding him with pillows and heating pads and rolled-up towels to prop up various limbs. We massage his hands and feet obsessively to prevent painful contracture. We change his diapers immediately so he doesn't get a rash. We've split his meals into nearly a dozen mini-feedings because his throat muscles don't work correctly and he coughs his food up if he's given too much at a time. We give him many, many medications. We tried to give him physical therapy, but he just moaned and slept through the exercises so we don't do that anymore.

Priscilla likes to stretch out on the bed right next to him and show him pictures on her phone. Most of the time, he doesn't pay attention. On occasion, however, he moans in a meaningful way, and we're reminded that he's really here. He's not a body without a soul. Our work isn't for nothing.

This morning, it's just me and my dad, and that's a little unusual. Technically, we're all responsible for one shift: my mom has the night shift, from midnight to 8:00 A.M., I have the day, from 8:00 A.M. to 4:00 P.M., and Priscilla has the evening, from 4:00 P.M. to midnight. But this is where everyone congregates. Also, it's difficult to move him without help, and we must come running if we're needed. Well, *I* have to come running. I never call for anyone's help when I'm caring for him on my own. I don't feel like I have that privilege.

It's 11:00 A.M., one of his feeding times, so after changing his diaper, rotating him to his other side, and cranking the top half of his bed up so he's relatively upright, I exchange my soiled latex gloves for clean ones, lift his feeding tube away from his tummy where we keep it tucked out of the way, and set it on top of a white towel. Then I fill a large plastic syringe with liquid food from a can. It's thick and brown and has an unpleasant smell—I tasted it once, and it's decidedly nasty—but it contains all the calories and nutrition that he needs. It's keeping him alive.

I uncap his feeding tube and am about to insert the syringe when he grabs my wrist with surprising strength. When I look at his face, I find him staring straight at me. His eyes are focused and clear, aware.

"Hi, Ba," I say, a smile bursting over my face. He hasn't interacted with me at all before now.

He moans low in his throat. Is that hello?

I can't help but feel excited. He's been here all this time, but I've missed him so much. "I'm feeding you, but when I'm done, we can look at pictures if you want."

I try to insert the syringe into his feeding tube again, but he tightens his hold on my wrist and shakes his head.

"What is it, Daddy?" I ask.

Grimacing, he lets go of my wrist and motions with his hand. No one here knows sign language, but that hand signal, shaking his fingers from side to side, is universal.

Stop. No more.

"But it's been hours since you last ate," I say, still not fully comprehending what he's communicating.

He squeezes his eyes shut and makes that hand motion again.

Stop. No more.

"If you're not hungry now, I'll feed you later, okay?"

He turns his face away from me, but I see the moisture tracking slowly down his cheek. My dad is crying.

One last time, he motions with his hand: *Stop. No more.*

I don't know what to do, so I quickly put everything away, tuck his feeding tube back under his hospital gown, and run to the adjoining bathroom, where I sit on the tile and hug my knees to my chest.

My breath comes in short pants. The light is so bright it's making me dizzy. I'm still wearing latex gloves, so I peel them off and toss them into the trash bin. My skin has absorbed the sharp chemical scent of the gloves, and even though they aren't close to my face, the smell is nauseating me, filling my mouth with saliva. I tuck my hands behind my knees to smother the scent, and I rock back and forth and tap my teeth together, trying to return to a tolerable state of being.

Stop. No more.

Dear God, what are we doing?

He doesn't want this.

He wants us to stop.

But if we stop, that means . . .

No, I can't do that.

Even if I could, my family would never allow it. Worse, they'd condemn me. They'd *exile* me.

I can't lose my family. They're all I have.

It's too much. I can't stand my thoughts. So I start counting in my head. I get to sixty, and I start back at one. Over and over until I don't need to rock anymore, until my jaw is tired, until I'm numb.

Finally, I find the strength to push myself to my feet and open the door. My face is hot, and there's loudness in my ears. I feel like something enormous has happened, like the entire world has shifted on its axis. But my dad's room looks just like it did before. He's sleeping just like usual. He looks exactly the same. Old. Frail. Tired, even in rest.

I walk to the dresser that doubles as our medical supply table and examine the chart where we record my dad's information throughout the day—how much we fed him, when, what meds he was given, did he have a bowel movement, et cetera. The next entry is supposed to be a feeding. That's the schedule. That's the pattern.

It wasn't my decision to give him the feeding tube. I had reservations. But I didn't speak up when I had the opportunity. I never speak up. So this is our path now. We're all trapped, just like he's trapped.

We have to see this through.

Swiping at my eyes with my sleeve, I prepare a fresh syringe for my dad, and when everything is ready, I connect it to his feeding tube. He's deep asleep, so this time, he doesn't stop me.

I slowly depress the syringe, pushing life-sustaining nutrients into his body. I care for him, even knowing that my care prolongs his suffering.

I'm sorry, Daddy.

TWENTY-FIVE

Quan

IT'S LATE, AND THE ONLY LIGHT IN MY BEDROOM IS THE GLOW cast by my phone's screen as I talk to Anna. This has become a ritual of sorts, catching up with her at the end of the day right before I go to sleep.

"How was today?"

"Long," she says, and I can hear just how long from the beaten sound of her voice.

"How'd you like that video I sent of the octopus punching fish?" I ask, hoping to distract her.

"Such an asshole," she says with a soft chuckle. "I got your message while Julian and his mom were visiting today. They wanted to know why I was laughing, and I didn't know how to explain."

An uncomfortable sensation crawls up my spine. "Julian . . . that's your ex?"

"Yeah, that's him. His mom is friends with mine."

"How was seeing him after so long?" I ask carefully. I don't want to act jealous. I want to be fair and calm and rational. But I wouldn't mind punching him in the face.

"It wasn't as awkward as I thought it'd be. We just acted like we're back together."

My stomach muscles flex like I've been punched in the gut. "Are you?"

"No." She makes an amused sound. "No, no, no, no, no, no, no."

"Does he know that?"

She releases a long sigh. "I guess we haven't had that talk yet."

"Anna . . ."

"I know. I need to. It's just hard. It seemed so clear to me that we were over. I never expected that he'd actually want to continue where we left off after he . . . you know."

I know I shouldn't, but I can't help asking, "After he fucked half of San Francisco?"

She draws in a sharp breath and says, "Yes," and I regret it instantly.

"Sorry, I shouldn't have said that."

"It's true, though," she says. "I've been meaning to talk to him for a while. But it never seems like the right time. Or else I'm exhausted. Sometimes, it's all I can do to get out of bed. I accidentally took a two-hour shower yesterday. I didn't mean to. I just . . . lost track of time. At first, my mom was afraid I fell or something. Then she yelled at me for wasting water." She laughs, but it's the saddest-sounding laugh I've ever heard.

"Why's it so hard?" I ask.

"My dad is miserable, Quan," she whispers.

"But you're helping him be less miserable, right?"

She's quiet for a long time, and when she finally speaks, her voice has that husky, quavering quality that means she's on the verge of tears. "I don't know how long I can do this."

I hear so much hurting in her words that my own eyes sting. It doesn't entirely make sense to me. If our places were reversed, I don't think I'd feel the same way. I like taking care of people. I like being needed. But Anna's pain is real.

I can't brush it aside just because I don't understand it. I can't place judgment on it. Pain is pain.

I know what it's like to hurt and for others not to understand.

"Can you take a weekend off, then? We can go out and see stuff, or we can stay in. Whatever you want. Just as long as we're together," I say. The more I think about it, the more I like the idea. I haven't had Anna to myself in ages.

"I can't," she says wistfully. "I can't leave Priscilla and my mom to take up the slack while I go have a vacation. That would be wrong."

"You guys are going to have to take breaks every now and then. You can't keep going like this forever, or you'll get burned out. I'm worried about you."

"Thank you," she says.

I take a frustrated breath. "You don't need to thank me for worrying about you."

"I know. But it means a lot to me that you do," she says. "My cousin Faith, the health guru, might come one of these weekends. She's really good friends with Priscilla, and the two of them would make a party of it, taking care of my dad and gossiping the whole time. I wouldn't need to be here. But no one can count on Faith. She's like the wind. She blows in when she blows in. Anyway, I'm tired of talking about me. How are you? How's your company? I realized the other day that I don't know anything about it. Priscilla asked if you sell T-shirts out of your trunk, and I couldn't tell her yes or no."

I throw my head back into my pillow as I groan inwardly. "No, I don't sell T-shirts out of my trunk. Here, this is us." I text her links to our website and one of our social media pages, and when she makes an impressed *ooooooh* sound, I relax somewhat.

"These clothes are adorable," she says, and then she gasps. "I want that rainbow dress in adult size. And one of those T. rex–in–a–tutu T-shirts."

"I'll see what I can do, but I'm pretty sure the biggest size we have for that rainbow dress is youth large."

"Darn," she says, but she laughs, too.

"Michael's in charge of design, but those T. rex–in–a–tutu shirts were my idea. They sell really well, actually. Turns out little kids just love T. rexes."

"Of course they do. *I* love T. rexes. It was such a good idea," she says. I can hear in her voice that she means it, and I want to reach through the phone and kiss her until she's dizzy. "Quan, there's an *octopus* in a tutu!"

"That's a new addition," I say, and I can't stop myself from grinning up at the dark ceiling.

"It looks like the same kind of octopus as in the documentary . . ."

"Yeah, I made sure it was the same kind. *Octopus vulgaris.*"

She sighs dreamily like I gifted her chocolates and roses and a trip to the opera, and my heart goes mushy. Those words from before fill my mouth, pushing to get out, wanting to be heard, but I hold them back. I can't say them yet.

"Looks like my company is getting acquired," I say. "We've started contract negotiations."

"Is that a good thing or a bad thing?" she asks.

"Good. There won't be too many changes in how we run things, but they'll help us reach a scale that we couldn't on our own. I won't be losing my job or anything."

"That's *great*. Who's the acquiring company? Have I heard of them?" she asks.

"I think you've heard of them. They're Louis Vuitton." *Tell that to your sister*, I think, but I don't say it.

"*What?*" Anna squeals. "Just wait until I tell Priscilla. My mom's going to flip out."

"Well, make sure to tell them it's not final yet. And I don't get discounts on their purses and stuff." My sister almost cried when I told her there'd be no discounts on her favorite designer handbags, but I figure it's good to be up front and set realistic expectations.

"Okay. I'll make sure they know it's not a done deal, and tell them not to hope for purse discounts. But I'm happy for you, and really, congratulations," she says, her words rich and warm and heartfelt. She's proud of me, proud that I'm hers, and it makes my heart feel like it's growing too big for my chest. "Are things really busy as you work on making this happen?"

"Thanks. Yeah, work has been nonstop meetings and phone calls and paperwork, but it's super exciting. I've felt bad, though, because things are going well for me, and you're . . ."

"Don't feel bad. I don't want other people to go through what I am. I like knowing that things are going well for someone," she says.

"I wish things were better for you."

"I know you do."

We continue talking for a few more minutes, though we don't say much. Mostly, we're listening to the sound of the other's voice, drawing comfort from it.

We eventually say our good nights, and I stare up into the darkness for a long while before I fall asleep. I can't stop thinking about the fact that her ex isn't technically her ex. They'd need to break up first for that to happen. I know she'd never cheat on me. I trust her. But somehow, my girlfriend has two boyfriends, and I'm *not* okay with that.

TWENTY-SIX

Anna

WEEKS PASS. WEEK AFTER WEEK AFTER WEEK, UNTIL IT'S BEEN two months since my dad landed in the hospital. He starts moaning at some point, a slow, rhythmic moan that goes on for hours. It's always the same. I must have inherited my perfect pitch from him, because his moans never vary from a perfect E-flat.

No one can figure out why he's doing it, but the doctor tells us not to worry. He's not in pain—of the physical kind. Priscilla, ever skeptical of expertise that isn't her own, becomes fixated on the idea that he's constipated and insists on giving him milk of magnesia. It turns out my dad is extremely sensitive to milk of magnesia, and we go through an entire bag of diapers—and a lot of gagging and nausea, on my part, which makes Priscilla glare at me—before his body settles down.

He moans the entire time. And continues afterward.

E-flat, E-flat, E-flat, E-flat, E-flat.

Priscilla and my mom grow frantic with worry. Because modern medicine isn't helping, they have an acupuncturist come to the house and treat him. They push herbal remedies into his feeding tube, put CBD oil under his tongue. They even pay a naturopathic doctor to give him vitamin C intravenously. It's obscenely expensive, but it doesn't work. Nothing works.

If anything, his moaning gets more vigorous.

I want to tell them to stop, that he's moaning because he doesn't want to live this way, and all their ministrations are torturing him. But I don't. I know it won't do any good. I'm not here to talk. I'm here to watch over my dad, to make sure he's never alone in his room, to see to his needs.

The sound of his moans gets to me, though, the constant reminder of *why* he's moaning, and it's not like I can put headphones on and ignore him. If he coughs or chokes, I need to know. I have no choice but to endure it. When my shift is over each day, I sit in the kitchen, close enough that I can hear if Priscilla needs my help, but far enough that his moans are muted.

It's not a true break. I know I'll be called upon at any moment, but at least I'm not directly absorbing his emotional pain into myself. Also, it doesn't smell like soiled diapers and Salonpas pain-relieving patches here.

I'm catching up on the hundreds of unread text messages on my phone—Rose performed on live Canadian TV and just signed a contract with Sony, the twelve-year-old prodigy is going to be in a Netflix movie, Suzie's violin cover of a popular rap song was chosen as the theme song for a new medical drama (ironic because she hates both rap music and medical dramas), Quan spoke with the head of acquisitions at LVMH and it was "rad," Jennifer is checking up on me, saying she's worried about me—when my cousin Faith walks into the kitchen with a duffel bag and a rolled-up yoga mat in her arms. Her hair is frazzled like it always is, and she's wearing her regular uniform of leggings and a baggy shirt over a fancy workout bra that crisscrosses in the back like a spiderweb, the kind that I can't wear because I get lost in the straps.

"Hey, Anna," she says, smiling at me in her sweet way. She likes everyone, genuinely cares about everyone. "How are you? How's your mom? Where's Priscilla?"

"Is that Faith?" Priscilla calls out from the other side of the house.

Instead of answering with words—I'm literally too tired to speak—I push a smile onto my lips and point toward my dad's room.

Faith has only taken a few steps when Priscilla barrels into the room and gives her a big hug, saying, "You're *here*. I can't believe you didn't even text me ahead of time."

"My schedule opened up, so I drove here straight from Sacramento. You're looking good, Prissy," Faith says as they separate, using Priscilla's nickname that I hate. I'm not sure if it's because of the negative meaning of the word or the fact that I'm not allowed to use it.

"No, I'm not looking good, but I love you for lying. I've gained five pounds since I've been here. There's nothing to do but watch Dad and eat, and her booty call gave us tons of food." Priscilla waves toward me with that last part, and it takes me a few seconds before I understand she means Quan.

I shake my head, trying to remember how to form words so I can correct her, but it takes me too long.

"*Your* booty call, Anna?" Faith asks in shock. "What about that super cute boyfriend you had?"

"They're in an 'open relationship,'" Priscilla answers for me, putting finger quotes around the words *open relationship*.

Faith's mouth hangs open.

"You should see the new guy." Priscilla waggles her eyebrows suggestively. "He's covered in tattoos. Our mom thinks he's a drug dealer."

Faith's surprised expression gradually transforms into a sly grin. "Good for you, Anna."

That irks me enough that I finally find my voice to say, "He's not a drug dealer. He's in the apparel business."

"He sells T-shirts out of his trunk," Priscilla says in a mock whisper.

"He doesn't," I say, irritated that she discounted Quan so easily—even though I did the same thing in the beginning. "His company is called MLA, and they're getting purchased by Louis Vuitton."

"Seriously?" Priscilla asks. In the next instant, she's pulling out her phone, typing "MLA clothing" into her search engine, and scrolling through the website. "This is him?"

"Yeah," I say, and my annoyance is completely overshadowed by nervous anticipation now. She's going to be impressed. She has to be impressed.

Please be impressed.

All she says is, "Interesting." She clicks through different pages on the website, evaluating, judging. "Has he signed a contract with Louis Vuitton?" she asks in a neutral tone.

"He said they're in negotiations. It's not a done deal yet."

"I thought so." Coolly putting her phone away, she says, "Just so you know, these things rarely go through. In case he's not aware, tell him not to get his hopes up. Nice website, though."

I slump back into my chair, disappointed and inexplicably angry. Why does she have to put everyone in their place like this? Why can't she just be happy for him? For me?

"How long are you staying?" Priscilla asks Faith.

"I don't have anything until Monday, so I thought I'd stay over the weekend to play with you and then leave early Monday morning, like five A.M.," Faith says with a twinkling smile.

"You don't want to leave Sunday night like a normal person?" Priscilla asks.

Faith shrugs. "You know how I am with sleep. I thought I'd do night shifts, too, so your mom can take a couple days off?"

"Oh my God, you're an angel. I'm going to kiss you," Priscilla says as she leans close with her lips puckered.

Laughing and batting Priscilla away, Faith says, "No kisses needed." Her expression softens when she looks at me, though a smile still plays at the corners of her lips. "You should take the weekend off and go see your fashionista boyfriend."

"You should go when you have the chance, Anna. I have to fly back to New York in a couple weeks to do some stuff, and you and Mom are going to have to watch Dad by yourselves," Priscilla says.

It's what I've wanted, a chance to leave this house, but now that it's here, I feel bad jumping at the opportunity. I shouldn't want to leave. I should want to stay. A good daughter would stay.

And what's this about Priscilla leaving for New York? She never mentioned this before. The thought of caring for our dad during all my waking hours by myself fills me with dread. The moaning... I'll have to listen to it for sixteen hours straight, only to sleep, wake up, and listen to it for another sixteen hours.

"How long will you be gone?" I ask.

"Just a week or two. Some stuff came up in the office, and they need me to sort it out," Priscilla says in an offhand manner. "I'll come back as soon as I can, but, yeah, you should really take the weekend off while you can. Don't worry, I'll be back before Dad's party."

My face goes cold as the blood drains from it. *A week or two.* I honestly don't know if I can handle that. I'm trying as hard as I can, but I'm not holding it together well. As it is, I've been crying as I get out of bed each morning, knowing what I have to look forward to, what I'm going to do, what our dad wants.

"Okay," I say. When I remember, I smile at Faith and say, "Thank you. Really. It's so nice of you to—"

"Of course," she says before I can finish, squeezing my hand. "I've been meaning to come. It just hasn't worked out until now. You know how it is."

I don't know how it is, but my head bobs in a circular kind of nod anyway. What I do know is that she has absolutely no obligation to be here, not like Priscilla and me. She's only my dad's niece. We're his *daughters*. He raised us, fed us, loved us. Caring for him now is something we must do.

Even if it breaks us.

Gratefulness overwhelms me, and tears swim in my eyes as Faith and my sister leave the kitchen, headed for my dad's room. It's been so long since I've been free that I don't even know what I'll do with the time she's giving me.

Practice violin in circles and circles?

No.

I type out a message to Quan: *My cousin came. She's HERE. Do you have this weekend free?*

He replies instantly, *I did, but not anymore! Can I come get you tonight? Like right now?*

Yes, please, I say.

Heading out. See you soon.

I hug my phone to my chest for a moment, wishing it didn't take so long for him to get here. Then I head up to my room. My plan is to hurry through a shower, pack my things, and make my bed before meeting Quan outside, but when I get into the shower, I lose track of time.

This has been my only sanctuary since I've been here. When I'm in the shower, no one can yell "Anna, come help me pull Dad up" or "Anna, go get me the bag of diapers from the garage" or "Anna, take the trash out for me" or "Anna, watch Dad while I go to the store" and expect me to drop what I'm doing, stop my thoughts mid-thought, and jump to their bidding with a happy smile. I'm showering. I can't hear them. They have to wait until I get out.

Even after my hair is washed and all of me is soaped and clean, I linger, resting my forehead against the tile on the wall. I might be crying. It's difficult to tell if it's water or tears running down my face, but I feel it in my chest and my throat. I feel it in my heart.

I shouldn't be so glad to go. But I am. Even worse, I never want to come back. I want to run and keep running.

TWENTY-SEVEN

Anna

I WAKE UP FEELING ACHY AND DISORIENTED, MUCH LIKE I'VE been sick and my fever just broke. My mind is slow to catch up, but I recognize my surroundings. I'm safe, in my bed, in my apartment, and that's such a luxury.

My head throbs dully when I sit up, and looking down, I see I'm wearing street clothes—a sweater dress and leggings. I get my phone from the nightstand to check the time and am confused to see it's past five P.M. Didn't I leave my parents' house later than this? How did time go backward? I have a zillion unread messages on my phone, but when I scroll through them I start to feel nauseated so I quit.

I fumble my way out of bed, and because I don't plan on going anywhere anytime soon, I change out of my street clothes and into my pajamas. I pull on my ugly fuzzy bathrobe, too, glorying in the softness, and plod out of my bedroom. The light is on in my living room, so I head there to investigate, instead of going to the bathroom like I planned.

And Quan is sitting on my couch, frowning over his laptop screen as his fingers fly over the keypad, efficiently typing away. The sight is unexpected but entirely welcome. I love how comfortable he seems in my space, barefoot and wearing a faded T-shirt and loose sweatpants.

He glances my way, and a wide smile brightens his face and makes him beautiful. "You're up."

"Hey." I scratch behind my ear and ask, "What day is it?"

Laughter spills from him. "It's Saturday. You slept for"—he checks the time on his phone—"seventeen hours straight."

"That explains why I feel like roadkill," I say, trying to keep my tone light even though I feel a sense of loss. This is my vacation. And I just slept half of it away.

Quan sets his computer aside and comes to my side, running his hands up and down my arms. "Want anything? Hungry?"

"I might be hungry. I really need to brush my teeth, though. Be right back." I cover my mouth self-consciously and hurry to the bathroom, where I go through the long process of brushing, seven seconds for each tooth, seven seconds for each corresponding part of my gumline to stimulate blood flow so I don't lose all my teeth before I'm fifty, meticulous flossing, mouthwash with fluoride. It takes forever, but this is how I live with the periodontal disease brought on by all my tooth tapping.

When I'm done, I return to the living room. Quan isn't there, but I hear him puttering around in the kitchen. Peeking around the corner, I find him poaching eggs at the stove. On the counter next to him, there are two packages of ramen noodles and two empty soup bowls.

"You're making me ramen?" I ask.

He looks at me over his shoulder. "It's the only thing you have. I thought about ordering delivery, but I figured you'd be starving and this is fast. Want something else?"

I swallow past the ache in my throat. "No, this is perfect."

He smiles and turns back to his work, scooping the eggs into the bowls, emptying the packets of soup powder into the pot of boiling water, and then putting the noodles in to cook.

Not long after, we're sitting across from each other at my tiny table, our knees pressed together, my feet on top of his because I'm cold and he's warm. Steam curls up from the noodles, and the poached egg looks yummy. The white part is firm, but I can tell the yolk will be runny. I lower my chopsticks to the bowl but hesitate before touching anything. I don't want to ruin it just yet.

"Something wrong?" Quan asks, a spoonful of ramen halfway to his mouth.

I shake my head. "No, I'm just . . . happy."

He tilts his head, aiming a confused smile at me.

I try to smile in return, but my lips don't want to comply. I don't know how to explain how wonderful it feels to be cared *for*, even in this small way, after all this time tending my dad, how dark it's been, how lonely I've felt, even though I've been surrounded by family, the people who love me most.

Even as I think that, I find myself wondering, *Do they really love me, though? Can they, when they don't know who I truly am?*

That's part of why I'm so exhausted, I realize. I've been masking nonstop for months, for my dad, but also for my mom and Priscilla. I don't usually notice because I see them for a few hours, a day or two max, and then I get to leave and recover.

It's like pricking yourself with a needle. Do it once, and you're okay. You can ignore that it even happened. Prick yourself repeatedly without giving yourself time to heal, and soon you're injured and bleeding.

That's me. I'm injured and bleeding. But no one can see. Because it's inside where I hurt.

Be that as it may, is it fair to recognize my own pain in the face of my dad's suffering? Self-loathing washes over me, and I ridicule myself, here in the privacy of my mind. It doesn't make me feel better. It's not supposed to.

We finish the noodles and clean up, and then I curl up with Quan on the couch. He browses through the documentaries for something I haven't seen, but it turns out I've watched them all. If it's narrated by David Attenborough, I've watched it at least five times. In the end, we find ourselves sifting through B-rated (or below) science fiction films.

As I'm reading the descriptions for *Llamageddon* and *Sand Sharks* out loud, and laughing with a mixture of awe and horror, Quan gets his phone out and takes selfies of us.

"I realized I don't have any pictures of us together," he says.

"We haven't taken any before now," I say, surprised that it took us so long.

He smiles at me, and there's warmth and understanding there. "We were too busy." He flips through the pictures until he comes to a horrible one where I look like I'm snorting. "Now, this one has phone wallpaper potential."

"Absolutely not." I snatch the phone from him and quickly delete the picture, even going so far as to delete it from his deleted pictures folder so it's truly gone forever.

"Oh, come on," he protests even while he laughs.

I snap a picture as I kiss his cheek, and there it is. The best of the bunch. His smile is wide, completely unselfconscious, and contentment radiates from him. As for me, there's something soft in my eyes as I kiss him, something that I can't put a name to. It's something good, though. Best of all, my ugly bathrobe isn't visible in the photo. I send the picture to myself, and then I nosily thumb through the pictures in his photo library.

"That's Michael," he says when I get to a picture of him and another guy. This must have been taken after kendo practice because they're both in matching sweaty black uniforms and gear. Quan's got his arm thrown over the other guy's shoulder, and their heads are wrapped in white bandanas, their helmets tucked under their arms.

"Michael . . . as in Michael Larsen, the ML of MLA?" I ask.

Quan grins. "That's him."

The next picture shows Quan surrounded by a pack of little kids in full kendo armor. The next is a snapshot of two little kids as they spar. Another sparring photo of kids. Another. Another. Little kids in kendo uniforms, grinning. A selfie of Quan and a little boy who's missing one of his front teeth. Another selfie with another little kid in glasses. Quan and kids in T. rex T-shirts in front of the kendo studio. Quan getting hog-piled. Quan with kids crawling all over him. He's trying to look aggrieved, but he's smiling too hard for it to be believable.

"You like kids," I observe.

His expression immediately grows serious, but he nods. "I do." After the briefest hesitation, he asks, "Do you?"

I shrug. "They're okay. I'm not good with them like you clearly are." I flip through more pictures, and I find one of kids striking poses in trendy MLA outfits that include T. rex shirts, plaid skirts and shorts, and newsboy hats for everyone. "Was this for a company photoshoot?"

"Yeah, I had my kendo kids model for us. It was so much fun," Quan says, and he smiles at the picture like a proud parent.

"That's not the kind of thing that I'd generally think of as 'fun,'" I say with a laugh. "Isn't it like herding cats, getting kids to listen to you?"

"Nah, I mean, I don't bark orders at them and expect them to obey. We were just goofing around together, and the photographer snuck in some shots."

"You're going to be a good dad someday," I say with absolute certainty.

I expect him to laugh or be modest about it or say something like *I hope so*. Instead, he stiffens, and he's distant from me even before he gets off the couch and walks over to the balcony. I can't fathom why he looks so lost as he stares down at the street below.

"What's wrong?" I ask as I approach him slowly, my heart skipping with unease.

He tucks his hands into his pockets and hangs his head. For the longest time, he says nothing, and I can hardly breathe as I wait. It has to be me, what I said. It's always me. And like always, I don't understand why.

Without lifting his head, he asks, "Do you want kids someday?" His voice is oddly gruff, vulnerable, and it sends shivers over my skin.

"I honestly don't know. I haven't thought about it a lot," I reply.

He takes a long inhalation, exhales. "I can't. Have kids, I mean."

I stop several paces away from him, my mind reeling as the meaning of his words hits me.

"I should have told you before now. I'm sorry," he says, his voice even rougher now. "I tried. But the words wouldn't come out."

"You don't need to apologize. You're telling me now," I say.

He draws in an unsteady breath and swipes a hand over his face and across his scalp before he clasps the back of his neck. There's such defeat in his posture that it feels like part of my heart is tearing open, and I close the distance between us and reach up to rest my hand on top of his. He flinches at first, but then he pulls me close and presses his cheek to mine.

Holding him tight, the way I like to be held, I ask, "D-did it happen when you were sick?"

"Yeah."

I don't know what to say now, so I touch him, his back, his neck, his cheek. I kiss his lips softly, hoping to comfort him, but he doesn't kiss me back.

He pulls away and is quiet a moment before he says, "I get it if this changes things. For you. For us. But I guess I would like to know either way, so I don't . . ." His words trail off, and he doesn't finish.

"So you don't what?" I ask.

His gaze meets mine, and he says, "Anna, I'm in love with you."

My breath catches in my lungs, and my chest expands, expands, expands.

"I'm not asking you to say it back if you don't feel it, but I want to know if I have a chance. Or has what I told you made things impossible? I understand if that's the case, and I'd never hold it against you," he says, and the steadiness of his words makes them sound like a promise.

A completely unnecessary promise.

I reach up and stroke his stubbled jaw, because I feel the need to touch him. "This doesn't change anything for me."

A pent-up breath gusts from his chest, and he pulls me closer and presses a hard kiss to my temple, holding me like I'm precious, like I'm important.

"I love . . . being with you. You're the one person who I can really be myself with. But I don't know if I'm in love with you yet," I confess.

Julian and I exchanged those words. He started it with a casual *love you, babe* over the phone, and it seemed like I should say it back, so I did. But it didn't mean anything.

With Quan, I want the words to matter, like his words matter to me. I've tucked his *I love you* into my heart, where I can carry it forever, safe and treasured.

A smile slowly forms on his lips as he searches my face, and he leans down to kiss the corner of my mouth. "You said 'yet,'" he whispers. "That means you think it's going to happen."

"I do."

"Maybe you already do," he says, kissing his way down my neck. He opens my robe to expose that sensitive spot where my neck meets my shoulder, and when he scrapes his teeth over my skin, I gasp and cling to him.

"I might. I've never felt this way with someone before."

"You think I have?" he asks in a low voice by my ear, making me shiver.

"You've been with so many people. I guess I thought—"

"They weren't you, Anna," he says simply.

He kisses me with hungry strokes of his tongue, and I'm swept away, weak with longing. I sneak my hands under his shirt, so I can feel his hot skin against my palms. I love the way his muscles tighten and bunch as I touch him, the way he kisses me deeper.

"I want it to be tonight," he says, running his hand up my inner thigh, cupping the flesh between my legs possessively. "Me, inside you."

"Are you sure—" My voice breaks when his fingertips slip beneath my underclothes and touch me intimately.

I haven't touched myself in any way over the past two months. I haven't wanted to. But now, with Quan, my body is coming to life, soaking his fingers.

"Want you so bad," he groans before he sucks on my neck and circles my clitoris with gentle teasing motions that are *so close* to being what I need.

I seek out his mouth and kiss him as I arch into his touch, rubbing against him, trying to turn the caress into something that works for me. But no matter what I do, I'm left unfulfilled and aching.

"Bed," he says roughly. "Need to get you in bed."

Without warning, he picks me up and carries me to my bedroom, where he lays me down on the mattress. He touches the side of my face almost reverently and kisses me, but his kisses are different all of a sudden. They lack the intensity from earlier. They're tentative, distracted.

He goes to shut the door, shrouding us in darkness, and when he doesn't return to me right away, I sit up in bed. I can see his silhouette in the middle of the room, standing, motionless. Something is wrong.

"Are you okay?" I ask.

"Yeah," he says, but there's undeniable tension in his voice.

After a long drawn-out pause, I hear hushed sounds as he removes his clothes, the unzipping of his pants, the soft brushing of fabric against skin, the muted thuds as his garments hit the ground, so I undress as well. I am not the kind of person who enjoys being naked, and the coldness of the air on my skin makes me anxious as I wait for him.

The mattress depresses next to me, and I sense his nearness. I feel a charge in the air in the instant before he stretches out beside me.

He gathers me close, warms me with his own heat, kisses my forehead, and my mind and body unravel and relax.

I expect to feel the insistent prodding of his erection against my belly. But I don't. He's gone soft in the minutes since we came in here. And now that I'm paying attention, I notice the fine tremors claiming him.

"You're shaking," I whisper.

"Things suddenly got really noisy in my head," he says.

"What are you thinking?"

He releases a heavy breath. "Stupid stuff."

I edge forward and kiss the first thing I encounter—his nose. Then his mouth, his beautiful perfect mouth. "I think stupid stuff sometimes. What kind of stupid stuff is it?"

"That I have a lot to prove tonight, to you, but mostly to myself. That I need to please my woman like a man should," he says.

My heart clenches painfully at his confession. "You do please me."

"You know what I mean," he says, and he grabs my hips and pulls them flush with his, where his sex remains flaccid. "How can I with this? So fucking embarrassing." His voice is gruff with mortification, and I hate that. I never want him to feel that way with me.

"You're not a robot. You're a person. You have nothing to be embarrassed about," I say firmly. "It's not like you can dick me to orgasm anyway. I don't work that way."

He makes a choking sound before he breaks into laughter. "I can't believe you just said that."

I grin before I laugh along with him, strangely proud of myself. "Well, it's true. *You're* the one who made sex between the two of us about *me*. For my part, I've always been more interested in *you* liking it."

"We have the same exact problem," he says. "How is it that I'm only realizing that now?"

"Because we're so different."

He hugs me tighter and presses his cheek against mine, and for a stretch of time, that's all we do. We breathe together.

"Where do we go from here?" he asks.

"I don't know. Where do you want us to go?"

He kisses me on the lips, the chin, my jaw, and nips my ear. The sharp bite of his teeth, coupled with the heat of his breath, covers me in goose bumps. "I want to kiss you."

"Just kissing?"

"Just kissing." His mouth opens against the side of my neck, and his tongue touches my skin, making my breath catch.

"Kissing is good," I hear myself say.

"Very good."

His lips find mine, and he licks me, sucks on my bottom lip, before plunging his tongue deep, claiming my mouth with a drugging kiss. His hands rove over my body, squeezing my curves, palming my breasts. He teases my nipples until I'm gasping into his kiss and digging my nails into his shoulders as my body responds to him helplessly. My inner muscles tighten and clench on nothing, and I move my legs restlessly, run the soles of my feet along his calves. That's when I feel him, hard now, between my legs. When I roll my hips, my sex strokes over his length, and he breaks the kiss as he makes a hoarse sound.

"Quan, you—"

"Just kissing," he repeats before he takes my mouth in another deep kiss.

That works for me, so I lose myself in the moment. I stroke his tongue with mine, I revel in the taste and texture of his mouth, I glory in the feel of his body against my body, against my hands, against my sex. I arch my back, and the tip of his length dips inside me. It's so tempting, so good, that I push into the sensation, taking more of him.

He stills my movements with a firm hand on my hip. "I should—we should—a condom."

"You said just kissing," I murmur before I brush my lips across his, giving him tiny teasing kisses.

"This is more than just kissing." As if to prove the point, he flexes his hips, and we both moan as I take another inch of him.

"Do you want to stop?" I ask in a breathy voice.

"Fuck no."

"Then don't." I kiss him lightly and undulate my hips, loving the feeling as my body stretches to accept him.

He makes a pained sound as he pushes in deeper, pulls out a fraction, pushes in again. "You don't want me to use a condom?"

"I got tested after Julian . . . changed our relationship. Because I thought he might have started seeing other people before he told me," I manage to say. It's hard to focus when he's just inside me like this. Instinctively, I crave a more complete joining, even though I know it won't satisfy the ache in my body. "I don't have anything. Do you?"

"I don't have anything." He kisses me, but only briefly, like he can't help himself. "Are you sure?"

"Ye—es." The word turns into a moan as he pushes in the rest of the way.

Breathing hard, shuddering, gripping my hip tightly, he says, "Nothing has ever felt as good as you do right now."

His words make me light up with happiness despite the fact that I have very little responsibility for what he's enjoying at the moment. It's not like I dutifully practice Kegels every day to optimize my vaginal muscle tone for his maximal pleasure. For lack of anything better, I say, "Thank you."

A rough laugh cracks from his chest. "You're the only person who could make me laugh at a time like this."

Smiling into the dark, I say it again, whispering in his ear, "Thank you."

He laughs as he kisses me, and I feel his smile on my smile. I wrap my arms around him, wondering how I don't light up the room when I glow like this.

He moves between my legs with a slow sinuous movement of his hips, pulling away and returning to me like waves on the seashore. It's so sexy that I wish the lights were on. I want to see him moving against me. I can't help arching into the motion, claiming as much of him as I can. I'll never orgasm this way, but my body craves what it craves. It craves him.

Our position changes slightly as he urges me onto my back and captures one of my hands. I don't understand what he wants until he eases it between our hips and whispers, "Make it feel good, Anna."

Unease threads through me. I can't shake the feeling that it's wrong. I hide my face against his neck, saying his name in protest.

"So I'm not alone," he says, and there's such stark vulnerability in his voice that I can't deny him. He matters more to me than the voices in my head.

Here in the safety of his arms, here in the dark, I touch myself. And I cry out as I tighten around him.

"Just like that," he whispers, kissing my temple, sucking on my ear, biting my neck, licking the sting away.

I do it again, touching myself exactly the way I need, and I can't help the sound that rises from my throat. Pleasure concentrates low and sharp, irresistible.

"More," he encourages me, moving inside me now, retreating and returning with gaining momentum.

I can't stop. Perhaps this is what I've always needed without really knowing it, to love myself without shame and without reservation.

He praises me with dark words, tells me he's proud of me, tells me what I'm doing to him. He asks me if it's good, when he has to know. I'm crying out nonstop as I climb higher and higher, lifting my hips to meet his every thrust, clenching down uncontrollably.

"Are you with me?" he asks in between ragged breaths. "I'm close. I don't know if—"

I pull his head down so I can kiss him, and he groans and kisses me back. Grasping my ass with both hands, he pulls me closer as he drives into me faster. It's that touch of desperation in his actions that ruins me.

All my muscles contract as I stiffen, arching into him. At the same time, I feel myself opening wider, getting softer, trembling. I want to tell him that I'm with him, I want to tell him what's happening, but all I can say is his name.

I call out his name as I reach the pinnacle. I call out his name as I convulse around him, raw repleted sounds trilling from my lips. I call out his name as I'm completely undone.

TWENTY-EIGHT

Quan

THERE IS NOTHING BETTER THAN ANNA COMING APART around me, crying my name over and over again. Nothing in the whole world.

She tries to kiss me, to move with me, but her convulsions are too strong. She's lost all coordination, and I fucking love that.

I'm right on the edge, but I hold back and slow down so I can draw this out. I'm going to be the best she's ever had. I need that. She's never, ever going to forget tonight.

When her tight grip on my cock relaxes and she sighs and withdraws her hand from between us, I force myself to stop. Gritting my teeth, I pull free of the warm clasp of her body and turn her around onto her knees. My name is a question on her lips, and I reassure her with kisses on her neck, her shoulder. I run my palm up and down her back before tilting her hips upward, positioning myself at her entrance, and pushing slowly into her.

The feel of her taking me inch by inch, the sound of her soft moans, is almost more than I can take, and against all odds, I harden further. Sensation courses over my scalp and down my spine, and everything that I am concentrates low, clamors to rush into her. It's pure desperation, pure need, but I refuse to give in. I follow her arm down to her hand and press it between her legs as I kiss her neck, silently demanding she touch herself.

"I don't know if I can," she says. "I already—"

"Just try it?" I whisper, smoothing my hands along her sides, massaging the curves of her perfect ass as I fight the urge to move. "If it's too much, stop."

The slippery sound of her fingers flickering over her clit reaches my ears at the same time that she gasps and locks down on my cock, making my abs clench and my hips jerk involuntarily. It feels so fucking good that I can't resist drawing back and repeating the motion.

"Is it too much?" I ask. I try to hold still, but my hips move without my permission, stroking into her with a steady rhythm.

"No," she says, her voice pitched high with urgency.

She rocks back sharply, meeting each of my thrusts, and our bodies slap together loudly as her cries come faster and faster. When she reaches for me and kisses me over her shoulder with wild sweeps of her tongue, moaning against my mouth with every breath, I know she's close, and it gives me the deepest sense of satisfaction.

I cover her tits with my palms and tweak the tight points of her nipples, and her body tenses like she's been struck by lightning. Her breath tears. She trembles in my arms, drawn so tight she's a hairsbreadth from breaking. I keep kissing her, keep teasing her nipples, keep stroking my cock into her relentlessly, because that's what you do when something's working—you keep doing it. I keep doing it until I'm nearly delirious with the need to come.

And then it happens. She cries out. She comes hard, like she's releasing a lifetime's worth of tension, and it fills me with elation. I might not be whole, I might not be perfect, but I can be what Anna needs.

Holding her as she falls apart, I let go. I fall with her.

TWENTY-NINE

Anna

EARLY MONDAY MORNING, QUAN AND I SIT IN HIS CAR OUT-side my parents' house. It's 7:56 A.M. A good daughter, a good *person*, would run inside and take over for her mom, give her those extra four minutes.

Me, I want my four minutes.

My weekend away should have given me the energy to tackle this. Indeed, I slept through most of my vacation—most of Saturday and then half of Sunday as well—and when I was awake, my time with Quan was easy and relaxed.

Yesterday, we went to the pancake house by my apartment for brunch, and we took selfies with mountains of fancy pancakes in the foreground. After that, I showed him my favorite places in the city—a café with the best espresso, an art gallery where they don't mind if you eat your lunch on the benches and admire the work, a park that presents different modern sculptures every month. Every-thing was within walking distance of the Davies Symphony Hall, my world is small after all, but Quan never mentioned it. He never asked me about my music. I'm grateful for that. When we got home, I promptly fell asleep on the couch and didn't wake up until late evening. I was starving but still exhausted, so Quan ran out for takeout and we watched the documentary *My Octopus Teacher* as we ate. Then we cuddled, which led to kissing, which led to touching, which led to my bedroom and another night of the most glorious sex.

But even after all that, I don't feel well rested or restored. There's a knot in my stomach and dread in my heart.

I do not want to go into that house.

"Are you going to be okay?" Quan asks.

I put a smile on without thinking. "Yeah." That might be the truth, so it's not quite a lie. It feels like one, though, and I correct myself, saying, "Maybe. I don't know."

He considers me for a moment before saying, "I'm worried this isn't good for you. Is there any way you guys can get help? You're clearly not hurting for money, so—"

"It has to be me. It has to be family," I say firmly.

"I mean, yeah. I get it. But you're not doing well. Anna, I think you were only awake for eight hours the entire weekend."

Wincing, I say, "I'm sorry. That wasn't a cool thing for me to do when we were supposed to be spending time together."

He releases a frustrated sigh. "I'm not complaining. I'm *worried*."

I slump back in my seat and stare out the window at the house. "There's nothing we can do about it. It's hard for everyone, and I need to tough it out just like everybody else."

He begins to reply, but the time on the clock changes to 8:00 A.M. Gathering my things from the floor by my feet, I say, "I have to go. Text me when you get to work?"

"Yeah, I'll text you," he says in a resigned voice.

I lean across the center console and kiss him on the cheek. I should make it fast and run into the house, but I linger. I press my forehead against his temple for a moment. "I'm going to miss you."

Somehow, I find the motivation to pull away, leave the car, and cross the dew-moistened lawn. With one last wave at him, I let myself into the house.

As I shut the front door, the weight of this place descends on my shoulders. There's sunlight pouring in through the many windows, but it *feels* dark. I take my shoes off and walk down the cold marble hallway toward the kitchen, where I toss my things on one of the island stools before heading to my dad's room.

The smell reaches my nose before I've even reached the door, and I cough to clear my sinuses. It doesn't help. As soon as I take another breath, the scent coats my nasal passage and throat. When I walk inside the room, my mom's back is to me as she busily changes my dad's diaper. He's on his side with his back to me, too—and other parts of him that I never imagined I'd see when I was younger.

"Hi, Ma, Ba," I say, bright and chipper like I'm overjoyed to be here, like I've been taught.

"Come help me turn him," my mom says instead of hello.

I head to the other side of the bed and smile when I see my dad's eyes are open. He's not moaning. That has to be a good sign. I lightly touch his arm. "Hi, Daddy."

His body sways as my mom wipes him down on the other side, and he squeezes his eyes shut and grimaces. He's not in physical pain. My mom is efficient, but she's gentle. But I understand what's going on.

He hates this.

And so it resumes. I help change his diaper even though I know the process brings him shame. When we're done, my mom leaves, and I feed him even though I know he doesn't want to eat. I realize we're the same, the two of us. Neither of us can speak. Our lives are both dictated by other people.

THE NEXT WEEK, PRISCILLA ANNOUNCES THAT SHE HAS TO FLY back to New York City for two weeks. She leaves a day later.

Then it's just me and my mom.

And my dad, of course.

All of us are trapped in this enormous echoing house. We're together, but each of us is painfully alone.

The days grow impossibly long and gray, and I settle into a sort of numbness as I go through the motions. Gradually, the mistakes start happening.

My musician's hands, usually steady, begin to drop things. A syringe full of liquid food. A pail of warm water during bath time. A jar of moisturizing cream. My spatial awareness decreases abysmally, and my body starts to look like a bruised peach as I run into more and more things. My ability to focus disappears. I forget things. I zone out midsentence. I walk straight into closed doors.

Caring for my dad becomes even more stressful as I worry that I'm either forgetting to give him his meds or accidentally giving him twice the proper dose. I make a point of writing everything down, but what if I wrote something down and then forgot to actually do it? I arrange the syringes and measuring cups at the beginning of the day in such a way that I can tell if I've given a feeding or dose of meds. My mom hates it because it looks cluttered, but she tolerates it for me.

Text messages and phone calls from Quan make my days bearable. Photos of Rose's cat help, too. She's recently given it a horrible haircut that makes it look like a stegosaurus, and its hate-filled stares photograph well. She and Suzie check in on me from time to time, asking how I am. They care about me and offer kind platitudes like *Awww, so sad to hear things are so tough* or *I wish there was something I could do to help*, but I know they don't understand what I'm going through. No one does, not even Quan or my mom or Priscilla.

This is difficult for me because of a failing unique to myself, and yes, I believe it's a failing. I want to be the kind of person who finds meaning in caring for those who need it. That kind of person is *good*. They are heroes who have all my respect.

I'm just not that kind of person.

My dad's suffering wears on me in a way I can't explain. His pain, the way he's trapped in his bed, trapped in his life, when it's not what he wants. Knowing that this could potentially go on for years. Knowing that everything I do only makes it worse. Knowing that it's hopeless.

Near the end of the two weeks, my mind works almost nonstop trying to figure out how I can escape from this. I can't use my career as an excuse to leave. I'd just play in hellish circles. Maybe if I had a small accident and broke a leg? No, I could still manage while I was in a wheelchair. It would just make things more difficult. I'd need to break both my hands, and I can't bring myself to do that. If I didn't heal correctly, I'd never play again, and what if that inconceivable day came when music spoke to me again? What would I do then? Would my life even be worth living?

What I would really like is a lobotomy. I don't want to feel anymore. I would give up all the joy in my life so that I didn't have to feel the way I do right now. I'd do it in a heartbeat if I could be certain that I'd still be able to fulfill my obligations afterward. That's all that matters now, seeing this through.

As it is, I live for the hours when I sleep. Eight precious hours before I have to do it all over again. But I often wake up in the middle of the night and cry as I fist my hands and stare up at the ceiling, silently screaming, *I don't want this. I don't want this. I don't want this.*

Guests come to visit, including Julian and his mom, and I smile at them like I'm supposed to. My mom loves to entertain visitors in my dad's room while I work in the background. She praises me then, tells her friends how I've put my career on hold to care for my dad, how self-sacrificing I am, what a great daughter I am.

Normally, I'd drink in her approval like manna from heaven, but I can't in this circumstance. If they only knew . . .

What they see is not who I am. It's the mask that they love, the mask that's suffocating me.

Julian's mom is the most impressed of anyone, and when he begins messaging me more and more, I believe it's her doing. She wants me for a daughter-in-law—she pulls me aside during a visit and tells me so herself. I smile and tell her that would be a dream come true. What else could I say?

A cynical voice in my head suggests that perhaps what she wants most of all is for me to care for herself and her husband this same way someday. The thought fills me with cold terror. I don't think I would survive doing this again.

At the end of Julian's latest visit, he lingers behind in my dad's room with me as my mom leads his mom and a small group of friends from their church out.

I'm turning my dad to his other side, propping pillows around him to keep him comfortable, when Julian says, "You're really good at this. I was surprised to see it."

"Thanks," I manage to say, keeping my voice light as I flash a quick smile at him. It's a compliment. I should act flattered. But that's not how I feel.

I feel like screaming.

When my dad looks properly situated, I go to check the spreadsheet to see if I've recorded everything. Then I count the syringes and measuring cups, trying to confirm that I haven't forgotten anything or given double doses.

As I'm forcing my scattered brain to do the math, Julian approaches me from behind. He runs his hands down my arms and leans down to kiss my nape. Goose bumps stand up on my skin. But they're not the good kind. I don't want this. I don't like this. Not from him.

But I don't move away from him. I don't say anything.

What *can* I say?

All I've said since I've returned to this house is *yes* and *yes* and *yes* and *yes* and *yes*.

"Can you get away one of these weekends?" he asks. "It's been a long time since we've been together, just the two of us."

Holding still and measuring my words very carefully, lest I upset him, I say, "I'd feel bad leaving my dad's care to just my mom and Priscilla."

"Priscilla left him to you and your mom," he reminds me.

"She didn't have a choice. There was important stuff she had to do. She's not on vacation." *I'm* the one who had a vacation, with Quan, and I owe it to Priscilla to stick around when she needs me.

"When can we be together, then?" he asks. His breath is hot and humid on my neck, and I fight the urge to cringe away from him.

"When my dad gets better," I say, even though I know he's never going to get better. He was never going to get better.

Julian steps away from me, and there's a harsh undercurrent in his voice when he asks, "Are you mad at me? Because I opened up our relationship?"

I turn around, shaking my head. "I'm not mad at you." It's the truth. I'm not mad. Anymore. And I moved on. But I don't know how to tell him that. He'll be angry. His mom will be angry. That will make my mom angry, which will make Priscilla angry, and they'll start pressuring me, pushing me, making me feel worse and worse and smaller and smaller, all because they believe they know what's best for me better than I do. I can't deal with that. Not right now.

Please, not now.

I've fallen into darkness, and I don't see a way out. But I'm fighting. I'm trying. I'm trying as hard as I can to do what's right, to be what people need. I don't have anything more to give. I wish I did.

"I learned something while we were apart," he says.

"What did you learn?" I ask dutifully.

"I met a lot of women. I admit I had a lot of sex. Some was amazing—I mean *really* amazing," he says, smiling in a reminiscing way. I hate him for that smile. "Some wasn't so amazing. But I don't regret any of it. Because it helped me to see that it was just sex. None of those women were like you, Anna."

He tucks my hair behind my ear for me, and the sensation of someone else touching my hair sends discomfort through my nerves. I ignore it, as I'm supposed to.

"I want someone in my life who'll be there for me no matter what, even if I'm sick and bedridden. You always see things my way. You put me first. You don't push me to do things I don't want. Being with you is *easy*. Do you know how special that is? I want us to be together again, just us. No more exploring. I know what I want," he says.

I make myself smile. It feels twitchy and wrong, but he doesn't seem to notice it's not my best work. He smooths his hands over my hair, like I'm his favorite pet, and I tense my muscles and bear it as his words make me combust inside with silent rage.

When we were together, I *didn't* always see things his way. I *pretended* to. I put him first, even above myself, and after being with someone who truly cares about me, I see how wrong that was. I never fought for myself, and that suited him just fine because he got everything he wanted out of our relationship. From the looks of things, he wants more of that.

There was a time when I thought this was what I wanted. But I don't. I don't want this at all.

And I don't know how to say it. I can't be the one to end this. My family would be so upset with me.

But if *he* ends it . . .

"I saw someone," I say with a suddenly dry mouth. "While you and I were apart."

He stiffens abruptly and blinks at me like he doesn't believe it. "You did?"

I wet my lips, nervous now. But an open relationship works two ways. It wouldn't have been fair to expect me to sit at home while he had sex with every woman he saw. Even so, I try to minimize my wrongdoing by saying, "One person."

"Do I know him?" he asks, sneering ever so slightly.

"No."

That seems to appease him somewhat. "Did you guys . . . Was it *good*? Did you *like* it?" There's a mocking edge to his voice as he asks his questions, and I get the distinct impression that he believes it's impossible for me to "like it."

I lift my chin, and though my voice isn't loud, I still say, "I did."

His expression darkens for a heart-stopping moment before it clears. "I suppose I deserved that."

"You did."

"Well, I hope he had fun while he could. It's over for him now," he says, grabbing my arms and pulling me against his body. "I'm the one you love."

He tries to kiss me, but I turn away so his lips land on my cheek.

"My dad is right there," I say.

"He'd be happy for us," Julian says.

As he's trying to kiss me again, my mom pokes her head in the door. "Your mom says it's time to go soon," she says, and her expression is carefully blank, even though she must have seen what she was interrupting.

He grins at her like they're sharing an inside secret and kisses my temple before stepping away from me. "I'll call you later, okay?"

"Okay," I breathe.

He leaves the room and follows my mom down the hall, and I stand there, frozen in place. If my mom hadn't come at just the right time, I probably would have let him kiss me. I might even have kissed him back. Not because I want to, but because I feel like I have to—in order to make everyone happy.

Everyone but me.

My dad starts moaning, his regular E-flat moans, and my heart sinks. My everything sinks. I check the time. Not medicine time. I go to his side and touch his forehead. Cool to the touch. No fever. I check his body positioning to see if anything is off. There's nothing obvious.

"What's wrong, Daddy?" I ask.

He doesn't open his eyes to acknowledge me, but his brow furrows and his moans continue. There's nothing I can do other than hold his hand, so that's what I do. His hand remains limp. He doesn't hold me back. He never does.

In a way, he's been gone since he had his stroke. He's still alive, but I lost him months ago. Perhaps I've been mourning all this time without realizing it.

Can you hurt without knowing it?

When he falls asleep and stops moaning, the tension in my body eases, but I still hear those E-flats in my head. They repeat on an endless loop.

My mom enters the room quietly, checks the spreadsheet to see if I've kept on track, and sits on the sofa next to the bed. "Everyone just left." When I don't say anything, she adds, "They said good things about you."

I don't have energy for this, but I force myself to smile like I mean it and say, "That's nice of them."

"Especially Chen Ayi," my mom says, referring to Julian's mom. "From what I saw a little bit ago, it's obvious you two are back together again. I'm relieved. That other . . ." She shakes her head and wrinkles her nose.

"Quan's been really good to me," I say, feeling like I need to defend him.

"Of course he's good to you. He knows how lucky he'd be to have you. Look at you. Look at him. But Julian is good to you, too," she says.

I don't understand why Quan would be lucky to have me. I'm a mess. My life is a mess. I haven't even been able to tell him that I love him.

But I think I do.

I think I've fallen hopelessly and irrevocably in love with him, like seahorses and anglerfish do.

"You need to talk to that Quan," my mom says. "He's not a bad person. He deserves for you to treat him with respect. Be kind when you end things."

Tears blur my vision, but I hold them back. "He makes me happy, Ma."

My mom sighs and gets up to come to my side. "He's a phase. You don't marry boys like that."

"He doesn't feel like a phase."

"Trust me, okay?" my mom says. Her voice is gentle, her expression caring, and I'm reminded that she loves me. She doesn't have a Make Anna Miserable agenda. She wants what's best for me—unless it conflicts with what's best for my dad or Priscilla. Then I'm a lower priority. Because I'm youngest and female and unremarkable. That's just how things are. "You're young. You don't know the value of what you have. But *I* know. Julian will take care of you, Anna. You need that. You knew how we felt about your music career, but you chose it anyway. Now you have to be realistic."

"I'm not good at anything else," I remind her.

When my parents first signed me up for violin lessons, I think they did harbor the hope that I was a prodigy and would go places. When special talents never arose, they kept me in lessons because it would look good on my college applications if I was "well-rounded."

That's how it worked for Priscilla. She performed a violin solo at Carnegie Hall when she was in high school, and that experience, coupled with her exemplary academic record, got her into Stanford, where she majored in economics, and then went on to receive an MBA. Everyone was horrified when I announced that instead of following in Priscilla's footsteps, I wanted to use my musical training to be an actual musician.

"You didn't try anything else," my mom says with a distasteful twist of her mouth. "You could have taken over my accounting business. I would have been happy to hand it to you."

"I'm *horrible* at math. Besides, I'm doing okay now," I say, hopeful that I've finally proven to her that my one rebellion was truly the best choice for me.

My mom pins a hard look on me. "You know your success is temporary. Soon you'll be back to struggling to pay your rent."

My throat swells, and I bite the inside of my lip so the small physical pain can distract me from my turbulent emotions. I hold my dad's hand tighter, stroke my thumb over his pockmarked knuckles. He doesn't hold me back.

"You know I tell you these things so it'll hurt less when you hear it from others," my mom says softly.

Swallowing past the tightness in my throat, I nod.

"Mom is tired, so I'm going to sleep now." She strokes my hair much like Julian did earlier, and I hold still and let her, even though it feels like ants are crawling on my scalp. It's how she demonstrates affection for me. When I was young, I lashed out when people—my grandparents, aunts, uncles, et cetera—tried to touch me this way, and I was chastised and punished for it. It hurt people's feelings and made them feel rejected, a terrible sin, especially between a child and an elder, so I learned, by necessity, to grit my teeth through it. I grit my teeth now. "You're a good girl, Anna. What we're doing is hard, but you don't complain. You always listen. You make me proud."

With one last pat on my head, she leaves. Tears swim in my eyes before falling onto the back of my dad's hand. I wipe them away with my sleeve, but they keep falling.

I don't make a single sound as I cry.

THIRTY

Quan

"SO GOOD TO MEET YOU IN PERSON AT LAST," I TELL PAUL RICH-
ard, head of LVMH Acquisitions, as I shake his hand.

"Likewise." He flashes a polite smile at me, and after unbutton-
ing his suit coat, he sits in the chair across from me at the restaurant
table.

I've been looking forward to this meeting all week. It's our last
meeting before we finalize the terms in the contracts. After that,
we're signing.

Michael Larsen Apparel is going to be an LVMH Moët Hennessy Louis Vuitton company.

But this guy is giving me strange vibes. I don't know what it is
exactly, but something isn't right.

A waiter offers to fill his water glass, and he waves them away.
"No need, I won't be long." Focusing on me, he says, "You probably
have lots of questions, so let me reassure you that yes, we want Michael Larsen and the MLA brand under our umbrella. We're de-

voted to making this happen. And I must say, your leadership of the company up until now has been impressive."

"Thank you," I say, thinking maybe I was wrong about him. "It's been really exciting getting the company off the ground. I'm looking forward to working with your team as we continue to grow."

"It would be a learning experience for you, I'm sure," Paul says, and there it is again. That strange vibe. "Especially given your limited experience."

I sit up straighter in my chair as alarm shoots up my spine. "That hasn't been an issue for us so far."

Paul makes a point of adjusting the diamond cuff link on his pristine white sleeve before saying, "Let's cut straight to the chase. You're not the right person to lead the company post acquisition. We're going to instate a CEO with the proper credentials, but if you're interested, we would like you to head the sales team."

My body heats up until I can feel my neck burning beneath the collar of my T-shirt and sports jacket. "We were assured since the beginning that Michael and I would remain in our current positions."

"Michael definitely needs to remain," Paul says.

And I understand what he's not saying: Michael is essential. I'm not.

"You and Michael Larsen are family, is that correct?" he asks.

"Yeah."

Watching me steadily, he says, "I know it would be easy to take this personally and turn the deal down, but you need to ask yourself if that would be the best thing for Michael. I'm telling you now, if you do that, you won't hear from us again. This is a once-in-a-lifetime offer." Before I can say anything, he gets up, buttons his suit coat, and checks his watch, frowning like our two-second meeting ran long. "I'm going to have the lawyers put a pause on the contracts. A week should be enough time for you to think things over. You have my contact information. I hope I hear good news a week from Monday."

He leaves, and I sit there alone. For the first time in my life, I really understand what it means to "lose face." The waiter approaches and asks if I'd like anything, and I can't turn my face toward them. I can't stand being seen right now. I can't look anyone in the eye.

I haven't eaten and I like this place, but I throw a twenty on the table and go, keeping my head down. Outside, I plow down the sidewalk until I reach my bike and then I jump on it and hit the streets. I don't know where I'm going, but I'm going to get there fast.

As the world flashes by quicker and quicker, I think, *Fuck that guy.* Michael and I made this company—*both* of us. I know what I did, what I accomplished. I'm not replaceable. Michael won't let them break us apart. We're partners. We stay together. MLA was fine before they came along. We'll be fine without them.

I'd rather burn it all down than hand it to that jackass.

Michael would burn it down with me if I asked him to.

We're that close. Closer than brothers.

But I'd never ask him to do that.

And I'd never ask him to give up his dreams. Not for me.

I turn onto the freeway and push my bike to its limits as I weave in and out of the traffic. I can get a speeding ticket for this—if a cop can catch me. At this point, I'd welcome the chase.

I want to break rules, destroy things, watch smoke blacken the sky. I don't give a shit if I get hurt in the process. Maybe I even crave the taste of pain. It couldn't rival this gaping sense of betrayal.

But there's someone who *would* care if I got hurt, someone who likes it when I drive with my hands precisely at ten and two and signal at every turn.

My heartbeat is crashing in my ears, my blood is rushing, rage is howling in my chest, but still, when I think of Anna, I slow down.

When I realize I'm headed south on the 101, I'm not surprised that I'm going straight to her. My compass always points to her.

THIRTY-ONE

Anna

TODAY IS MY DAD'S BIRTHDAY. THAT MEANS I'M SUPPOSED TO perform, and I'm not remotely ready. I haven't practiced at all. Tonight should be interesting. I predict it's not going to involve me actually playing the violin, but I haven't figured out how I'm going to accomplish that yet. Appendicitis would be convenient.

Priscilla returned last week, but that doesn't mean things have been any easier. Her New York trip must not have gone well because she's been foul-tempered and caustic to everyone but Dad, whom she's been treating more and more like a newborn, speaking to him in baby talk, kissing his face all over, and pinching his cheeks as she tells him how adorable he is. I don't think my dad appreciates it. In fact, I'm fairly certain he hates it. He's a proud old man, not an infant. But I don't say anything.

The party is scheduled for this evening, but my uncle Tony has been here since early morning. He tried to tell my dad about the costly divorce their doctor friend is going through because he had an affair with a thirty-year-old and got her pregnant, but my dad moaned/slept through the story. After that, Uncle Tony got out aviator-style reading glasses and a book—*Ringworld* by Larry Niven. He's spent most of the day quietly reading at my dad's bedside.

In his mid-sixties, Uncle Tony is the youngest of my dad's siblings and the least successful. He can't hold down a job for longer than a few months and lives off intermittent unemployment checks and family handouts. All my life, my parents have used Uncle Tony as a model for failure, saying things like *Don't pursue a career in music or you'll be like Uncle Tony.* But he comes to see my dad every week, is unobtrusive and doesn't expect to be entertained, and always brings Ferrero Rocher chocolates. Now and then, he gives a red envelope with precious wrinkled twenties in it, to help take care of his brother.

I'm returning to my dad's room with a new bag of diapers from the garage when I see Priscilla outside the doorway looking in.

"I don't know why he bothers coming," she says, speaking in a low voice so it doesn't carry into the room.

"He comes to spend time with Dad." It's obvious to me.

She sneers. "He's so lazy. He could try harder to get Dad to talk, or show him videos, or FaceTime their friends, or give him a massage, or wash the dishes. *Something.* But all he does is sit there."

"Sometimes it's really hard just being here," I say quietly. I think he's doing as much as he can, and I don't expect more from him. I can't understand why she looks down on people when they're trying their best.

Her lips curl and her nostrils flare with disgust as she looks sideways at me. "You would say that. You don't interact with Dad either, and you've been so sloppy lately that you might as well not be here."

The sharpness of her words takes my breath away, but it's the look on her face that stabs straight into me, damaging me in ways I can't describe. *I'm* the one she's looking at that way, *I'm* the one she finds revolting, and I've been giving all I have. I'm struggling not to break into pieces.

She just doesn't know.

"It's hard to do those things when he doesn't *want* to talk or watch videos or FaceTime people. He wants all of this to *end*," I say, trying to make her understand.

The wrinkles of disgust on her face deepen. "Does he want that? Or do *you*?"

"I want it if he wants it," I confess in the barest whisper. I'm so tired of him hurting, so tired of making things worse for him. *So tired.*

Her eyes widen into round saucers, and I know I've shocked her, horrified her.

Without a word, she grabs the bag of diapers from me and sails into the room, aiming a broad smile at Uncle Tony as she thanks him for the chocolates. He nods at her, pleased, and returns to his book.

I hang around the doorway awhile, waiting for her to issue commands like she always does. Everything should still be okay if she orders me around. But she doesn't.

She's acting like I'm not even here.

I turn around and walk away from the room. I need to be alone and figure out what to do, how to fix this. She's my sister. I need her to love me. I *need* that.

I shouldn't have said anything, I know that. But I've been doing that for so long that it feels like the words are piling up, pushing to get out, demanding to be heard. *Please, please*, I want to scream, *please understand me.*

Stop judging me.

Accept me.

Down the hall, my mom opens the front door and lets a whole troop of people inside—out-of-town relatives and their families and a handful of her friends from church. They're smiling, exchanging greetings, and handing her red envelopes, which she tucks into her pocket for safekeeping. Everyone wants to help take care of my dad in some way, and money is the easiest way to do it.

I try to slip into a bathroom and hide, but it's too late. I've been seen.

"Anna, come say hi," my mom says, beckoning me toward her with her hands.

My face is hot and I'm on the verge of tears, but I put on a smile. I remember to wrinkle the corners of my eyes. I fumble through greeting them all. I'm horrible at remembering faces, and there are different ways to say aunt and uncle in Cantonese depending on if they're on my mom's side or my dad's side, their age relative to my parents, and whether or not they married into the family. In the end, my mom has to reintroduce me to everyone, and I parrot back the titles that she gives me, only with abominable pronunciation that makes people laugh. My mom laughs along with them, but there's a hard edge to her face that tells me she finds my failure humiliating.

By the time that's over, my heart is hammering and my head hurts. I need a quiet place. I need time. As I'm closing the front door, Julian and his mom walk up the front steps. I didn't invite them, so Priscilla and my mom must have done it. I really wish they hadn't. It takes energy to be with him, and I feel like I'm scraping the bottom of my resources.

Numbly, I note that he looks good today. Well, he always looks good, but today he looks exceptionally good. He's dressed in well-fitting khakis, a white button-down shirt with no tie, and a navy blue sports coat, and he's having a great hair day. His chin-length locks look like they've been professionally styled with a round brush and a hair dryer and then flat-ironed, but I know he rolls out of bed like that. Julian is lucky in many ways.

My facial muscles don't want to respond, but I make them cooperate through a force of will. I say the right things with the right amount of enthusiasm. I hug Julian and his mom and show them to the backyard, where caterers have set up a big white tent and a dozen round dining tables on the grass. The sun's only begun its descent, so the sky is still bright and the illumination from the Christmas lights suspended overhead is subtle. The flower arrangements are beautiful—fresh hydrangeas in shades of magnetic blue and magenta—and there's a long buffet table filled with food from my dad's favorite restaurant. In the back corner, a bartender is setting up a wet bar.

This is what happens when Priscilla organizes an event. Everything's perfect.

For other people.

For me, it's a test of my endurance. Every minute, more guests arrive. The tables fill up. The noise escalates. Activity levels escalate. I shake hands with unfamiliar people and hug familiar ones. I make small talk, pushing my brain to its limits as I follow the conversations with careful attention, reason through what I think people want to hear as quickly as I possibly can, and then say it with the correct delivery, which involves facial expressions, voice modulation, and hand motions. I'm a marionette, hyperaware of all the strings I need to pull in order to give a convincing performance.

All the while, my cousins are tossing a football back and forth at the far end of the yard. A baby is crying, and her mommy is trying to distract her by pointing out the football. Bees are buzzing on the camellias. The air smells like grass, flowers, Chinese food, alcohol, and the smoke from the next-door neighbor's barbecue.

I haven't been moisturizing my skin properly, and as I sweat, my face stings. My hand grows clammy, and Julian lets me go so he can wipe his palm on his pants.

"I can't tell if that's you or me," he says with a laugh. "I'm a little nervous tonight."

"Why?" I ask, because that's unusual for him.

His chest expands as he draws in a big breath, and instead of answering the question, he asks, "Want a drink? I could use one."

"Sure." Now that he's mentioned it, dulling my overloaded senses with massive amounts of alcohol sounds like a fantastic idea. Maybe I'll have an entire bottle by myself.

I follow him to the wet bar, and as he's ordering us two glasses of red wine, I can't help noting how attractive he is. But I could say the same of a Monet painting, and I don't have a burning desire to possess one. Julian isn't Vivaldi for me. He doesn't captivate me. He's not my safe place.

There's only one man like that for me, and he's not here. I wish he was. At the same time, I'm glad he's not. I'm pretty sure my mom doesn't want him in her house. Priscilla doesn't respect him at all. The rest of my family would probably hate him on sight.

As Julian hands me a wineglass and tips the bartender, the crowd quiets. Priscilla rolls our dad outside in his wheelchair. There's a knit cap on his head, and he's wearing a black cardigan backward over his hospital gown. A fleece blanket covers his legs and is tucked neatly under his feet. His head is propped up with pillows, but he still lists slightly to the side as he blinks groggily at his surroundings.

"Thanks for coming, everyone. Dad is so happy you could make it here to celebrate his eightieth birthday with him," Priscilla says proudly.

People clap and crowd around him, and there's a steady hum of conversation as everyone tries to get a family photo with him in it. I see my mom in the middle of the throng, dressed to the nines, makeup on, talking animatedly with guests, entirely in her element. This party, I realize, isn't for my dad. He appears to have fallen asleep.

"Where did Priscilla go?" Julian asks.

I look around, and when I don't see her, I say, "She's probably getting 'fresh air.'"

His mouth crinkles like he's tasting something he doesn't like. "I guess I'll wait until she gets back, then."

"Wait for what?"

He just smiles at me and shakes his head before sipping from his wineglass. "My mom said she spoke to you."

I'm not sure what he's talking about, but I nod. "It's been really nice of her to visit so often." That seems like the right thing to say.

He gives me a skeptical look before he takes a sip of his wine. "You told her you'd love to have her as a mother-in-law."

A bad sensation settles over me. It feels like all the small lies that I've told to please people are catching up with me, and a moment of reckoning is coming. I'll have to deal with everything eventually and make tough choices. But I can't today. Not here and now, not while everyone is watching.

"I did. I like her a lot," I say. My cheeks are tired from all the smiling I've done today, but I smile again for him.

"You know what that means, right?" he asks, reaching out to tuck my hair behind my ear.

I try my hardest not to flinch as the nerve endings in my scalp protest his touch. My smile stays in place, but my heart is beating so fast I'm light-headed. I can't remember his question, but I know how I'm supposed to respond. "Yes."

A wide smile breaks out across his face, and I know I've said the right thing. I'm relieved and terrified at the same time.

THIRTY-TWO

Quan

THE STREET WHERE ANNA'S PARENTS LIVE IS SO CROWDED that I have to park a block away and walk. Someone is having a party.

Normally, I wouldn't mind. I'd enjoy stretching out my legs and imagining people having a good time. But tonight, all I can think about is how badly I need to see Anna. I feel like shit, and there's only one thing right now that can make this better. Her.

I need her in my arms. I need to breathe her in.

As I get close to her house, however, I see that the driveway is packed with cars. The party is *here*.

Two things occur to me at once: First, this must be her dad's birthday party. Second, she didn't invite me.

That definitely feels like a stab to the gut, but I tell myself it's okay. I get it. I need to work harder at winning her family over. But how the hell am I supposed to do that if she doesn't invite me to stuff like this? I should be in there buttering up the old folks, making golf dates with anyone who plays, and becoming best friends with her cousins. Most important, I should be at Anna's side.

But I'm not. I'm out here while she's in there.

I slow to a stop in front of her neighbor's house and debate turning around and going home like a reject, but that's when I hear her sister.

"Thanks for helping me get my dad into his chair, Faith." There are trees and bushes in the way, so I can't see her clearly, just a glimpse of her profile as she lifts a cigarette to her mouth. The smoke blows directly my way, and I suppress a cough.

"No problem," replies Faith, who's completely hidden from view. "It was easy with that Hoyer Lift device. I never saw one of those before today."

"Easy, yeah, but you definitely need two people. I didn't want to ask Anna. She's been so airheaded lately that she might have dropped him," Priscilla says, and there's a bite in her tone that makes me stiffen. I have to clench my teeth together to keep myself from defending Anna.

"You're so tough on her," Faith says, and I want to hug her in gratitude.

"Maybe I am, but I expect a lot from people. You don't think I'm tough on myself, too?" Priscilla asks.

"I know you're *toughest* on yourself."

Priscilla's hand lifts, and the end of her cigarette flares ember red as she draws on it. A fresh cloud of smoke wafts my way. "I quit my job while I was in New York."

"*What? Why?* I thought you loved your job."

"I've been due for a promotion for three years, and they just gave it to this new guy who took over my projects while I've been here. I had to fly to New York to fix *his* problems, and they promoted him over me. Fuck them. I might sue."

"That's horrible," Faith says. "I can't even imagine that on top of everything else you're going through. Have you ever thought of trying therapy?"

Priscilla laughs bitterly. "Yeah, right. Anna went to therapy and now she thinks she's autistic. What a load of crap. Not for me, thanks."

There's a pause before Faith muses, "Anna might be autistic?"

Priscilla makes a scoffing sound. "No."

"I don't know. She was such a weird kid, so quiet. I don't think she had a single friend when—"

"I'm not listening to this," Priscilla says.

"Oh, come on, you don't think—" Something drops and shatters into pieces on the sidewalk directly in my line of sight. "Crap."

Instead of running away to avoid being seen—the hell with that—I step forward. "Need help with that?"

Priscilla and this Faith whom I've never met jump in surprise.

"Sorry. I didn't mean to scare you," I say.

"You must be Quan," Faith says as a huge grin takes over her face. "I've been wanting to meet you. I'm Faith." She steps toward me like she wants to shake hands, but glass crunches beneath her shoe.

"Nice to meet you," I say as I come forward and crouch down to gather up the broken pieces of glass. The champagne flute is still mostly intact, so I put all the shards inside it. When I'm done, there's nothing but a wet spot left from the champagne.

Priscilla takes it from me with a smile that doesn't quite reach her eyes. "Thanks, Quan. You must have come to see Anna."

Before I can say yes and apologize for showing up uninvited,

Faith grabs hold of my arm enthusiastically. "She's out back. She'll be so happy to see you. Come on, let me take you there."

Priscilla looks like she wants to say something, but in the end, all she does is aim a nauseated-looking smile at me as Faith leads me around the side of the house, past the garbage bins, where Priscilla chucks the broken glass, and to the backyard.

I can hear the people before I see them, laughing, talking, coughing, screaming (there is one very pissed-off little kid here). When we round the corner, it takes me a second to process it all. It looks like they're celebrating a wedding, not a birthday.

"Let's see here. Where is she?" Faith says as she scans the crowd.

Someone says, "There's Priscilla," and soon her mom waves at her, summoning her toward a table on the far side of the tent where her dad is sitting in a wheelchair.

"I have to go. Feel free to eat and drink. The bar's right there," Priscilla says, pointing to a nearby corner where there's a short line of people waiting for drinks before heading away.

I'm about to thank her when a loud clanging draws everyone's attention to a good-looking guy who's banging a fork against his wineglass. "Attention, please, everyone. Attention," he calls out.

Anna is next to him. She's wearing a simple black dress, and her long hair is down. She's the most beautiful thing I've ever seen.

I step toward her just as the dude sets down his fork and takes her by the hand.

A friend of hers?

No, that guy's body language doesn't say "friend." I don't like that guy's body language *at all*, not while he's holding *my* girlfriend's hand.

"First, I wanted to wish Xin Bobo a happy birthday," he says as he lifts his wineglass toward Anna's old man.

At the table with Priscilla and Anna's dad, Anna's mom pats her husband's shoulder before smiling graciously and lifting her champagne flute.

"Zhu Xin Bobo shengri kuaile," the guy says before drinking from his glass, along with everyone else in the tent. "Next, since everyone's gathered here, I wanted to share some news with you all."

I go completely still. My feet feel like they suddenly weigh a thousand pounds. This can't be what it looks like.

"Who is that guy?" I ask Faith in a low whisper.

She looks at me with wide eyes and lifts her hand away from her mouth to say, "Julian."

My heart stops beating as I stare at Anna's face and try to read the situation. She's smiling up at that piece of shit, hanging on his every word. Her cheeks are flushed, her eyes sparkling. So fucking gorgeous.

"Anna and I are getting married," Julian announces.

THIRTY-THREE

Anna

"WE HAVEN'T SET A DATE OR ANYTHING YET, BUT I THINK sooner is better than later so that the important people in our lives can attend. Isn't that right, Anna?" Julian says.

For an inappropriate length of time, all I can do is gaze at him and smile. That's the only outward reaction that feels acceptable when everyone is watching me.

Inside, I'm melting down.

He said we're *getting married*. How is that possible? He never even proposed. If he had, I would have said no. I don't love him. Right now, I might hate him.

Words pile up in my mouth, demanding to be spoken. Things like *No, you misunderstood* or *We're never getting married, and I'm not sorry.*

But I see my mom press her hands to her chest as happy tears track down her face. Priscilla wipes her own tears away as she excitedly bends close to our dad's ear, no doubt telling him about my upcoming nuptials. Julian's mom smiles at me like this is the happiest moment of her life.

And I can't do it. Not in front of an audience.

Later, I tell myself. *I'll do it later.* When it's quiet, when there aren't people all around, when I've had time, when I've caught my breath, when my head doesn't feel like it's exploding.

I find my voice, and I say, "Yes."

Applause breaks out, loud whistling. Silverware clinks against glasses, and Julian smiles at me, looking like I've given him the moon. As he leans down to kiss me, my peripheral vision catches sight of a familiar face.

Quan.

He's here. He witnessed that. He looks like someone just tore his heart out.

Julian's lips touch mine, and I freeze. I don't kiss him back. I can't.

What have I done?

He doesn't seem to notice that I didn't kiss him back as he pulls away and lifts his glass toward me.

"To us," he says.

I clink my glass with his and tip my head back to drink. What else can I do now? I swallow even though the wine tastes like vinegar in my mouth.

When I'm done, my eyes immediately seek out Quan. But he's gone.

Pure, undiluted panic shoots through me. I can't let him leave like this. I have to explain. I have to make him understand.

"I'll be right back," I say to Julian, and I hurry around to the front of the house.

I don't see him on the front lawn or the driveway, so I run to the sidewalk. It's starting to get dark out, but I see him. He's there, walking fast, walking away from me.

"Quan," I call out as I chase after him.

Instead of turning around to face me, he walks faster. "I can't do this right now, Anna."

"It's not what you think."

He keeps walking, so I run after him. When I grab his hand, he yanks his arm away from me like I've burned him, and it feels like a smack in the face.

"Quan—"

He whips around abruptly. "I really can't do this right now. I'm not—" He drags in a breath. Down at his sides, his hands curl into fists. "I'm not thinking straight. I don't want to say things that—I don't want to hurt you."

"I'm sorry," I say. "I'm not marrying him. I just couldn't say it while everyone was watching. Plus, my mom and his mom want this so bad that I—I—I . . ."

"*I* was watching, too, and I saw my girlfriend tell her entire family that she was marrying someone else. Do you have any idea how that feels?" he asks.

"I know it was wrong of me. I really am sorry. I'm going to fix this," I say, pleading with him. I'm not in control of my life. He has to know that.

"Then fix it now," he says. "I'll go in there with you, and you can make a new announcement. Tell them I'm the one you're with. *Me.*"

I don't know what to say. I can't do what he's asking. Everyone wants me and Julian to be together. If I'm going to go against their wishes, I have to find another way to do it, something quiet and clever. I'm still figuring it out, but I'm fairly sure it involves getting

Julian to call it off. They can't pressure me then. They can't make me say yes.

"Or can you only be with me in the dark? Are you ashamed of me, Anna?" he asks in a rough voice.

"*No.*"

"Then why do you act like you are? Why can't you speak up for me?"

My throat locks, and I shake my head ineffectually. How can he expect me to speak up for him when I can't even speak up for myself? I'm not allowed to. Why can't he see that?

When I don't answer him, his features droop with disappointment. "This isn't working. I can't do it anymore."

A jolt of adrenaline makes my heart squeeze, and my senses stand at red alert. "Do what?"

"*Us.* You're breaking my heart, Anna."

I can't bear the sadness in his eyes, so I look down at my feet and do my best not to make a sound as my tears fall. I hate that I'm hurting the person I love. I hate that there's *nothing* I can do about it. I hate how trapped I am in my life. There's no winning for me. I'll never be able to please everyone.

"I'm going to go," he says.

Everything inside me rebels at his statement, and I bunch the fabric of my dress in my hands as I fight the urge to reach out and stop him. There's an invisible barrier around him now, and I'm not allowed inside it.

"I don't want you to go," I say, and it feels like the words come from my very soul, they're so true.

Instead of answering, he turns around and continues down the sidewalk to his motorcycle. Without looking back at me once, he puts on his helmet, climbs on, starts the engine, and drives away.

I watch him until he's gone, and even then, I stare at the intersection where he turned and disappeared from view. That's it. We're over now. He's broken up with me. I'm not ready for a future where I never see him again. Yes, I still have my family. But what do I have to look forward to now? Where is my safe place now?

He's just a man. I shouldn't feel so empty with him gone. But I know I've lost something important, something essential. Because I haven't just lost him. I've also lost the person that I am when I'm with him—the person behind the mask.

I've lost *me*.

"Anna, are you out here?" I hear Faith call out behind me.

I can't find it in me to move or tell her where I am. I don't want to be found. It's quiet out here, and I want to be alone.

But footsteps come my way, and soon she says, "Here you are. Are you okay?"

Feeling tired to the marrow of my bones, I look at her over my shoulder and nod.

"Priscilla said it's time for you to play," she says hesitantly.

My throat is almost too swollen to speak, but I manage to say, "Okay."

"You look so sad, Anna. Did something happen?"

I don't have the energy to answer her question, so I shake my head and walk quietly to the house. As I'm opening the front door, I say, "Getting my violin."

She flashes an uncertain smile at me and heads back to the party.

My feet feel impossibly heavy as I make my way up the stairs to my room, where my violin case is resting on the floor underneath a pile of dirty laundry. I kneel on the floor, brush everything off the instrument case, and after a small pause, open it. There's my violin.

It's not a Stradivarius and isn't worth millions of dollars, but it's mine. It's good. I know its sound, the feel of it, the weight of it, even the smell. It's a part of me. Running my fingers over the strings, I remember all the trials and triumphs that we've gone through together. Auditions, opening nights, my introduction to Max Richter's recomposition of Vivaldi's *Four Seasons*, my *obsession* with his recomposition, the performance that put me on YouTube, the circular hell of the piece that I can't finish . . .

It's a shame I have to break this violin tonight.

But I don't see that I have a choice. I can't play. If I try, I'll just humiliate myself in front of my harshest critics—my family. The mental problems that I'm facing aren't worthy of their respect or even a cursory attempt at understanding. In their minds, I need to identify the problem, find a solution, and get on with it. It should be that easy.

So I'm doing that now, just not in the way they'd prefer.

I take my violin from its case, relishing the familiar way its curves fit into my hands, and I hug it. *I'm sorry, my friend*, I whisper in the safety of my mind. *I'll fix you afterward.*

After tightening the bow, I apply rosin. There's no need. I won't be playing tonight. But that's part of the ritual. It has to be done.

Then I walk from my childhood bedroom, down the hall, to the top of the staircase. Gripping my violin tightly by its neck, steeling my heart, I prepare to throw it down the stairs with as much strength as I can muster. It's a hardy instrument, and I can't just dent it. It must be injured to the point where it's unplayable. That's the entire point of this.

I count to three in my head, throw it, and watch as it sails through the air. There's a moment when I think it'll bounce down the stairs and land on the ground without a dent and I'll have to throw it again and again, maybe jump on it a few times like it's a trampoline before it sustains suitable damage. But my violin does the unexpected upon contact with the marble floor.

It shatters into tiny pieces.

Gasping, I drop my bow, run down the stairs, and frantically sweep up the fragments with my fingers. The neck broke clear in half, and the body of the violin is nothing but splintered bits of wood. It no longer resembles an instrument. One of the strings snapped. The others lie limp and lifeless on the marble at the base of the stairs along with the pegs and bridge and unidentifiable debris.

There is no way I can fix this.

This violin will never sing again.

Uncontrollable sobs spill from my mouth. I can't stop them. I can't silence them. The hurting inside me will be heard now. It won't stay quiet.

"Anna, Priscilla says you should—"

I look up to see Faith taking in the scene with her mouth hanging open. I don't try to tell her the lie that I prepared in advance, that I "accidentally" dropped it.

My violin is dead. I killed it with my own hands.

I took a beautiful innocent thing, and I murdered it. Because I couldn't bring myself to say no.

I've destroyed everything good in my life.

Because I can't say no.

Because I'm still trying to be something I'm not.

"I'll be right back," Faith says before hurrying out.

I'm almost hysterical with tears and trying to piece my violin together like a 3D puzzle when Faith returns with Priscilla in tow.

"Oh my God," Priscilla says as she considers the carnage. She considers me for a tense moment before she seems to lose some sort of internal battle and continues in a resigned voice. "Stop doing that. You're not going to fix it, and you'll just give yourself splinters. And relax, okay? It's not the end of the world. Mom wanted to get you a new one anyway. I've been talking to a bunch of dealers."

"You were going to get me a new violin?" I ask, letting the violin shards fall from my fingers to the floor.

"Yeah, I think I've found the right one. We're negotiating the price right now," she says.

I know I'm supposed to be grateful that she's not ignoring me anymore. I'm supposed to say thank you for the violin.

But it feels like someone lit a fuse inside me. I'm burning, about to explode.

I can't stop myself from asking, "You were going to buy it without asking me what I thought?"

"Mom wanted it to be a surprise. Plus, she didn't want you involved. She knew you'd get your heart set on the most expensive one, and that's not how you get a good deal. Don't worry, I tried out the one I like, and it fits me fine. It'll be comfortable for you, and you know I have good taste," Priscilla says, like I'm upset over nothing and I need to see reason.

But matching a violin to a violinist is a tricky task. Not only does it need to have the right fit and weight, but the unique voice of the instrument needs to resonate with the musician's ear. No one can hear that but *me*.

Most important, I didn't *want* a new violin. I liked my old one, the one that's nothing but scraps now. If everything had gone according to plan, they'd have replaced my old one and expected me to play it regardless of my wishes on the matter.

And I would have. With a smile on my face, no less.

Because I can't say no.

Priscilla rubs her forehead tiredly. "What are we going to do now? You can't perform tonight with that."

"Do you still have your old violin from high school?" Faith asks her helpfully.

Priscilla's eyes widen, and she grins like the sun just came out. "I *do*. It's on the shelf in my closet. You're an *angel*. Thank you." She smooches Faith directly on the lips and bounds up the stairs.

Laughing and smearing an arm over her mouth, Faith runs to get a plastic container from the kitchen and then crouches down next to me to help me with the mess. "The timing is perfect, isn't it? Priscilla told me about the violin they're getting you. It's Italian and very old. That's all I'll say."

I look down at the violin pieces on the ground, too overwhelmed to put my thoughts together. Everything is wrong. *Everything*. I tap my teeth over and over, trying to get back to normal, but it doesn't help. This wild hurting inside me won't go away.

This day, this interminable day. Why isn't it over yet? I need it to be over now.

Right now.

Right. Now.

RIGHT. NOW.

Priscilla hurries down the stairs with a violin case in tow and holds it out toward me like it's a prize. "There. Tune it up and come on out. Everyone's waiting for you."

I clench the remnants of my violin in my hands until the jagged ends pierce my skin and bite out the words, "I can't play."

Priscilla heaves an annoyed sigh and looks heavenward. "Yes, you can."

"I *can't* play," I repeat.

"You're so *frustrating*," Priscilla says through her teeth. "You need to do it for Dad. It's his *birthday*."

"What's going on in here?" my mom asks before she appears on the opposite end of the hall and walks toward us, followed by Julian and a handful of curious relatives.

"She's refusing to play. She dropped her violin, so I gave her my old one. And she still won't do it," Priscilla explains.

"*I can't play*," I repeat again. "I told you why, but you won't—"

"You want to know how to deal with your anxiety? You tune your violin, you take it out to the stage, and you play your song one note at a time until you're done. That's it. You just do it," she says. She even smiles, like it's funny that I don't understand something so obvious. After extracting her old violin from its dusty case, she holds it out for me to take. "Go out there and do it, Anna."

This is the end for me. I don't wage any internal battles against myself. It's *not* as simple as she says. Not for me. And she won't even try to understand. She just wants me to do what she says, like I always do.

"No." I say it firmly and deliberately despite how strange it feels on my tongue.

For the span of a heartbeat, two, she looks at me like what just happened defies comprehension. Then she hisses, "You're being a spoiled little—"

"*I'm not doing it*," I say in a raised voice so she *has* to listen to me.

Priscilla visibly recoils at my public show of disrespect, and my mom utters a sharp, disapproving, "*Anna*."

"You see what I'm dealing with?" Priscilla cries.

"You won't play for Ba?" my mom asks, looking bewildered at the idea. "You need to play his song for him. This might be your last chance." Her expression collapses with pain, and tears shine in her eyes.

I shouldn't be able to hurt more than I do, but I feel like I absorb her pain into myself and add it to my own. It's unbearable. I can't contain it all. I feel myself breaking open as I say, "My last chance was months ago. He's not listening now. He doesn't want any of this. We're torturing him because we can't let him go."

"Don't say 'we.' *You* don't have that problem. *You're* tired of taking care of him. *You told me you want him to die*," Priscilla says, pointing a finger at me as that sneer from before twists her face.

My mom gasps and covers her mouth as she stares at me in horror. All the people standing in the room stare at me the same way. Shame and humiliation swamp me.

"I've been trying as hard as I can, but it's not enough," I say in a choked voice. "I can't keep going on like this. I'm tired, and my mind is sick. *I need help.* Can we please get help so we don't have to do this alone anymore? Why does it have to be just us?"

"You know what?" Priscilla says. "Since you're so 'sick and tired,' why don't you pack up and leave? You haven't been doing anything anyway, and I've been cleaning up after you nonstop. You'll make everything easier for me if you go back to your apartment and sit on your ass there."

Her words feel like the worst kind of treachery, and wild hurting tears through me. I told her that I'm sick and I need help, and she threw my words in my face. There's no recognition of what I've done or how hard I've struggled to be here for everyone, including her. It's nothing to her.

Why have I been tormenting myself like this, then?

I shove the remains of my violin in the plastic container and run up the stairs to my room to pack my things. I have to get out of here.

"Hey, are you, uh, okay?" Julian asks from the doorway.

"*I'm fine.*" I don't mean for it to happen, but my words come out as a shout.

He looks at me like he doesn't recognize me. He's never seen this side of me before. No one has, not since I learned to mask. But now my mask is just as shattered as my violin is. I messed up. I talked back. I said no. People know about the awful thing that I told Priscilla.

You want him to die.

I'm no good anymore.

I can't be loved anymore.

Working as fast as I can, swiping at the tears streaming continuously down my face, I shove my clothes, clean and dirty, into my bag. Then I move to the bathroom and get my toiletries. As I'm forcing shut the zipper on my bag, there's a jingling sound as Julian pulls the keys out of his pocket.

"I'll take you back to your place," he says.

The thought of being trapped in a car with him for an hour right now is intolerable. There's no way I can deal with that. "I need to be alone. Thank you, but no," I say with what remains of my control.

And there's that word again. I feel like I have nothing good left in my life, but at least now I can say *no*.

He looks at me like I'm being ridiculous. "Anna, we live five minutes apart from each other, and we're *getting married*. I can't let you leave here without me."

"I don't want you to take me." The words come out forcefully, but slightly slurred. I'm losing the ability to talk as I crash from all this overstimulation, I can feel it. "And I don't want to marry you. You didn't even ask me, and you announced it to my entire family."

"I asked. You knew what I meant," he says, as if it was so obvious.

"No, it wasn't entirely clear. And I don't want to be with you anymore. I'm breaking up with you, Julian."

He flinches back in shock. "What the heck? That's totally an overreaction. Be reasonable, Anna."

There's a lot I want to tell him, things like how to propose to someone so they know it's happening or not to have your mom ask for you or to double-check with your partner before you make an engagement announcement. But I'm running out of energy and my tongue doesn't want to move.

In the end, all I can do is look him straight in the eyes and say, "No."

Throwing my bag's strap over my shoulder, I go. Everyone's returned to the party, so I make it out the front door without incident. From there, I walk to the nearest park, and I order a ride home to San Francisco.

THIRTY-FOUR

Quan

I BREAK EVERY SPEED LIMIT AS I RIDE AWAY FROM ANNA. I don't care if I get in an accident. Maybe part of me even wants it to happen.

I've lost everything. My job, my girlfriend, my fucking manhood, it's all gone, and I don't know how to deal with the wreckage that's left over. The wreckage that is me.

Five years ago, nothing could have shaken my confidence this way. I walked my own path with swagger, covering myself with tattoos, giving the world the middle finger. But success seduced me. *People* seduced me. And since then, I've been fighting to be the man they think I am without even realizing it.

That fight is over now. I don't have anything to offer anymore. No fame, no fortune, no future. When I raced to see Anna, what I needed was reassurance that those things don't matter, that *me,* the person I am, is enough.

That didn't happen.

When I reach the city, I head straight for the liquor store. My plan is to buy ten bottles of booze, hole up in my apartment for days, and drink until my brain sloshes around in my skull. But when I'm stuck at a red light, I catch sight of my gym. Through the windows, I can see a bunch of people on the treadmills—an old guy, a hot chick, some rich ladies in neon-colored yoga outfits, and a ripped dude who looks like Rambo. They're running, sweating, completely lost in their physical suffering. The light turns green right as I notice the empty treadmill by the wall, and I make a split-second decision and pull over.

Inside, I put on the spare workout clothes that I keep in the locker that I rent from the gym and claim that last treadmill. The trainers—cool guys, I know them all because I've been going here for a long time—try to chat and shoot the shit, but when I crank up the speed on my machine and start running, they get the idea and leave me alone. I don't want to talk. I don't want to listen to music. I don't want to watch the TV. I only want to run.

So that's what I do. For hours.

When I catch myself thinking about Anna and my job, I run harder, like I can escape everything if I'm fast enough. That works for a while, but I can't run full-out forever. Eventually, my strength fades, and I slow down enough that thoughts creep back to me. The events of the day replay in my head. Learning that the LVMH deal won't go through unless I step down. Seeing Anna smile as that guy announced their engagement, seeing him kiss her.

Tears threaten to spill down my face, and I swipe at my eyes like sweat is stinging them and max out the speed on the machine again. I run and I run and I run. Until I can't anymore. And then I drag myself home, sleep, eat, and repeat the same cycle on Saturday.

Sunday morning, my body is sore. But not sore enough. I need a longer, more grueling run, something that'll push me to my limits and truly clear my mind.

As I load up on granola and high-calorie healthy shit and ice my knee, I watch YouTube videos of people running the Grand Canyon in a day. Apparently, this is called a "rim to rim to rim" or R2R2R run because you go from one rim to another and then back, for a total of more than forty miles. Everything that I see cautions runners that this is not for the faint of heart, lots of planning is needed, you might die, blah blah blah. I'm not exactly mentally stable right now, so this seems like the best idea I've ever had. Impulsively, I book myself a ticket on the next flight to Phoenix, Arizona, arrange a car rental, nab a room at the hotel close to the South Rim due to a last-minute cancellation, and go to the airport, planning my route and water logistics on the way there.

After all, what do I have to lose?

Not a single fucking thing.

When I arrive in Arizona a couple of hours later, I go shopping for all the stuff that I'll need, like a hydration pack, lightweight layers of clothes, trail food and energy packs, sunblock and lip balm, a hat, a headlamp, et cetera, and then I make the long drive to Grand Canyon Village, check into my hotel room, and head to bed early.

My alarm gets me up at two A.M., and I'm at the trailhead by three A.M. It's still dark out, I know I'm being foolish, I know I should have prepared more, but I don't hesitate before venturing onward.

I only want to run.

And I'm determined to set a new record.

THE VIEW THAT EMERGES AS THE SKY BRIGHTENS IS DAZZLING.
Majestic cliffs plummet sharply to the earth in shades of sunrise,
greater than time, greater than man. I feel minuscule in the best of
ways. My problems seem insignificant; my pain, trivial.

Elevation drops steadily while I descend through billions of years
of rock into the depths of the canyon, and I make it to the halfway
point in a little less than three hours feeling good and strong and
invigorated. I've never breathed air this fresh or felt this connected
to nature. My knee hardly aches. This is exactly what I needed.

But as I begin the trek back, things change. The air gets hotter,
heavier. My knee protests. There aren't any more water-refill stations,
so I cut back and conserve. It's okay at first, but as the sun beats
down on me mile after mile, thirst gets to me. My energy ebbs. I
start to feel light-headed. If I'm going to continue, I *have* to drink
my water.

It's warm after being carried on my back all day and the nozzle
from my water pack tastes like sweat, but it's exactly what my body
needs. I try to drink it slowly, but no matter how much I take in, it's
not enough. I empty my water pack right as the trail steepens.

I've made really good time so far, though. If I can keep up the
pace for this last stretch, the hardest stretch, there's still a chance I
can set a record. I *need* to set that record. I need to show everyone
what I'm made of. That dude with the diamond cuff links, Anna,
that asshole Julian who thinks he's marrying her, her family, my
family. Most of all, *me*. I need to show myself I can do this. I need to
win.

All I've got at this point is me. I have to be enough.

So I push myself to go faster.

The trail steepens even further. According to the research I did before coming out here, I'm now fighting an elevation of five thousand feet. It sounds intimidating, but I've done interval training. I know I can do this.

When it's not a thousand degrees out and I'm fully hydrated and I haven't already run thirty miles.

The sky darkens as a storm gathers, but the heat doesn't lessen. Instead, the air gets thicker, just like in a sauna, and I feel like I'm carrying the weight of the world on my shoulders as I run up an endless staircase, a staircase headed straight for the clouds. Still, I plow on, one step at a time, ignoring dizziness, exhaustion, and the deepening ache in my knee. If I have to reach the sky itself, that's what I'll do.

A dramatic landscape surrounds me, but I'm too sick to appreciate it. I'm alone, so I definitely can't share it. I'm aware, vaguely, in the back of my mind, that I'm wasting this experience. But I'm blinded by the need to win, to set the record, to earn the cold, comforting knowledge that I'm not only enough, but better, the best.

I'm essential, damn it. I'm worth standing up for. My body isn't what it was, but look what it's going to do.

My quad muscle cramps, and I almost trip and career off the edge of the trail and into the canyon. I manage to catch myself, and digging my fist into my cramping thigh, I try to keep going, even though it hurts like a motherfucker. The muscle cramps tighter, and I collapse against the side of the cliff. Groaning through my teeth, painfully aware of every passing second, I stretch my thigh until the muscle loosens. When I try to walk on it, it immediately threatens to lock up again, so I let myself rest. I don't have a choice.

I'm out of water, but maybe food will help. I get an energy bar from my pack, chew it into gooey peanut-buttery globs with my dry mouth, and choke it down. It doesn't sit well in my stomach, and after a couple of minutes, it all comes back up. As I'm vomiting behind a bush, the sky cracks open, and rain pours down on me in a heavy deluge. Within moments, it's freezing cold, and I shiver nonstop as I pull on a parka.

This is the real challenge of running the Grand Canyon. You don't just fight against your mind and body and the trail. You fight against nature itself, the heat, the cold, the punishing rain.

Determination rises inside me. It's getting close, but I can still set the record. So what if it's dangerous and stupid to run in the rain? No risk, no reward.

I push away from the cliff, and I make myself hobble onward. Everything hurts, my knotted-up quad, my knee, my lungs. I can barely see through the rain, but I keep going.

Until I slip. This time, I do fall. Right over the edge. But I'm ridiculously lucky. I don't go far. I fall into a soft bed of wet grass. I'm scratched up but not really bleeding. Nothing is broken—just my pride. And my heart.

Anna would be so upset if she saw me like this. She'd be even more upset if she knew why I was doing this to myself.

Thinking about her makes my eyes burn, and I'm too tired to fight the tears. I let them mix with the raindrops falling on my face.

Even as much as I hurt, I don't regret loving her the way I did—the way I *do*. With our relationship, I was all in until it was clear it wasn't the same for her. With MLA, I was all in, too. The company could tank or go on to be successful without me, and I'd still be proud. I did my part to the very best of my ability. Nothing can take that from me.

It's not winning the race that's important.

It's this moment right here, when I'm lying in the mud staring up at the dark sky with rain falling in my eyes.

It's facing the pain, facing failure, facing myself, and finding a way to make it to the end.

I rest my knee and thigh, giving my overworked muscles time to recover, and when I notice the pool of water forming on a section of my parka, I lift the waterproof fabric and drink it all.

The rain lightens into a drizzle, then a fine mist, before stopping altogether, and I get up and make my way back to the trail. I don't need to check the time to know there's no longer any chance of setting a record. I can't run anymore today anyway, not responsibly. If I pass out and get eaten by wildlife or airlifted to a hospital, that doesn't count as finishing.

I find a long stick, and I use it to take the weight off my bad leg as I hobble up this never-ending staircase to the clouds. When the sun sets, the canyon glows red like it's on fire, and I forget to breathe as I take in the view. I wish someone was here to see it with me. Next time, I'll do this right. I'll train better for the elevation changes, I'll bring more water, I'll ask someone to come with me.

The trailhead comes into view, and even though I didn't set a new record, I feel an overwhelming sense of accomplishment. It wasn't pretty. I threw up, I fell, I cried like a little kid, but I made it. I finished.

I did my part. I'll keep doing my part.

I finally feel like me again.

I RETURN TO SF THE DAY AFTER I DO THE R2R2R. THERE'S NO sense in staying. It's not like I'm going to do that run over again for kicks. My body can't handle it. I feel like I've been run over by a truck and then pounded by a gang of pissed-off gorillas.

I'm looking at maps of the Grand Canyon on my phone while

icing my knee and popping ibuprofen like candy when the intercom buzzes. I have a visitor.

Instantly, even though it seems like I knew her in another lifetime, I wonder if it's Anna. There's no chance that we're going to get back together again. I'm not signing up to be her secret lover or some shit while she keeps seeing that asshole. But my stupid heart doesn't care about that. It jumps like an excited puppy because I might get to see her again.

I make my creaky joints take me to the intercom, and I don't let myself hesitate before pressing the button. "Hello?"

"Let me up. We need to talk," says a familiar male voice—Michael. Definitely not Anna. Yeah, I'm disappointed, but I knew this talk with Michael was coming. I've had time to come to a decision and make peace with it.

Without a word, I push the button to let him into the building, unlock the door to my apartment, and limp back to my couch so I can continue icing my knee.

My doorbell rings in a few minutes, and, like I knew he would, Michael tries the door. Upon finding it unlocked, he lets himself in and comes to sit on the sofa next to me.

"Hey," I say, looking up from my maps. "What's up?"

"Seriously? 'What's up?'" Michael asks. "Where the hell have you been? Things are in full swing with the acquisition, and you email me out of the blue saying 'Taking time off to go running, be back Wednesday'? I tried calling you a hundred times."

"Sorry, there isn't reception in the Grand Canyon."

Michael's eyes bug out like he wants to murder me.

"I take it you want to talk about the new condition on the LVMH deal," I say.

"Why didn't you tell me? I had to hear it from one of our lawyers. He was panicking," Michael says.

"There's nothing to panic about," I say calmly. I can't say I feel *good* about LVMH's decision, but it doesn't tear me up anymore.

Michael runs his fingers through his disheveled hair and breathes a sigh of relief. "I knew you'd have it figured out."

I smile at how confident he is in me. He's a good friend.

"So what did you do? How are we working around it?" he asks.

"We're not working around it. I'm going to step down," I say. He opens his mouth, looking like he's about to have a blowup of some kind, so I add, "In the beginning, I *was* pissed about it. This isn't what I envisioned, you know? I wanted it to be you and me until the end. But that doesn't make sense. This is a great opportunity, and I want you to make it as far as you can possibly go."

"You're talking like you're already gone," Michael says in disbelief.

"Well, I'm not. I'm sticking around until everything's transitioned over to the new guy, whoever he is. Probably some nice old dude with white hair and a house in the Hamptons. But after that I'm going to leave the company, yeah." It would suck being demoted while taking orders from the guy who took over my old job. Not going to happen. I'd rather clean outhouses. Maybe I'll get into the restaurant business. I can see myself doing something like that.

"If that's the case, then we're turning them down," he says.

I release a long breath. "I knew you'd say that, but you need to be rational about this. Not only are they going to give us both a shitload of money, but they're going to—"

"No." He gets off the couch and paces agitatedly around my living room as he yanks at his hair, giving me angrier and angrier looks every few steps. "If you think for one second that I'm going to let them kick you out, then you have no fucking clue."

I take the ice pack off my knee and get up so we can talk this out. "Listen—"

"Sit back down and put that ice back on your knee. You've been running yourself to death, haven't you?"

"I'm fine." But I do sit down and put the ice pack on my knee. "Can you stop being all dramatic about this? This is the right thing to do. I *want* you to go ahead with the acquisition."

He looks at me like I'm speaking nonsense. "I like two things about working at MLA. One"—he holds up a finger—"I get to design clothes for kids, and two"—he holds up a second finger—"I get to work with this awesome CEO who also happens to be my best friend. If I lose you, my job automatically loses half the appeal. I'm not letting that happen. This is our company. We call the shots. That means you stay."

I shake my head, frustrated because he's not listening, but also, secretly, proud. This is why he's my best friend. It's also why I wouldn't be able to live with myself if I let him pass on this opportunity. "That isn't what's best for the company. You need to take a step back and look at things logically. With the international distribution channels—"

"I'm not listening to this," Michael says, getting up and striding to the door. "I'm going to go talk to our lawyers and tell them we're pulling the plug."

Before I can protest any further, he leaves, slamming the door shut behind him.

I release a resigned sigh, and feeling a little dirty, I pick up my phone and call his wife.

She picks up on the fifth ring. "Hello?"

"Hey, it's me, Quan. Michael just left here a minute ago," I say.

"Oh, okay. Thanks for letting me know."

"Did he tell you that LVMH won't go through with the acquisition unless I step down?" I ask.

"He did, yes."

"Well, he's trying to stop the acquisition from going through even though I'm willing to step down. You can't let him do that, Stella," I say.

"You want your share of the buyout?" she asks.

"*No.* That's not it at all." If someone other than her asked that question, I'd be insulted, but I know she doesn't mean anything by it. She just wants the information. "I want the company to become a global brand. I want Michael to make it big. This is the right choice."

"I disagree," she says in a reasonable tone. "Your leadership is half of what's made the company as successful as it's been. It's brash and effective, and you have meaningful relationships with your employees. Another CEO wouldn't be able to get them to rally for him the way they do for you. Your business partners love you, too. I don't think they'd want to work with MLA if someone else was at the helm. Plus, have you seen the magazine articles featuring MLA? The press loves featuring you and Michael together."

I let my head fall back against my couch cushions and groan in exasperation. "I don't know why they insist on dragging me into that stuff."

"You're part of the company's brand, Quan," she says simply. "I was very disappointed when I heard LVMH wanted you to step down. It was clear to me then that they don't know what they're doing in MLA's case and will probably destroy something special if they have the chance. Please don't ask me to convince Michael to go through with the acquisition. He'd be miserable, and it's not the best thing for the company. I can't endorse your choice."

I press a palm to my forehead, torn between temptation and duty. As an econometrician, Stella doesn't look at problems through an emotional lens. I was positive she'd find me expendable.

But she doesn't.

Instead, she's saying exactly what I wanted to hear.

I was prepared to step down and do the right thing. Now I don't know what I should do.

"You make it sound so rational to pass on this," I say.

"That's because it is." There's a beeping sound on the line, and she adds, "That's him. I have to go. Bye, Quan."

"Bye, Stella."

I hang up and toss my phone onto the couch. I was prepared to move on and focus my energy on something else. I'm not going to waste my life trying to prove myself to stuck-up assholes with diamond cuff links. I don't need to prove myself to *anyone*. I'm done with that.

But it looks like I still have work to do where I am. I haven't finished my part yet.

THIRTY-FIVE

Anna

THE FOLLOWING DAYS GO BY IN A STRANGE BLUR. I FEEL LIKE I
sleep away most of my time, but it's not a good sleep that leaves me
feeling rejuvenated and well rested. It's fractured, an hour here, two
hours there, and I toss and turn through most of the night, soaking
my pajamas with sweat.

I should be caring for my dad, but I'm an outcast now. I can't return to the house. Ironically, it's a relief to be away from Priscilla, my
mom, my dad, that room, and the E-flat moans. But guilt and a deep
sense of rejection plague me constantly. I'm not better off than before. I might even be worse. Food doesn't taste good. I can't focus
enough to read. I can't escape into music.

I miss Quan.

When I'm awake, I watch documentaries so David Attenborough's voice can keep me company or I look at pictures of me and
Quan on my phone. I want to, but I don't let myself message or call
him. I hurt him. I let my fear of people's opinions control me.

And what good did it do me?

My life is in ruins now. But that's because it was built on lies in the first place—*my* lies. Perhaps this was always going to happen. Perhaps it *needed* to happen. I can't bring myself to apologize to my family for speaking up for myself when they finally asked for more than I could give.

If there's someone I need to apologize to, it's Quan. I said the words the night of the party—"I'm sorry." But I couldn't make it right. I couldn't claim him in front of everyone the way he deserved, and I'll regret that forever. If I could do it over again, I'd be proud to tell everyone he's mine.

Except he's no longer mine.

I *can* give him a better apology, though. The more I think about it, the more certain I become that I need to do it. I fixate on it until one day—I'm not even sure what day it is; a glance at my phone says it's Sunday—the need for action propels me into the shower, where I scrub two weeks' worth of grime from my body.

When I'm clean and dressed in fresh clothes, I do the fifteen-minute walk to Quan's apartment. It's a boxy eight-story building that I've only been to once before, and that was the underground parking garage the first night my dad was in the hospital. I've never seen the inside of his place. There's probably a list of Bad Girlfriend Attributes with that on it.

I'm building up the courage to call him and ask him to let me into the building when a guy in sweaty exercise clothes opens the front door and gives me a double take from the doorway.

"You're Anna," he says.

"Do I know you?" I'm not good at remembering faces, but his is pretty enough that I feel like I should know if I've met him before.

"Ha, no. We've never met, but I've seen pictures of you. I'm Michael." He doesn't try to shake my hand, but he does offer a guarded smile. "Here to see Quan?"

I duck my head self-consciously. "Yeah."

"Why?" he asks.

I squirm in my shoes for an uncomfortable moment before saying, "I need to apologize to him."

After a short hesitation, he smiles at me and steps aside to hold the door open for me. "He's in 8C, since you don't look like you're familiar with this place. Knock. He never hears the doorbell."

"Thank you," I say gratefully as I run inside.

The elevator ride is short, but it feels long because my heart beats so hard. I know what I need to do to show him how I feel, and it's terrifying. But if it works, if this makes a difference, it's worth it.

When I reach a door labeled 8C, I straighten my dress, tuck my hair behind my ear, and lift my chin before knocking. Three times like I mean it.

Because I really do mean it.

I'm not just going through the motions. No one pressured me. No one pushed me. I knocked on the door because *I* intended to. I'm standing here because this is exactly where *I* mean to be.

It's me, Anna. There's something I need to say.

THIRTY-SIX

Quan

I'M STANDING IN THE SHOWER, ENJOYING THE EXHAUSTION IN my muscles and the stinging spray of hot water on my skin after my run with Michael—I sold him on the R2R2R run, and we're planning to do it together as soon as we're both ready—when I hear the knocks on my door. I groan and crank off the water before wrapping a towel around my waist. Michael must have forgotten his keys here or something.

When I open the door, I'm not at all prepared to see Anna standing there. Her color is off, washed-out almost. I can tell she's nervous. But there's a fierce glint in her eyes and a stubborn tilt to her chin. She looks like she did in her YouTube video right before she played the first notes on her violin. She's absolutely beautiful. For a full two seconds, the breath is knocked out of me.

"I wanted to talk to you, if that's okay," she says. "To apologize."

That word, *apologize*, makes everything come back to me, and I tighten my grip on the door handle as my need to keep looking at her wars against my need to shut the door in self-preservation. "You already apologized. You don't need to do it again."

"Does that mean you've forgiven me and you'll take me back?" she asks in a hopeful tone. Her smile is light, but her eyes remain dark, uncertain.

"Anna . . ."

She looks over my shoulder into my apartment. "Can I come in?"

I indicate the towel around my waist and try to gently turn her away by saying, "Now's not a great time. I was in the middle of—" Her face drops and her eyes gloss over as she backs away, and I can't help it, I open the door wide. "Come in."

Her expression immediately brightens, and she walks past me and enters my space. It's the first time she's been here, I realize. I don't know how I feel as she considers everything. It's decently neat because I finally had a cleaning lady here, and the place came furnished with all these contemporary-style couches and decorations and things. None of this represents me, but it's bright and airy, especially in the daytime like this.

"It's nice here. Thanks for letting me in," she says, being so damn polite that this is ten times more awkward than it should be. We broke up, but it's still *us*.

She falls silent then, and my gaze drops to her hands, where she's mangling her purse's shoulder straps. I feel like I need to comfort her somehow, to calm her down, and I clasp my hands behind my back so I don't do something stupid like hug her. My arms get twitchy at the thought of it. They ache to hold her.

I forcefully remind myself that we're over. No self-respecting guy would get back with her after what she did.

"I'm sorry," she says suddenly. "I'm *so* sorry for what I did. It's because I have trouble speaking up, especially in public, and especially when my family is involved. I know that's a horrible excuse, but it's true. I'm determined to change, though. I promise you that I'll never do something like that again where you're concerned—if I have the chance. I'll draw a line around you, and I'll protect you and stand up for you and speak up for you when it's right. I'll keep you safe. And I'll do the same for me. Because I matter, too."

Her words, the expression on her face, her body language, it all begs me to give in. Part of me wants to. But a bigger part of me remembers all too well what it felt like when she let another guy announce they were getting married and kiss her in front of her entire family, a guy she told me she was going to break up with. "I know you mean what you're saying. At least you do right now. But, Anna, when the time comes, I don't trust that you can actually do it. I just don't. You're *ashamed* of me. Because I'm not like fucking Julian."

She sucks in a sharp breath. "I'm *not* ashamed of you," she says forcefully as tears spill down her face. "I don't want you to be like Julian. I want you to be just as you are. I *love* you. I don't know how I would have gotten through these past months without you. Every day in that house is hell for me, watching my dad suffer, watching him hate his life, and keeping him alive anyway. It destroyed me bit by bit until there was almost nothing I wanted to live for. I've been swallowed up in sadness and pain and hopelessness and every different kind of self-hatred that exists. But you've been my bright spot. You've pulled me through. The only good thing this broken heart of mine can feel is love for you."

Her words hit me so hard that I feel shell-shocked. I know she's telling the truth. I can hear it in her voice, and it matches what I saw with my own eyes. I take several steps toward her before I realize what I'm doing and stop myself. "I didn't know how bad it was," I whisper, addressing the first part of what she said and not the second. I don't know what to say about her admission of love. It's what I've wanted, but I'm afraid there isn't a path forward for us.

She looks away from me and wipes at her face with the back of her hand. "I didn't know how to talk about it. Good people don't feel that way about taking care of the people they love. It should make me feel . . . happy, purposeful, things like that."

"Your dad's case is different," I point out. "I don't judge you for feeling the way you do."

"My family does," she says, and her face wrinkles with such intense hurting that I take another step toward her. "But I'm going to learn not to care what they think, what *anyone* thinks. I have to. Because I can't go on like this."

She drops her purse to the floor then and squares her shoulders as she looks at me with intense resolve.

"I can't make you trust me, but I can show you how much I trust *you*," she says before she pulls down the side zipper to her dress.

"What are you—"

She pulls her dress over her head and carelessly drops it to the ground, and my tongue lodges in my throat. I can't guess what she's doing. That would require thinking. All I can do is watch as she reaches behind her back, unclasps her bra, and lets it fall away from her tits. Biting her bottom lip, she reaches for the waistband of her underwear, pushes them down to her ankles, and kicks them to the side.

I greedily drink in the sight of her naked body, her tits and dark nipples, the curve of her belly, the flare of her hips, the cloud of wild curls between her luscious thighs. I've never seen this much of her. Because we've only had sex in the dark.

Breathing rapidly and visibly shaking, she searches about my apartment until she finds what she's looking for and heads there. To my bedroom. My legs follow her without my telling them to, and I watch, completely stunned, as she pulls open the blinds on all the windows, sits on my unmade bed, and scoots back until she can rest her head on my pillow.

She shuts her eyes and turns her cheek toward my pillow, breathing deep like she's pulling my scent into her lungs. "You wanted me to tell you . . . or show you . . . what I like," she says. "It's hard for me, so please . . . be patient with me."

"You don't need to do this. I never—"

"I want to," she says, and even though she's nervous, her words are firm with certainty.

She shifts restlessly on my white sheets, bunches the blankets in her hands, and finally, like it's taking all the bravery she possesses, she spreads her legs for me. A little at first, but then wider and wider. So I can see. Every fold, every line, every color, every secret, is bared to me, and I get drunk off of the sight.

Watching me from beneath half-lowered lashes, she pushes her hands over her belly toward her pussy, but before she touches herself, she loses her courage and squeezes her eyes shut, swallowing so hard I can hear the sound.

"There's a certain way I need to be touched," she says. "It has to be this way, or I can't relax and I can't let go."

After a period of time that feels like eternity, her fingertips settle on her clit, and I watch, transfixed, as she touches herself. Her breathing quickens and her hips rise, and I have never seen anything more sexy.

"There's a pattern," I hear myself say as I sit at the foot of the bed, unable to stay away. Of course there's a pattern. She's Anna. But it's not complicated. It's extremely simple. There's symmetry to it, with clockwise strokes and an equal number of counterclockwise strokes. I want to touch her that way so bad that it feels like a physical need.

Her face blushes a deep red color, but she nods. "I know it's strange, but—"

"What you need could never be strange. It just is what it is," I say. "What else do you need?"

I shouldn't be asking. I still don't know where we're going with this. But I can't help it. I have to know.

"You don't know?" she breathes.

"No, I don't."

"I need you to touch me and kiss me, so I'm not alone in this," she says, and it seems that she holds her breath as she waits for me to respond.

A full-on battle rages inside me. I want to do what she's asking. There's nothing I want more.

She's *naked*.

In. My. Bed.

But that would mean I'm ready to forgive her and risk letting her hurt me again.

I hesitate too long, and she covers her mouth to stifle a sob and moves to get off the bed. She turns her face away from me, but she's not fast enough. I see her devastation, and it's like a knife in my solar plexus. I pull her to me before she can touch her feet to the floor.

"It's okay," she says in a ragged voice. "I understand. I blew it. I don't deserve—"

I kiss her. Just once. I know I can chalk it up to a mistake, say it was done in the heat of the moment. I can still end us. But then I kiss her again, and her mouth is so unbelievably perfect that I can't help kissing her again, deeper. As soon as I taste her, I know it's over for me. I can't lose this. I understand what she was going through now. She's finally being open with me, just like I've been demanding from the start. It's hard for her but she's trying anyway, and that means everything to me. I forgive her. I'll risk anything for her. I kiss her with everything in me. Maybe I'm too rough, but she welcomes me. She kisses me back like she's been starving without me.

When I release her mouth and kiss my way to her neck, she shivers and asks, "Are you kissing me because you feel sorry for me?"

I bite her neck and slide my hand between her thighs. I touch her the way she showed me. "You think I do this when I feel sorry for someone?"

Her shoulders hunch forward, and her hips press sharply against my hand. Her mouth falls open on a soundless gasp.

"Do I have that right?" I ask, even though I think I know. She's drenching my fingers as she tries to get closer. "Is that good?"

Instead of answering, she pulls me down for a long kiss. Her hips undulate against my hand as she licks at my lips, sucks on my tongue, making needy little sounds that drive me out of my mind. She touches me hungrily, my face, my scalp, my shoulders. Her nails scrape down my back, hard, but not enough to break the skin, and every muscle in my body tightens. The instinct to lower her to the bed and drive into her is almost overwhelming.

The only thing stopping me is the brightness of the room. When we were together before, the darkness wasn't just for her. It protected me, too.

When she grips my ass over my towel, the cloth loosens precariously, and I barely manage to catch it with my free hand before it falls.

She doesn't seem to notice the conflict going on inside me. Her movements are urgent now, urgent but frustrated. I can feel it in the way she's touching me, like she's looking for something, trying to say something.

"Tell me," I say.

She kisses me harder as she trembles in my arms. I feel the press of her nails on my shoulders, feel the moisture flooding my hand, the tension in her body. She's close. But unable to fall.

"What do you need?" I ask her. I'm down for trying any kind of kink as long as it involves her and me together. I just need to know what it is in order to give it to her.

"I need—" She hides her face against my neck without finishing.

I whisper in her ear, "Ass play?"

"No," she says in surprise. "I need . . ." But she presses her face closer to my neck. "Why is this so hard?"

"Should we shut the blinds? So it's like before?" It's a little wrong, but I want her to say yes.

She looks up at me, and tears gather in her eyes as she shakes her head. "I *want* to do this when it's not dark. I want to be able to tell you when I—but I—I'm still so afraid—" Her chin wobbles, but she draws in an unsteady breath as a fierce light shines in her eyes. "I need—" She draws in another breath. "I need—" She wraps her arms around my neck and hugs me tight for a long shivering moment.

"I promise I'm down with it," I say.

She kisses my jaw and whispers in my ear, "I need you to fuck me."

Her words send a shock wave through me—*that* word in particular, because I know how difficult it is for her to say. My skin flashes with heat before an odd sort of hyperawareness claims me. It feels like everything's been leading to this moment, now.

I pull away from her, and I bring my hands to the towel around my waist. She's let me in all the way. I need to do the same. This broken body of mine isn't what it was, but it's what I have. It took me into hell and back. I can't be ashamed any longer.

Keeping my eyes on her face, I bare myself to her.

THIRTY-SEVEN

Anna

QUAN'S BODY IS INK AND LEAN RUNNER'S MUSCLES AND MAS-culine lines. He's beautiful.

His arousal juts out proudly, and it pleases me at an elemental level. That's a response to *me*. *I'm* the one he desires. The other part of him, the part that causes him so much self-consciousness, looks more or less the same as other ones I've seen in real life and in pictures. Perhaps it has a more uneven appearance. But I accept it, just as I accept him. Just as I accepted my imperfect violin.

I didn't expect this. I wasn't trying to make him do this, though I should have realized this was the natural consequence of what I was asking.

His trust humbles me and honors me. It makes me love him more.

"Can I touch you?" I ask, reaching toward him but stopping be-fore I get too close.

"Always," he replies.

When he takes my hand in his, I expect him to wrap my fingers around his sex. But instead, he guides me to a small raised line on his inner pelvic area, one of the places on his body that isn't covered with ink.

"That's the only visible scar left from the surgery," he says.

I run my fingertips over the two-inch mark. It's difficult to believe something so small had such a large impact. Because of this cut, because of that surgery, he's here with me now.

Bending down, I press my lips to his scar. I want him to know that I'm not disgusted, that I'm grateful for this scar, that I love it, that I love all of him. I brush my cheek against the firm length of his sex so he can witness my affection, then my other cheek. He's soft as velvet but burning hot. I press a chaste kiss to the head.

"Anna, you don't have to do that," he says in a gravelly voice. "I know you don't like—"

"This isn't a blow job. I'm just kissing you," I say, but then my lips part and I run my tongue over him. Once I've gone that far, it's the most natural thing in the world to take him into my mouth.

He flinches like I've electrocuted him. His chest billows. His stomach muscles ripple and tense, making the waves inked into his skin roll like real waves in the sea. But when he touches my face, his fingers are unbearably gentle.

As I suck on him, teasing the tip with my tongue before taking him deeper, his gaze doesn't waver from me. I'm pleasuring him, but we're doing this together. Neither of us is alone. I'm not just an accessory for his masturbation.

And unlike the other times I've done this, I find myself enjoying it. His hoarse sounds excite me. The barely contained violence in his body excites me. His every response excites me.

He didn't push my head down and take from me, knowing I couldn't refuse. He let me choose. And because of that, I could choose to give. That completely changes things.

I don't count the seconds as I caress him with my mouth. I don't hope for him to finish quickly so that I can do something else.

Instead, I feast my senses on him, getting drunk on the feel of him, his taste, his clean scent, the sight of him, the sound of his gusting breaths. Something awakens in me. I get wetter between my legs, and a sense of emptiness expands until I ache with it. When he pulls free of my mouth and takes my lips in a hard kiss, pushing my back to the bed as he covers my body with his, I'm almost mindless with wanting.

He strokes my sex with his fingertips. Exactly the way I need. Exactly. Because I showed him how. And I cry out as I arch into his touch. I'm right on the edge, but there's something I need, something he taught me to crave. I pull him closer, I try to force words past my lips, *that* word.

But he understands. He positions himself between my legs, and we both watch as the head of his sex penetrates me, pushing in slowly while his fingers continue to touch me. The feel of my body stretching to accept him, this extraordinary fullness, leaves me breathless. I want to savor this moment, to memorize every minute detail. When he retreats and thrusts back into me, finding the perfect rhythm, stroking me in all the right places in all the right ways, I clench on him helplessly. I'm captivated by the intensity on his face and the fluid flex and play of his body as he takes me, as he *fucks* me.

The darkness took this from me. My fear took this from me.

The pleasure heightens, and every part of me winds tight. I kiss him frantically, needing that extra connection to him as I climb and climb, as I hang at the precipice for a moment out of time. When the convulsions rip through me, I kiss him still, crying out with every breath I take.

The look he gives me as I shudder beneath him is dark with satisfaction and lust, yet full of tenderness, full of love, and I know that I'm completely safe with him, here in the light of day.

His motions hasten, his expression borders on pain, and with a sound of surrender, he drives deep, joining us tight as our hearts pound in tandem. I hold him, and I kiss him softly, and I smile, whispering "*I love you*" in his ear.

WE SPEND HOURS LAZING IN HIS BED, SHARING PILLOW TALK and smiling at each other as sunshine blankets our naked skin. He tells me the stories behind his water tattoos as I trace them with my fingertips. I tell him about my favorite pieces of classical music inspired by the sea, Wagner's overture to *The Flying Dutchman* and Debussy's *La Mer*, how they encapsulate moments of blissful calm and explosive violence. As usual, talking about music brings me back to Vivaldi's *Four Seasons*, and I have to mention the incomparable intensity of his *Summer* and *Winter* pieces, how they evoke the most magnificent and beautiful storms. He laughs when I describe storms that way, but he does it fondly. He says storms are great unless you happen to be stuck in one. He also says my passion for music is one of his favorite things about me and he's certain I'll play again when I'm ready. I hope he's right.

When hunger drives us out of bed and into the city in search of dinner, we hold hands and press close to each other, maximizing the points of contact between our bodies, like we need that extra reassurance after all that's happened. I'm craving noodles—those are my favorite thing in the world to eat—so he takes me across town to Chinatown, where they have the best noodles anywhere. We both get steaming bowls of spicy Taiwanese beef noodle soup, and when we're finished, our bellies are full, our sinuses are clear, our tongues are numb, and we're high on pain endorphins released in response to the chilis.

I'm drowsy, so he takes me to my place. We might watch documentaries, I don't remember. But there's a lot of cuddling because I can't stand to be separated from him, and I think he feels the same. We kiss, but not in a sexual way. We kiss to express our affection. I fall asleep against his chest, lulled by the steadiness of his heartbeat.

It is, by all measures that matter, a perfectly flawless evening.

So I experience a sense of inevitableness when I wake up the next morning to a phone call from my mom. Before answering, I know it's bad news.

She confirms it when she says, "Your father just passed away."

Part Three

After

THIRTY-EIGHT

Anna

AFTER HANGING UP THE PHONE, I FEEL . . . NOTHING. AT LEAST, it seems that way at first. I'm calm. I don't cry. I recognize I'm thirsty, and I'm able to get myself a glass of water and drink it without inhaling liquid into my lungs. But there's an unreal quality to everything around me. The water I drink tastes a little funny, metallic perhaps. The cup feels oddly heavy in my fingers. Was it always this solid? As I look at the glass, I notice the surface of the water is trembling very finely.

Quan hugs me, and I sag against him as I try to make sense of everything.

It's over. My dad isn't suffering anymore.

I believe this is what he wanted.

But he's really gone now.

No more secret candies in the car. No more listening to old-school music stuck in the tape deck together. No more attending my concerts. No more anything.

Loss grips me, but it's muted, perhaps because I've already mourned him so many times by now. How many times in the hospital? How many times since we brought him home? My heart has traveled this path until it's well-worn, and it's hard to see new tracks, especially when an immense sense of failure overshadows everything.

I didn't make it until the end. If I'd known it was only two more weeks, maybe I wouldn't have felt such an oppressive sense of futility. Maybe I could have held it together better and been less absent-minded and more functional. Maybe I could have found a way to play for him at the party, since it really was my last chance. Maybe my family would still think I'm the person I'd been pretending to be for so long—not perfect in their eyes, but still good enough.

I'm not sure if I'm welcome, but I go home to help with whatever I can. Quan offers to drop me off and come back later to get me, but I ask him to come in with me.

We walk hand in hand to the front door of my parents' house, and after letting myself in, I continue to hold his hand as we walk down the marble hallway. The house is colder than ever today, and the light pouring in through the windows is gray, drab.

We find Priscilla in my dad's room, where my dad's hospital bed is starkly vacant. This room is the master bedroom of the house, and without my dad's presence to fill it, it now feels ten times as large. Priscilla is organizing our dad's medications into ziplock bags and boxes, and she gives no indication that she notices our presence. She looks awful. Her eyes are puffy, her skin sallow, and I think she's lost weight since two weeks ago. She's skeletal. I can even see wrinkles on her face. This is the first time that she's looked the full fifteen years older than me, and I hate that.

So I swallow my pride and my own hurt, and I approach her. "Hi, Je je."

"There's a box of stuff you forgot here in your room," she says in her harsh way.

"I'll get it, thanks."

Instead of responding, she continues organizing the medications, content to ignore me.

"Do you . . . need help with that?" I ask.

She gives me a stony look and says, "No," before returning to her work. Only now, her hands are unsteady, and she drops a pill bottle to the ground.

I pick it up and put it on the table for her. "Can you look at me? So we can talk? Please?"

She lifts her chin and gives me her attention, but she doesn't speak. She waits.

"I'm sorry." It's hard for me to logically conceptualize what I did that's so wrong. I spoke the truth. I stood up for myself. *Why is that bad?* But if I hurt her, I regret that and I genuinely want to do better in the future. "I didn't mean to hurt you. I just—"

"You accused me of torturing him because I couldn't let go," she says, pointing an angry finger at me as her eyes tear up. "You're supposed to back me up. That's what sisters do. Instead, you betrayed me and disrespected me. In front of everyone."

She doesn't touch me, but my whole body flinches with every jab of her finger. "I didn't mean to betray you. I said *all of us* were torturing him."

"It wasn't my choice. I was just trying to do the right thing." Priscilla covers her face with her hands as her thin body quakes, and it breaks me. "You were supposed to understand. We were supposed to be in this together."

My heart wrenches, and I hug her, saying everything I can think of to make it better. "I'm sorry I hurt you. I'm sorry. I'm so sorry."

Eventually, she thaws and hugs me back, and I feel like I have a sister again. I feel like maybe everything's going to be okay.

But when we finally pull apart, she wipes her tears away and acts like we're finished. In her eyes, I did wrong, so I apologized. I love her. I don't want to cause her pain. But something important is missing.

I wait, and still, it doesn't happen. Turbulent feelings swell in my chest, raging to get out, and I can't swallow them down.

I promised to draw a line. Around Quan. And around me. Because I matter, too.

If I don't stand up for me, no one else will.

I have to do this.

"Aren't you going to apologize to *me*?" I ask.

She narrows her eyes at me. "For what?"

"For hurting me. For treating me the way you did. I told you I was struggling. That being here was making me sick. But I stayed anyway. Who do you think I stayed *for*? And yet you looked down on me because I didn't meet your standards. You didn't care that I was doing the best that I could. You—"

"If your best job is a shitty job, *it's still shitty*," she yells.

"Why couldn't we get help, then?" I ask, openly crying now. "He needed too much care, care that he didn't even *want*. This was too much for us."

"You mean it was too much for *you*," Priscilla says through her teeth, pointing at me again. "It wasn't too much for *me*."

That hurts, but the truth of it sends an odd calm over me. I sense Quan coming toward me. No doubt he's agitated by the things Priscilla's saying and wants to defend me, but I motion for him to stay away. I need to handle this on my own.

"I'm different from you," I tell Priscilla.

"Are you talking about your 'diagnosis'?" she asks sarcastically, putting finger quotes around the word *diagnosis*.

"I don't know if that has anything to do with this. Maybe it does. But you have to stop expecting me to be the same as you."

Priscilla rolls her eyes. "Trust me. I *don't* expect that."

"Then why are you always judging me and pressuring me to change? Why can't you accept me the way I am?"

"That's not how family works," she says through her teeth. "I *get* to judge you and pressure you because I want what's best for you."

"What's best for me right now would be an apology from you." I need her to love me enough to acknowledge when she's hurt me and try not to do it again. I need her to *attempt* to understand me. I need her to accept my differences. Hiding and masking, trying to please other people, trying to please *her*, has been destroying me, and I can't live that way anymore.

Her lips thin and curl. "I can't apologize when I didn't. Do. Anything. Wrong. *You* were the one who did."

"You don't care why?" I ask, feeling like I'm crumbling and sinking into the ground.

"I don't want your excuses, Anna," she says in exasperation.

I want to correct her and tell her they're reasons, not excuses, but I don't. There's no point in continuing with this. I see that now.

I have to choose. I can spend my time trying to make her accept me, either through bending to her will or bending her to mine, or I can accept myself and focus on other things. How do I want to spend my life?

I turn away from her and catch Quan watching my sister with his jaw clenched and his hands fisted at his sides. He's outraged, but when he switches his attention to me, sadness lines his face. She doesn't understand. But he does.

Taking his hand, I head away from the room. Out in the hallway, he looks at me and whispers, "Proud of you."

Before I can reply, my mom appears with Priscilla's violin case in her arms. "Give Je je time," she says.

I don't want to argue with her, but I don't want to make promises that I won't keep either, so I say nothing.

Her gaze lands on Quan, on our joined hands, and I think she's going to comment on us being together. I think she's going to voice her displeasure and ask where Julian is. But she doesn't. Instead, she hands Quan the violin case.

"Hers broke. She's too stubborn to take this, but you keep it in case she wants to play, okay?" she asks him.

"I will." Quan smiles at her, his beautiful smile that brightens his eyes and transforms his face, and I think my mom sees it then—why I love him. There's such genuine caring and kindness in him.

"Are you okay, Ma?" I ask.

She looks exhausted, but she nods. "We knew this was coming. Except for maybe Priscilla. She's blaming herself for not doing enough."

My mom's words give me pause. I don't like the idea of Priscilla blaming herself when she did all that she could, all that anyone could, really. But I guess that's how it must be when someone's standards are so impossibly high and their capacity for empathy so limited. They are cruel to others, and cruelest to themself.

An unexpected realization washes over me: I'm glad I'm not Priscilla.

"Do you need help with anything?" Quan asks, looking about my mom's immaculate house for something that might need his attention.

"No, no," my mom says, but she gives him a small tired smile. "There's the funeral, but I need to plan that. It's better if you two go home. Priscilla is . . ." She can't seem to find the right words, so she shakes her head. To me, she adds, "It would be appropriate if you played at the ceremony."

Hot tears well in my eyes. Not this again. "Ma, I don't think I—"

"Just think about it. That's all," she says quickly as she herds us toward the front door. "Go home. Rest. Eat. You're looking skinny. I'll let you know our plans."

As I'm leaving, she pulls me aside and surprises me by hugging me. She doesn't admonish me. She doesn't ask anything of me. She doesn't say anything at all. She just lets me know she cares.

That is all I've ever wanted.

THIRTY-NINE

Anna

I'D LIKE TO SAY THAT AFTER THE FUNERAL, I MOURN FOR A couple of weeks, and then I pick up my old life where I left off. I'd like to say that now that I've learned to stand up for myself and stop people pleasing, it's easy to overcome the creative block associated with my music. I'd also like to say that Priscilla and I are reconciled.

But if I said those things, I'd be lying.

Once the funeral is over, an intangible thread breaks in my mind, and I mentally collapse. I've learned since then that this is called autistic burnout. I can't remember the weeks immediately following the funeral at all. It's like I never lived them. The earliest post-funeral days that I can recall are from months later, and they involve me staring blankly into space or watching the same documentaries over and over while basically fusing my body to my couch. I don't do anything productive. I can't reason my way through any semi-complicated tasks, like getting the mail or paying bills or even checking my bank account balance online. I only manage not to get kicked out of my apartment through the miracle of autopay. Emotionally, I'm highly unstable. I switch between intense melancholy, rage (at Priscilla), and then exhaustion from the aforementioned melancholy and rage. I cry . . . a lot.

Rose and Suzie message me, but I rarely answer. I don't have the energy. It matters to me that they care about me. I appreciate them. But I have to go through this alone and find my way back to them later.

Similarly, Jennifer checks up on me, but I don't have energy to answer her either. Therapy can't help me when I'm like this.

FORTY

Quan

AFTER A FEW MONTHS, I MOVE IN WITH ANNA. I'VE BASICALLY been living there anyway, so it doesn't make sense to keep a place of my own. Because I can and want to, I take over the rent. She covers the utilities. It works out for both of us.

She's not well, I can tell, but we're slowly getting through this. I think I see her recovering bit by bit. When I come home after work, she's always happy to see me. She asks me about my day and listens as I tell her goofy stuff that no one else cares about, like the seagull I saw during my lunch-hour run who stole a dude's lunch right out of his hands or the mourning dove who tries to sit on her babies in the nest right outside my office window even though they're almost as big as she is.

I check up on Anna every day while I'm gone, sending her text messages filled with hearts or funny memes with octopuses and other creatures. When we're together, I hold and cuddle her a lot, because I sense she needs to feel loved. We don't have a lot of sex, though. It's kind of hard to have sexy thoughts when your girlfriend can barely keep her eyes open past eight P.M. and regularly wakes up in the middle of the night crying. I just take care of that kind of stuff in the shower. Don't get me wrong, I don't *prefer* jerking off in the shower to having sex with the woman I love, but I'm happy to wait until she's ready.

FORTY-ONE

Anna

IT TAKES ME A LONG TIME TO GET TO THE POINT WHERE I FEEL mentally strong enough to practice music. Months and months. But then I obsess over getting a new violin. I won't touch Priscilla's old instrument. I'd rather do any number of horrible things to myself.

Naturally, this is when my mom decides to drop by my apartment. I'm stunned when I hear her voice through the intercom one afternoon. "Anna, it's me."

I'm even more stunned when I buzz her in, and moments later, I open my door and see her standing there in white slacks, a cream-colored silk blouse, and an Hermès scarf artfully wrapped around her neck. She looks casual but stylish, but she's aged since my dad passed away. The new lines by her eyes make me sad. Priscilla must have returned to New York by now. That means she's been living in that giant house all by herself. She must be lonely.

"Hi, Ma. Uh, come in. Sorry it's so messy." If I'd known she was coming, I would have straightened things up more. As it is, I only had time to sweep my dirty dishes off the coffee table and stick them in the sink and haphazardly straighten the pillows and blankets on my couch. My bed's not made. The laundry is overflowing. My bathroom is a disaster. I pray for her not to go into my kitchen.

She perches herself gingerly on my armchair and looks around, spending extra time on the pair of men's running shoes in the corner next to an open duffel bag stuffed with clean workout clothes. There's a small pile of business management books on the end table next to her, and she scans the titles with interest. "Your Quan moved in with you?"

I sit on the couch and look down at my knees. "Yeah."

"You're happy with him?" she asks, and the way she says it, I feel like she honestly wants to know.

I can't help the soft smile that curves over my lips. "Yeah." Without him, I'm not sure I'd be holding it together right now. As it is, I miss him the entire time he's gone for work. When he messages me during the day, it makes me nauseatingly happy.

"Your music? How is that?" my mom asks. "How is Je je's violin working for you?"

I avert my eyes and shake my head.

"So stubborn, Anna," she says in a tired voice. "Here, I want to buy you this one."

She takes her phone out of her purse and shows me an email that Priscilla forwarded from an instrument dealer. In the body of the email, there's a picture of an elegant Guarneri violin. Guarneri was an Italian luthier during the 1700s who rivaled Stradivari, the creator of the famous Stradivarius violins. The most expensive violin in the world is a Guarneri. This is not *that* Guarneri, of course. According to the dealer, this Guarneri sustained serious damage on multiple occasions and has undergone extensive repairs, so its price reflects that. But it still costs as much as a house.

"Ma, it's too nice. I can't—"

She makes a scoffing sound. "It's not too nice for my daughter. Priscilla said the sound is very good. You'll like it."

An uncomfortable sensation crawls over my skin, and I hand the phone back to my mom. Speaking in a soft, measured tone and keeping my demeanor the way I've learned to around her, I say, "I love that you want to get me this. It means a lot to me. Thank you. But—"

"You won't play it if she picked it out for you," my mom observes, *seeing* me in a way I didn't think she could. "I was there, I heard what she said, it was not kind. But just forgive her already. Let it go. Let things go back to the way they used to be. She told me she's sad that she's losing you and Ba at the same time."

I recoil as a sense of injustice engulfs me. "How do you forgive someone when they won't say sorry? It's been months. She could have called me at any time, messaged, or stopped by. But she hasn't. She won't."

My mom makes a dismissive waving motion with her hand. "You know Je je."

"I do. She thinks it's okay to treat me that way. Based on how she's acting, she'll keep on doing it. *That's not fair to me*," I say, and I don't even try to hide how angry this makes me. I let my mask completely drop away.

I expect my mom to chide me for having an "attitude" around her, for not listening, but instead, she says, "You have to see it from her perspective."

"What about *mine*? I'm not being unreasonable. It's not like I'm asking her to cut off one of her arms." I'm asking for her to treat me as an equal.

"You're breaking our family apart, and there are only three of us now," my mom says, her eyes pleading with me to give in because

Priscilla won't. "I want us *together*. This Christmas, I want us to go on a nice vacation. You could bring your Quan. It's what Ba would have wanted."

"I don't think he'd want that if he knew how hard it is for me to be what Priscilla wants, what you all want," I say in a quiet voice. "I've tried to be different, to change for you, but it doesn't work. It just hurts me. I—I—" I consider telling her about my diagnosis and the hell I've been going through, but I remember how Priscilla reacted and I know it's hopeless.

"You're autistic," my mom says.

Surprise makes me freeze in place. I can't speak. I can't even blink.

"Faith told me. It's probably from your father's side. Like Uncle Tony," she grumbles, and for whatever reason that makes a laugh crack out of me. "I've been reading about it. I think I see it now."

She rests her hands on top of mine, but then hesitates, like she's not sure if she can touch me now. I turn my hands around and hold hers tightly, telling her without words that this is okay.

"I don't know what I'm supposed to do," she confesses. "I feel like I don't know you anymore."

"I don't know what we're supposed to do either," I say. "But maybe we can start over."

She squeezes my hands and nods. "You were difficult when you were little, very difficult, and I'm sorry I didn't know how to—what to—I thought I was doing the right thing for you."

"It's okay, Ma," I hear myself say. Part of me doubts this conversation is actually happening, but her hands feel very real in mine.

She gives me a searching look before saying, "Long before I came here to marry your dad, during the Cultural Revolution in China, I was sent to reeducation camps, where I worked and starved in the fields. Did you know this?" When I shake my head numbly, she continues. "Our family wasn't safe because Gung gung was a wealthy landowner. *I* wasn't safe. That's what I learned from them—it's not *safe* to be different." Speaking through her tears, clinging to me like I'm a lifeline, she says, "I pushed you to change because I wanted you to be safe. Do you understand?"

My throat swells, but I manage to say, "I think I understand." An old knot of resentment loosens in my heart. I needed to hear this. "How come you never told me?"

She releases a long, weary sigh. "I told Priscilla. I didn't want to burden you with ugliness from the past. I worry about you so much, Anna."

"I *want* to know things like this."

"I'll tell you more about it sometime. For now, I—" She sighs again. "I have to talk to your sister. She had to block off time on her calendar for it, do you believe it? She's that busy with her new job. A hundred hours a week until the merger goes through or something. I'm going to tell her to try therapy. I've been going once a week."

My jaw drops.

She laughs before she pats my hand and gets up. "I need to go. Maybe I'll have a cappuccino and a pastry in the park while I talk to her. It's the small things in life."

I walk with her to the door, and before she leaves, she hugs me firmly. She's wearing her regular perfume, but the scent is very light. She doesn't touch my hair. These are small changes, but I suspect she made them for me. I think she read about these things. I can't explain how much that means to me.

"I love you, Anna," she whispers fiercely. "No matter what happens, I hope you know that. Fight with your sister if you must, but *I* stay in your life. Talk to me, tell me when things are wrong, and I'll do my best. I can't lose you."

I'm too overwhelmed to say anything, so I nod and hug her tighter, soaking her scarf with tears.

When she finally leaves, I watch her until she disappears down the stairwell, and then I go to my balcony and watch as she gets in my dad's old Mercedes convertible and drives away. I imagine she's listening to the cassette that's stuck in the tape deck.

The bittersweet irony of the situation strikes me. I lost my dad and my sister, but somehow that gave me my mom.

FORTY-TWO

Anna

BECAUSE I REJECT THE NOTION THAT ALL THE BEST VIOLINS have already been made, that nothing from the present or future can compete with the past, I opt to buy a violin handcrafted by a modern luthier based in Chicago. It doesn't cost as much as a house thankfully, but it's not cheap either. I spend most of my savings on it. It's worth every penny, however. Its voice is sweet and bright and achingly beautiful, and I fall in love with it the instant I test it out, playing my first clumsy scales in nearly a year.

Once I bring it home, I'm determined to conquer the Richter piece. I've had so much time away. I should be returning to music well rested and full of fresh perspective. I vow that I'm going to master the piece within a month. Back before my Internet fame, it took me less time than that to gain fluidity with a piece of music. I should be able to do it, especially with this new violin.

It doesn't work that way. I immediately fall into the same mental trap as before, only it's worse now. I play in horrid, never-ending loops all day, and when I stop to rest, my mind is battered and drained in a way I've never experienced. Still, I'm determined to forge through. I tell myself that I *will* finish this, even if it's the last thing I ever do.

I end up pushing myself so hard that I burn out even worse than I did previously. I lose days and weeks. I lose functionality. This time, in addition to grief and rage, there's anxiety, desperation. The Richter piece is trapping me, ruining my life. I want to be free. Why can't I get free?

If I can't play my way free, there's one other way . . .

From there, I plummet into pure darkness.

But there's a light that keeps me from falling too far. That light is Quan. When I get up in the middle of the night, nauseated and silently sobbing and tempted, so tempted, to set myself free in the only way I believe I can, he senses something is off. He wakes up. He holds me. He asks me what's wrong.

I know he'll believe me. I know he won't look down on me and tell me to pull up my big-girl pants and tough it out. So I tell him the ugly truth of my thoughts and fantasies, and he cries as he rocks me from side to side.

FORTY-THREE

Anna

WITH QUAN'S URGING, I START SEEING JENNIFER AGAIN. SHE
refers me to a psychiatrist. I go on medication that saves my life.

I start to feel . . . optimistic. There are days when I even feel *good*.
Drugs don't clear my creative block, though. When I pick up my violin, I still play in circles, so I set it down. I understand now that I'm
not healed enough to play. I have to give my mind time.

I have trouble focusing enough to read anything of significant
length, so I find my way to poetry. A poem can be as short as two
lines, sometimes even one, but there's an entire idea contained there,
an entire story. That's perfect for someone like me. I quickly fall in
love with rupi kaur's work, reading a page here, a page there, as I
move about my day, sometimes as I fall in and out of sleep while
watching documentaries, specifically the "Cape" episode of David
Attenborough's *Africa* documentary. I watch it for the two-minute
scene where butterflies mate above the treeless peak of Mount Mabu

in Mozambique. I'm fascinated by the vivid colors and patterns of their iridescent wings and the dizzying number of butterflies fluttering in the blue sky. It looks like a world apart from the one where I live, one that I can only dream of going to.

When Quan discovers my new special interest, he surprises me by creating a butterfly garden on my tiny balcony. He puts pots of milkweed out and trains passion vine to twine around the railing. As spring turns to summer, my plants blossom with vibrant color, and the butterflies come. It's just like in Mozambique.

I sit on my balcony for hours, basking in soft rays of sunlight and watching as butterflies dance about me. They're not shy or afraid of me. Hummingbirds try to compete with them for nectar, and I laugh when my small butterflies battle against their larger opponents and win. Caterpillars hatch from tiny eggs and eat voraciously, chewing through each milkweed leaf in neat rows like when people eat corn on the cob typewriter-style. I name them all. Chompy, Biggolo, and Chewbacca, to name a few, and I bring Rock outside so he can hang out with us. I'm careful not to put him underneath the plants, though, and he's grateful. He doesn't want his new friends to poop on him.

Together, we observe as the monarch caterpillars form green chrysalises, darken, and then break free to reveal wings of dazzling orange and black. Later in the season, a different type of butterfly visits my passion vine. The Gulf fritillary is sometimes known as the passion butterfly. On the outside, its wings are plain brown and pearly white, but when they open up their wings, they're the sweetest tangerine color. Passion butterfly caterpillars aren't cute like my monarchs. They're dark and spiky, almost poisonous-looking, and their chrysalises are camouflaged to look exactly like dried-up leaves. But when I poke one, it wiggles and squirms, very much alive.

It seems dead, but it's just in transition.

I wonder if it's a metaphor for me. Am I also metamorphosing and changing into something better?

FORTY-FOUR

Anna

IT'S SLOW, BUT I FEEL MYSELF HEALING. I CATCH UP ON MY bills, pay late fees, sign up to autopay as much as I can. I clean my apartment. It turns out that decorative black ring around the bathroom sink isn't supposed to be there. (It's mold.) I do the laundry. I start to use my exercise clothes for their intended purpose, but nothing drastic. I jog for ten minutes a day and increase the duration little by little. Now and then, Quan and I visit my mom, but we can't drop in unexpectedly. At any given moment, chances are slim that she's home. She's not working as much as she used to, but she spends most of her time traveling with her friends. They're currently planning a trip to Budapest.

As the seasons change again, I experience an odd sort of restlessness. It takes me a while to realize that I want to listen to music. But not classical music. I want something completely different. I want . . . jazz. For weeks, I listen to all the jazz I can find, everything from Louis Armstrong to John Coltrane to modern artists like Joey Alexander, and eventually, eventually, *eventually*, I am inspired by their musicality. Eventually, I *want* to play.

This is when I finally let myself pick up my violin again, but I do it carefully. I ease into it, only allowing myself to play scales at first. I rediscover my joy of patterns. I rebuild the calluses on my fingertips. I play simple songs from my childhood to see if I can.

FORTY-FIVE

Quan

TODAY, OVER A YEAR AFTER TURNING DOWN LVMH'S OFFER, Michael and I are meeting with their new head of acquisitions. Apparently, several women accused Paul Richard of sexual harassment and the company replaced him.

"I'm so happy to meet you both in person," Angèlique Ikande says, smiling broadly as she shakes my hand and then Michael's. With her white pantsuit and statuesque build, she looks like a corporate Wonder Woman.

"Likewise," I say as I motion for her to join us at the restaurant table.

She folds her tall body into her seat and asks the waitress for a glass of sauvignon blanc before regarding us for a thoughtful moment. "I'd like you to know that I think my predecessor is a complete ass."

Michael breaks into laughter, and I can't help grinning as I lift my glass and drink to that statement of hers. I've been wondering about the purpose for this meeting, but Michael and I haven't allowed ourselves to muse about it out loud. Paul Richard left a really bad taste in our mouths, and neither of us is over it. Angèlique, however, is totally different. She's not stuck-up. Everything about her screams competence and honesty. It's hard not to like her.

"You might not be aware of this," she says, "but the MLA deal was my project, and Paul stuck his nose in it at the last minute. On behalf of LVMH, I'd like to sincerely apologize for his actions. But that's not the only reason why I'm here. The first thing that I want to do as the new head of acquisitions is finish what I started. I'd like nothing better than to bring MLA under the LVMH umbrella—and that means *both* of you. To let you know how serious I am, I'm upping our original offer by twenty percent."

Considering what the original offer was, twenty percent is a lot of money. I glance at Michael to gauge his response and smile when I find him doing the same thing to me.

"We're going to need to discuss this," I say.

"Of course," she says.

I half expect her to get up and leave just like Paul Richard did, but she settles in and actually has lunch with us. She asks about our summer product line. She's been keeping up with our social media accounts and is excited by the publicity we've been getting recently. To demonstrate how much she loves Michael's designs, she shows us pictures of her kids on her phone. I don't know if she did it on purpose or not, but it looks like her kids wear MLA exclusively and I can tell it pleases Michael. That's the quickest way to my heart.

When lunch is over, we shake hands and part ways, promising to get in touch soon.

"So?" Michael asks as he drives us back to our building. "What are you thinking?"

"I think she's prepared to up the offer by twenty-five percent, maybe thirty," I say in a neutral tone, even though my heart is pounding so hard I feel like it might break through my ribs.

Michael's wearing his sunglasses so I can't see his eyes, but I still know what he's thinking when he looks at me and then returns his attention to the road. "That's not what I was asking."

I shrug and try to play it cool, but a grin sneaks onto my mouth.

He must see it because he shoves my shoulder hard. "Asshole, you had me going there. You want to do it, right? It'll really happen this time. If we want it to."

"Okay, yeah. I want to do it. She gets us. Plus, she might be our number one customer." I take my phone out to compulsively check my email, adding, "Still, I need to see this written out before . . ."

At the top of my inbox is a new email from Ikande, A. There's a file attached. When I open it, I see it's the contract that we worked on with Paul Richard, except now it clearly specifies PER THIS CON-TRACT, QUAN DIEP WILL STAY ON AS CHIEF EXECUTIVE OFFI-CER OF MICHAEL LARSEN APPAREL & CO., SUBSIDIARY OF LVMH MOËT HENNESSY LOUIS VUITTON.

"What?" Michael asks.

"She just sent us the contract," I say. "It's exactly as she said."

"Shit. This is really going to happen now." Michael swallows, and his face turns greenish as he grips the steering wheel like he might faint.

"Deep breaths. Pull over and let me drive. Anna will kill me if I get in a car accident."

"I'm fine, I'm fine," he says, shaking it off and getting control of himself. "You sure you want to do this? We don't *have* to. But we should consider it serious—"

"Yes, I want to. I'm not going to let a grudge hold us back. We're ready. We're going to kick ass." I feel the rightness of this in my bones, and I know we're going to see this through. We're going to dress a whole shitload of kids in super-cute clothes, and we're going to have the time of our lives doing it.

Michael grins so hard he looks a little scary, but I figure I look the same way.

When I arrive at our apartment a few hours later, I can't wait to tell Anna the news. But I don't get the usual attack hug from her. As far as I can tell, she's not even home, which instantly makes me worry.

I take my shoes off and venture into our apartment, and there, on the kitchen table, is a homemade cake covered with burning candles.

"*Happy birthday.*" Anna jumps out from the kitchen, lifts her violin to her chin, and plays in front of me for the first time ever, a huge smile on her face.

It takes me a few seconds, but even as tone-deaf as I am, I recognize it's "Happy Birthday to You"—probably the most elaborate rendition of it ever played. So much happened today that I forgot it was my birthday. But Anna didn't.

The significance of what she's doing, the fact that *this* is the first time she's playing for me, hits me. If I wasn't already in love with her, I'd fall now.

When the song ends, she puts her violin away and smiles at me self-consciously, and I crush her to me with a tight hug and kiss her over and over. "Best fucking birthday ever. You played that whole thing. So proud of you. Love you, love you, love you."

She wipes the moisture away from my face with her thumbs and kisses me slower and deeper. "Love you."

Her hands slide down my chest to the waist of my pants, and my fly comes undone.

"Are you sure?" I ask, even though I'm praying for her to say yes. I want her so bad I could climb the walls. "We don't—"

"Birthday sex," she says, pulling her dress over her head and tugging me toward the bedroom.

It's been so long for both of us that birthday sex only lasts five minutes, but you can bet your ass those five minutes are downright epic. I tell her about LVMH afterward, and she squeals with excitement. Then we have cake for dinner. It makes us feel sick, and we eat leftovers to settle our stomachs, laughing with each bite.

Truly, the best birthday ever.

FORTY-SIX

Anna

I DECIDE IT'S TIME TO RETURN TO THE RICHTER PIECE. BUT THIS time, I give myself a hard talk first. I can see now that I can never go back to the way things were. It was foolish of me to think I could find a magic key to turn back time. The truth is art will never be as effortless as it used to be, not now that people have expectations of me. All I can do is go forward, and to do that, I must stop chasing perfection. It doesn't exist. I can never please everyone. It's hard enough just pleasing myself. Instead, I must focus on giving what I have, not what people want, because that is all I *can* give. I don't mask anymore if I can help it.

I begin the Richter piece for the last time. Practice is slow and arduous. I make many mistakes and I go back and correct what I can, but I don't go *all* the way back—except for one more time, which I regret. I hear the voices in my head, criticizing me, judging me. Oftentimes they get the best of me, and I finish practice feeling despondent. But I keep going anyway. Fighting the compulsion to start over, to seek perfection, to outwit the voices, is exhausting, and most days I can only manage for a few hours before I know my brain has had it. This is a necessary thing for me to learn, though. If I'm sensitive to my own resource levels, I can keep myself from falling sick again. A slow me is much better than a sick me.

In this manner, I make it to the end of the Richter piece. When I tell Quan, he pops a bottle of champagne and celebrates with me, even though I still have many other pieces to prepare for this record and upcoming tour. But one by one, I get through those as well. I go to the studio, and I record them, permanently saving my renditions in digital format even though they're not one hundred percent flawless.

It never gets easier. I fight every time I set my bow to the strings, but I stay true to myself.

I play from my heart.

EPILOGUE

Anna

TODAY'S THE DAY.

I'm performing for an audience today.

It's been over two years since my dad's funeral. It took me that long to heal and to fight. I often despaired that I'd never make it.

But here I am, behind the stage.

The crowd is small, only fifty people, but I'm so nervous there might as well be thousands out there. These are my people, though, the select few who came from all corners of the country (some farther) to hear me. They are honoring me with the precious gift of their time. As much as I battled through these pieces for myself, I also battled for them. I treasure this small group of people who understands me.

I hope my art makes them feel. I hope it makes them think. I hope it has an impact.

I get the signal that it's time, and I swallow my nerves and carry my violin onto the stage.

The lights are bright, and I don't let myself look up at them. There, in the front row, is my honey, Quan. He's beaming at me, holding a bouquet of red roses in his lap, and I'm so overwhelmed with love for him that I feel like my chest is going to burst open. Next to him is my mom. She's wearing an evening gown and her finest jewelry and proudly sitting with a group of her posh friends. On Quan's other side are two faces that I've never seen in real life, but I recognize them right away. Rose and Suzie, my good friends who tried to be there for me and didn't fault me for disappearing when my life got too hard. I'm excited to go out to dinner with them after this performance.

This group is small, but it's good. It's all that I need.

Feeling emotional and very much alive, I lift my violin to my chin, and I set my bow upon the strings.

I play.

AUTHOR'S NOTE

This book is a work of fiction, but it's also half memoir. To date, it's the most "me" book that I've written. That's why it's in first person rather than third, like my other books. The words came out easier when I said "I" instead of "she." But the personal nature of this book made it harrowing to write. Anna's struggles were mine. Her pain was mine. Her shame was mine. And I relived it every time I sat down to write. All in all, for reasons ranging from writer's block to autistic burnout, it took me more than three years to finish, but regardless of how this book is received, I'm proud that I made it through and proud of the story I told. Writing this author's note is a momentous occasion for me.

At the same time, however, writing this note is a bittersweet experience, too. I wrote the author's note for *The Bride Test* while I was in my mom's hospital room, keeping her company as she struggled from complications related to her lung cancer treatments. Even as sick as she was, she tried to talk to me, to connect with me. She made the time count. But that night was the last time she was really "herself." After that, her illness consumed her. Out of love, my family took her out of the hospital and brought her home, where my siblings and I cared for her around the clock. As my mom's sickness worsened, I suffered from suicidal ideation. I'm not sharing this because I want anyone's sympathy. I'm sharing this because I want people to know how real and serious caregiver burnout is. I'm lucky to be alive.

I feel like there's a conversation about caregiving that society isn't having. It's not something that people can freely talk about. No one wants to be seen as "complaining," and no one wants to make a loved one feel like they're a burden. But the truth is caregiving is hard. Not everyone is suited for it. I most certainly am not, and it has nothing to do with my being on the autism spectrum. There are many autistic people who work as nurses and doctors and other types of healthcare providers and derive meaning and satisfaction from it. Even those who like this kind of work can get burned out from the heavy physical, mental, and emotional tolls it takes on them, as we've seen among frontline workers caring for patients with severe COVID-19.

As a society, we need to have compassion for all people affected by illness and disability—and that means those who receive care as well as those who give care. We all matter, and no one should feel like they can't ask for help when they need it. If someone says they're hurting, please listen. Please take them seriously. Please be kind. If you're hurting, please be kind to yourself.

Do you need to talk to someone?
It's free to call the Samaritans Helpline (United Kingdom): 116 123

ACKNOWLEDGMENTS

Thank you, readers, for waiting for this book! For reasons that I suspect you can guess after reading *The Heart Principle*, I wasn't able to finish writing on time to publish last year. I'm sorry for any disappointment I may have caused—but also perversely happy if anyone likes my books enough to *be* disappointed when they don't release on schedule. I hope the wait was worth it.

This book was a *long* time in the making, so there are many people I need to thank individually or by name. First of all, thank you, thank you, thank you to my husband. I seriously wouldn't have made it here without your support. You lifted me up when I felt down (which was often—I'm sorry). You let me talk your ears off about this book even though I'm sure you were bored. You hugged me, fed me, managed our kids' pandemic schooling so I could write, and covered our tiny yard with milkweed and passion vine so I could watch the butterflies. I love you with all my heart.

Thank you to my baby sister, 7. I'm so lucky Mom and Dad accidentally conceived you during that Bermuda vacation, so I could have my best friend at my side my entire life (except for the one year, one month, and one day that I lived alone before you were born). Thank you for the dinners, donuts, butterfly cage, and the millions of thoughtful things you do. Most of all, thank you for *you*. Love you, em.

Next, I need to thank my writer friends for being there throughout this process: Roselle Lim, you are funny and wise and kind. Pictures of your cat give me life, lol. Suzanne Park, I'm inspired by you. How you manage to achieve all that you do and still be such a considerate friend is mind-boggling. A. R. Lucas, I treasure you. You tell me the hard truths that I need to hear, but always with kindness and compassion. Gwynne Jackson, I'm grateful for all the times you've listened to me pour my heart out without judgment. Talking to you is like getting a big hug. Rachel Simon, I'm so glad we've gotten to know each other over the past few years. Your friendship, honesty, and thoughtfulness mean a great deal to me. Mazey Eddings, your vivid personality made this past year much more bearable. Chloe Liese, I have such respect for you and your work. You make this world better. My mentor, Brighton Walsh, I wouldn't have had the confidence to hand this manuscript to my editor without your help. Thank you, as always, for your guidance.

When I was struggling fiercely to write this book, Julia Quinn advised me to give myself time, to take a year off if I could and let myself slowly rediscover my love of writing. It was precisely the advice I needed, but more than that, I felt seen and understood and unspeakably touched that someone like her would even speak to me. It was a small thing for her to do, but she positively impacted my life. THANK YOU, JQ!!!

Later on, I reached out to another romance writing idol of mine,

Jayne Ann Krentz, asking her how she managed to fill bookshelves with so many wonderful books of her own, and she, too, shared helpful advice with me. From her, I learned that I need to trust myself when I write and if there are recurring themes in my books, it's *okay*. I don't need to reinvent myself with every book so I can be fresh and new. In fact, those recurring themes may be the precise elements that inspire readers to connect with my work. I needed to hear these things, and I took them to heart as I drafted this book. THANK YOU, JAK!!!

Many thanks to Rebecca Ong, Nancy Huynh, and fellow wuxia fan Yimin Lai for helping me with the Chinese American representation in this book. It was a privilege to interview you. I'm sorry I was so annoying and bothered you with random questions at odd hours of the day.

Thank you to my old tae kwon do friend from college who is now a cardiothoracic surgeon, Dr. Burg, for connecting me with your urologist colleague, so I could ask him all my questions regarding testicular cancer and radical inguinal orchiectomy. Thank you, Dr. Witten, for sharing your time and expertise with me.

Thank you, Kaija Rayne, for reading this manuscript on short notice and offering feedback. I appreciate it.

Thank you to my agent, Kim Lionetti, for doing what you could to support me through my journey with this book even though your life was challenging as well.

Last but not least, thank you to the publishing team at Berkley—Cindy Hwang, Jessica Brock, Fareeda Bullert, and others—for being so understanding and patient with me. I plan to return to being a professional, deadline-keeping kind of author from here on out. I'm beyond grateful that you were as kind as you were when I dropped the ball, and I'm excited to work with you on coming projects.

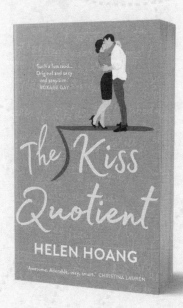